ZANE PRESENTS

DO WHAT YOU GOTTA GOTTA *Do*

Dear Reader:

We were introduced to the conniving vixen Aniyah Sanchez in Christine Young-Robinson's debut novel, *We Didn't See It Coming*. This scheming character took advantage of the wealthy Houston family and later served time for her criminal activities. Now she is out of prison and back on the streets with her eyes set on finding a rich man.

The novel takes readers on twists and turns through Aniyah's encounters with her Aunt Tessa, who comes to her rescue and attempts to keep her on the straight and narrow path. However, Aniyah has her mind focused on snaring Jarvis Powell Jr., whose father owns a chain of banks. Not trusting Aniyah, the senior takes extreme measures to ruin her budding relationship with his son, whom he sees as a victim. It's about power, money, family and greed and how one woman affects an established father and son bond. As always, thanks for supporting myself and the Strebor Books family. We strive to bring you the most cutting-edge, out-of-the-box material on the market. You can find me on Facebook @AuthorZane or you can email me at zane@eroticanoir.com.

Blessings,

Zane

Publisher
Strebor Books
www.simonandschuster.com

ALSO BY CHRISTINE YOUNG-ROBINSON
We Didn't See It Coming

ZANE PRESENTS

DO WHAT YOU GOTTA Do

CHRISTINE YOUNG-ROBINSON

STREBOR BOOKS

NEW YORK LONDON TORONTO SYDNEY

Strebor Books
P.O. Box 6505
Largo, MD 20792
http://www.streborbooks.com

ISBN 978-1-59309-627-4
ISBN 978-1-4767-8334-5 (ebook)
LCCN 2015934631

First Strebor Books trade paperback edition August 2015

Cover design: www.mariondesigns.com
Cover photograph: © Keith Saunders/Keith Saunders Photos

10 9 8 7 6 5 4 3 2 1

Manufactured in the United States of America

For information regarding special discounts for bulk purchases, please contact Simon & Schuster Special Sales at 1-866-506-1949

The Simon & Schuster Speakers Bureau can bring authors to your live event. For more information or to book an event, contact the Simon & Schuster Speakers Bureau at 1-866-248-3049 or visit our website at www.simonspeakers.com.

I dedicate this book to my oldest brother, Celess Young, Jr.

Dear Brother: I can still hear your voicemail in my head.
"Do What You Gotta Do."
Thanks for the inspiration for the title of this book.
I know you are in heaven doing the happy dance.

Acknowledgments

First and foremost, I would like to thank God for making me a miraclewriter4u.

To my parents, Celess and Ruby Young, thanks for always being there for me.

To my hubby, Joseph, thanks for being such a great husband, father, and grandfather.

To my children, Nishika and Rahim, you're my hearts. Thanks, daughter, for two wonderful and smart grandchildren.

To my siblings, Tynetta, Maxine and my twin, Christopher, you're my rock.

My heavenly siblings, Celess Young, Jr., Lonnie, and Charlene, I miss you so much, but I know you're smiling down on me.

To my mother-in-law, Ola Mae Smith, thanks so much for your love.

To my angel, Mrs. Witherspoon, I miss you.

To my agent, Dr. Maxine Thompson, thanks for believing in me as a writer.

To Zane and Charmaine, thanks so much for the opportunity to share my writing with readers. Words can never express how humble and grateful I am. To the Strebor staff and authors, I am honored to be in your company.

To the book cover designer, Keith Saunders, awesome job as always.

Thanks, Joan Dash (bestie), for always being there for me. Much love to Marvy Moore, Mercy Thomas, Pamela Williams, Victoria McCornell, Minnie Dix, Tia Wright, Carol James, Zina Jenkins, Angeleah Weldon, Tanji Dark, Tasha Martin, Johnathan Royal, Ricky Black, Zelma Whitener, Velma Patterson, Sharon Litaker, Tynetta Cohen, Felicia Young, Deborah Bush, Jo Ann Howard, Lavern Delima, Robin Duncan, Sylvia Grant, Yatifah Young, Vanessa Brown, Veronica Young, Connie Jenkins, Theresa Lewis, Yaphia Young, Deborah Pearson, Carmen Hampton-Julious, Summiya Young, LaShanda Shuler, Tanesha Reese, Renetta Pearson, Radisha Young, Ella Ray Jordan-O'neal, Latoya Mack, Vanette Delima, Tamara Mack Brailey, Shakeema Bryant Nix, Joelle McCornell, Ruth McFadden, Sylvia Santiago, Faverta Robinson, Jeanell Brown, Rose Branham, Rene' C.J. Davis, Catherine T. Yeiser, Barbara Jones, Sylvia Scott, Sandra Lambright, Rita and Paul Daniels, Jacqueline Bouvier Lee, Summiya Dash, Michelle Branch-Howard, Demetria Dash, and Towanna T. Morant.

Special thanks to my cousin James Moore for your uplifting spirit and positive energy and Darryl Profit for being like a brother to me.

To my family, neighbors and friends, thanks for your love and support.

Thanks, Eleuthera Book Club for the wonderful book recommendations and discussions.

To my author-friends, thanks for always showing me love.

Thanks to the bookstores, online vendors, media, and book reviewers.

I'm grateful for the readers whom I've met and look forward to meeting many more in the near future.

I know I may have missed someone, but it was not intentionally.

Please do not hesitate to email me at miraclewriter4u@aol.com and share your thoughts and views.

CHAPTER 1

At last, Aniyah Sanchez would no longer be like a lion locked up in a cage. After spending four years in a South Carolina prison for fraud and kidnapping, she was being released.

As she stepped out of her cell, a male prison guard whispered in her ear, "Fruitcake, I'll see you when you get back."

Sniffing the fish odor that escaped from his breath, Aniyah turned up her nose. *Didn't he know after lunch to eat a peppermint?*

"Goodbye, Slut," an inmate yelled from another cell to her.

"You better get your last feel, Officer Mann," another inmate added.

The inmates laughed throughout the ward, including the guard who sported a broken front tooth. He cupped Aniyah's left breast with his right hand. Then he took the club he held in his other hand and placed it between her legs.

"I don't think so!" Aniyah snapped her head, brushing him away. "Your time has expired."

During her prison term, she had fulfilled the guard's sexual needs in exchange for protection from conflicts that she had endured with other female inmates.

Aniyah, almost jogging, hurried ahead until she came to a point where she met up with another guard and other inmates that were being released.

Once the official documents were finalized, the guard let Aniyah out of the last door that gave her back her freedom. A chill ran through her body, but it quickly disappeared once the doors were slammed shut behind her.

Turning around, she took one last look at the place of residence she had called home. The fourth inmate in line wearing loafers donated by church volunteers, her feet made contact with the concrete ground.

Aniyah adjusted her eyes to the sunlight that blinded her. She pulled down on her red spandex dress that had risen up to her hips. It was the same dress she had worn before she became a part of the prison system.

Her once slender hips stretched the dress to its limits, but Aniyah strutted as if the garment was brand-new. She faulted her excessive weight gain from her no longer being able to shake her hips in the nightclubs. In prison, she mostly sat on her rear in her cell or in ongoing therapy sessions.

Under her armpit, she carried a plastic bag of her belongings and a pair of pumps. Her hands free, she twisted her flowing black hair up in a bun.

Other released inmates stopped to say farewell to each other, but Aniyah kept walking, too afraid that she might be called back by one of the guards.

Two female inmates ran past her, once they saw familiar faces of loved ones waiting to take them home. Aniyah was not looking for any family to come to her rescue. She would not know her father from any other black man on the streets. He was her mother's one-night stand with no name.

Julia, her mother, had died two months ago in Mexico, during the time dyed eggs were given to inmates for holiday treats. Aniyah remembered the day the warden delivered the news to her. Guilt troubled her, since she had run away from home at the age of sixteen, leaving her mother behind to suffer a broken heart.

The only family she had left was her mother's sister, Tessa Sanchez-Chavis. And she was not counting on her self-righteous aunt to come to her rescue.

Where am I going? I have no idea.

As the heat beamed down on her forehead, sweat dripped down her neck. The spandex dress felt like rubber against her body.

"Rosie Aniyah Sanchez." She heard the name echoing in her ears.

Her eyes lit up, when she recognized the familiar voice. She locked eyes with her aunt. The solemn look on her face turned into a bright smile. "Aunt Tessa."

She studied her aunt, noticing how much she had aged. Streaks of gray highlighted Tessa's jet-black hair. Aniyah, elated, ran into her aunt's arms. "I can't believe you're here."

"You're family," her aunt said humbly in her Spanish accent, giving her niece a kiss on the cheek.

Together, they strolled to a parked black Mercedes-Benz.

Admiring her aunt's ride, before prison life and without hesitation, if a man were driving the Benz, Aniyah would have easily flagged down the ride. She would have unraveled her bun to let her hair fall past her shoulders, propped one hand on a hip and batted her dark brown eyes. Then she would have worked her charm on the man behind the wheel, giving him her middle name instead of using her first name, Rosie. Played him for a sucker.

After all the counseling, her former lifestyle of being an escort and manipulating people, especially men, was supposed to be her past, but only time would tell.

Tessa unlocked the car door, hopped in and quickly Aniyah

jumped in and took a seat on the butter-colored leather seats. A free ride from her aunt would do.

"How did you know I was getting out?"

Tessa reached over and gave her niece another loving hug. Then she became emotional. "I've been keeping up with you. And although I can't forget what you did to the Houstons or me, you're still family. I have made peace with it."

"How about your lawyer-hubby, Baron?"

"He's Mr. Chavis to you from now on. And, he'll never forgive you for what you did to the Houston family, nor him," Tessa admitted with a hint of bitterness.

"It's not like it was *his* money." Reaching down between the seats, Aniyah picked up a bag of boiled peanuts. She cracked open the peanuts, tossing a few in her mouth. While chewing, she continued to speak. "The Houstons are garbage people. Mr. Houston was a male whore. How can you defend him?"

"Don't speak of the dead in a bad way," Tessa argued. She recalled working as a young woman in the home of Rupert Houston, owner of Houston Commercial Construction Company. He was a man who loved to have his way with his beautiful female workers.

Aniyah sucked her teeth. "Mr. Houston can rot in hell. And so can his spoiled-ass daughters." She slouched back in the seat.

In past years, Aniyah had crossed paths with her aunt's prior boss, Rupert. Her greed for money led her to become his mistress. He had promised her a false dream on Lake Murray, South Carolina, to later do away with her.

Aniyah vowed to get revenge on him. To keep her quiet, Rupert included her in his will.

Aniyah took a few more peanuts, folded the bag, and placed it back where she got it. "I still say you were more loyal to his spoiled-ass daughters than you were to me."

Staring at her aunt as she drove, Aniyah wanted to grab and shake her. Rupert's unexpected death had left her a happy and wealthy young woman, instead of his three daughters, until Tessa discovered her wrongdoings. Instead of living the life of royalty, Aniyah had landed in prison.

Tessa sensed Aniyah was still bitter. "I believe in doing what's right. You had no right to do wrong."

"I didn't want to be a maid like you and mama. I could have sent plenty of money to Mama." Aniyah lowered her voice. "Now she's dead."

Tessa was surprised. "I asked the warden to not tell you about Julia."

"You should have come and told me yourself."

"I didn't want you to be hurt. You couldn't go to Mexico to your mama's funeral."

"Did you go?" Aniyah asked sadly.

"I went to visit her in her sickbed a month before she went to her heavenly home. She wanted so much for you to come to her bedside. I simply couldn't tell her that I found you. You were in jail for doing bad things. It would have destroyed her. I stayed by her side to the end."

Tears flowed down Aniyah's face. "I'm glad you didn't tell her."

Tessa softly patted her niece on the hand. "Your mama loved you with all her heart."

"I know...I miss her." Aniyah wiped away her tears.

"Let's go shopping. You don't need to dress like you're a loose girl." Tessa had witnessed her niece's dress code. The dress had risen up on Aniyah. It resembled a tunic shirt.

"I'll go shopping. But I'm not throwing away this dress."

"It's too little."

Aniyah saw her aunt glancing at her. She tugged at her dress, trying to cover her exposed thighs. "So I gained a few pounds. No big deal."

"After shopping, you'll trash it."

"This hot dress stays with me."

Tessa concluded that it was going to be a long day for her. The sooner she took her niece shopping and got her settled, the sooner she would be rid of her. She sighed. "Aniyah, you have always been difficult."

"I think for myself. No one tells me what to do."

After shopping, Tessa drove Aniyah to a two-story apartment complex in nearby downtown Columbia.

Aniyah looked out at the buildings as Tessa parked. Startled, she said, "This is where you and Baron live now. What happened to his house?"

"We still have our home. This is where you're going to rest."

Aniyah's voice escalated. "Are you for real? Here?"

"I'm sorry, but there's no way Baron will let me bring you into our home."

"I'm your niece. He can now trust me."

"I'm afraid not."

Aniyah marveled. She heard the nervousness in her aunt's voice. She was flattered that her aunt thought of her as a threat. In the past, she had seduced her aunt's husband, prior to their marriage, in order to manipulate him to get to his client's fortune.

They got out of the vehicle, carrying shopping bags by the handles. Aniyah followed her aunt to the front door. Unlocking it, they entered the one-bedroom apartment.

She proceeded to the middle of the living room, while Tessa, clenching her handbag, stayed put near the door.

Aniyah felt her aunt's eyes piercing her, well-informed that she was uncomfortable being alone with her, but her attention was focused on her living arrangements. Next to a small wooden table, she tossed the bags that she held on a futon. Then she headed to see where she would sleep; leaving her aunt on edge to figure out if she would show any signs of psychotic symptoms.

Inside the bedroom, Aniyah spotted a four-drawer chest and twin-sized bed that was the bottom half of a bunk bed. *Secondhand crap.*

"I hope you like it." Tessa dropped the other bags on the linoleum floor.

Aniyah mumbled under her breath, "No bigger than a jail cell."

Returning back into the living room, Aniyah decided not to complain. She was convinced without her aunt rescuing her, she might be sitting on a bench like a homeless person.

Aniyah grinned. "It's good."

"There's food in the refrigerator. I've stocked it with a few things, sodas and sandwich meats. In the cabinets, there're cans of corn, black beans and a five-pound bag of rice."

"Any steaks, lobster tails or shrimp?"

Tessa laughed. "There're frozen foods, and chicken for you to cook. Tonight you can heat a frozen chicken TV dinner."

Aniyah went directly into the kitchen adjacent to the living room. She looked in the freezer to see that few products loaded the freezer, including one ice tray. She slammed the door shut. Then she opened the refrigerator section. Removing a can of orange soda, she snapped it opened and took a swallow, quenching her thirst.

Tessa entered. As she watched her niece's every move, she noticed the spandex dress Aniyah wore had risen up her thighs. "I say you should change into something more appropriate."

Aniyah tussled with the dress. "Stop looking at my clothes. It'll fit fine once I lose a few pounds. I'll get sexy-looking again." Shaking her hips, Aniyah looked around the kitchen, noticing something was missing. "Hold up...no microwave?"

"You can use the stove to heat a TV dinner."

"Whatever." Aniyah rolled her eyes.

"Change your style of dressing. Start off fresh by getting yourself decent work. And, find a good man that you can start a family with," Tessa lectured with an air of sophistication.

Aniyah stared at her aunt as though she were a hated prison guard. She had not thought about a job. She twirled around. Cheerfully, she said, "I can use a money man."

"It's nothing like making your own money."

Aniyah walked past her aunt, stepping back into the living room. Tessa followed behind her while Aniyah searched for any sign of communication technology.

"No telephone in here?"

Tessa shook her index finger at her. "When you get work, you can buy one."

"If you want me to get a job, at least get me a cell phone."

"For now, no phone. I'll be coming by to check on you."

Aniyah slouched down on the futon. She shoved her fist into the cushion, feeling the steel frame underneath. "I hate being broke."

"In due time, you'll find work. Make your own money."

"I have no skills. No one will hire me."

"There has to be something you like to do or you can go to college."

"Aunt Tessa, getting out of jail is not the same as getting out of high school. I didn't just graduate. No college for me."

"You know how to clean."

Aniyah jumped to her feet. Her mind went to the days she was forced to clean the toilet in her jail cells. Enraged, she yelled, "Hell to the no. I'll die before I scrub another toilet."

"It's an honest living."

"Never!" Aniyah snapped as she sat back down. "I'll find something else to do."

"Start looking for some kind of work."

Aniyah banged her fist on the table. "I need money now."

Tessa eased her way near the door. Digging in her purse, she pulled out a few bills. "This should be enough to get you by."

Aniyah hurried over to her, snatching the money out of her aunt's hand. Before she shoved the bills down in her bra, she counted up to a hundred.

"The rent on this apartment is paid in full for three months. By then you should've found work."

"Give me a break. That's not enough time."

"You must have work by then. Baron won't allow me to give you any more money after that."

"He rules you."

"Nonsense. We agreed on that decision."

"Tell him what you want…you're his wife, Mrs. Tessa Sanchez-Chavis. Stop being too easy."

"I'm loyal to my husband. He's a good man. I won't let you ruin my marriage. Three months it is." Tessa peered at her through hooded eyes.

Aniyah heard the authority in her aunt's voice and said no more. She was not about to let three months turn into get-out-right-now.

"In the drawer, there's a nightgown for you to rest in." Tessa jingled her car keys as she made her way to the door. "I must go. I must prepare dinner for my husband."

"I need to eat, too."

"Heat your dinner. I pray you'll turn your life around. My sister would want that for you. I'll see you in a few days. And for God's sake, don't go anywhere near Milandra, Noelle or Kenley Houston.

Baron and I have agreed not to disturb them about your release. They're in a good place in their lives."

Aniyah chuckled. "The fake sisters are history to me. I'm going to be in a much better place then, them uppity snobs."

"I have faith that you'll do fine, once you find work." Tessa noticed she still had the apartment key in her hand. "You'll need this." She tossed the key to Aniyah. "Don't lose it."

Following her aunt outside, Aniyah watched as she got into her vehicle. "Weak bitch," she hollered, once Tessa drove away.

Back into the apartment, Aniyah slammed the door behind her. She stood in the middle of the living room, sniffing the stale odor. She screamed, "I'm still in jail. The one time my Aunt Tessa could do right by me and she put me in a hellhole."

Aniyah went into the bedroom. She bounced on the bed. "Dead mattress," she fussed. "Aunt Tessa is going home to her fancy bed. I've got to sleep on a board for a mattress. Once again she shouted, "Weak bitch. Get a job, no way. My job will only be to find me a man with money. You and anyone else that gets in my way, will pay for treating me like I'm beneath you."

CHAPTER 2

Awakened by the tightness of the spandex dress that clung to her body, Aniyah felt as if she had taken a nap in a pair of Spanx shapewear.

Out of bed, she wiggled her way out of the dress. She removed her bra, wiping away the puddles of sweat in the crease of her breasts. Fanning herself, she went straight to the television that sat on top of the chest, and turned it on.

The ten o'clock news broadcasted a photo of a long-haired, blonde white woman wanted by the police for fraudulent checks. Aniyah was relieved *her* past troubled life was old news to the media.

Bare on top and in her underwear, she went into the kitchen and turned on the oven. From the freezer, she opened a chicken TV dinner. She pulled off only the plastic film that covered a brownie for her dessert, put slits in the film over the peas and potatoes. Then she shoved it in the oven.

Aniyah sucked her teeth at the pink enameled tub. The tub was nothing close to a jetted Jacuzzi, but it had to do; she longed for a hot bath.

She adjusted the chrome knobs, letting warm water flow into the tub while she hurried back into the bedroom.

She pulled a beige nightgown out of the drawer. Holding it up, she mumbled, "Old granny clothes. No rich man will ever see me in this."

Back in the bathroom, she saw that the running water had filled the tub halfway, and turned it off.

Once she slipped out of her underwear, Aniyah cautiously eased her right foot into the tub, making sure the water wasn't hot. She sat down, letting all of the tension of prison life fade away. Happy she no longer had to share a bathroom with female inmates.

Aniyah closed her eyes, ready to get lost in her thoughts, but out of nowhere, a booming sound blasted in her ears, making her feel like she was bathing in the middle of a music concert. A lover of dance, she moved her body, splashing water onto the floor.

Not hearing any footsteps from the apartment above, she was curious where the noise was coming from. Relaxation was no longer on her mind. Aniyah stood to her feet. She made her way out of the tub. Dripping wet, she grabbed a towel, wrapping it around her body. Then she ran to the door.

Looking out of the peephole, she was not able to see a thing. She unlocked the door, using the door as a shield and stuck her head out. Right away she noticed a young man with sandy hair, cornrows tight against his scalp, dressed in jeans and a navy blue tee shirt. He held a beer can in his hand. Instead of slamming her door shut, Aniyah spoke. "Hi. What the hell is going on with all the music?"

Her neighbor focused his eyes on her, trying to get a glimpse of her figure, while he busy shoved his T-shirt down in his pants. "My man, Floyd in the next building is throwing a party for the peeps. Get dressed and join us."

Aniyah's eyes lit up. "Two minutes. I'll be there."

"What's your name?"

"Aniyah."

"I'm Lenvy, but everyone calls me, Gold. Check it out." He pointed to his teeth.

Rolling her eyes, Aniyah shut the door in his face. *So ghetto. Not my kind of man.*

Running into the bedroom, she went through the bag of clothes her aunt had purchased for her. She got dressed in a red skirt and a white blouse that could easily be worn off the shoulder. Next, she brushed her flowing hair down the side of her face.

The smell of her food cooking took away the foul odor of the apartment. Aniyah ran and shut the oven off. She let the TV dinner stay in it to keep warm for later.

Out of the kitchen and back into the bedroom, she sorted through her bag from prison. She grabbed a tube of lipstick. Amazing to her, the lipstick was still good. Aniyah smeared the deep burgundy color onto her lips. "I'm back." She smiled into a mirror hung behind a closet door, then swung around, admiring her hips. "A little plump in the bump doesn't hurt."

Grabbing the key, Aniyah stuck it in the deep pocket of her skirt. Then she dashed out of the door. Her GPS system was the loud vocals from the music.

At the next apartment building, people stood outside, chattering as if it were the middle of the day.

Aniyah strutted, holding her head up high.

Lenvy spotted her quick. "Hey, Pretty Lady, get on up these stairs."

At the sound of his voice, Aniyah looked up and saw him looking over a balcony from the second-floor apartment. She realized that was where the music was coming from.

Aniyah made her way up the stairs, saying "excuse me" to people conversing. Young women who appeared to be in their early twenties looked her up and down.

Reaching the top of the stairs, Lenvy put his arms around her waist. He led her into the party scene as if she were his woman. Aniyah did not pull away from him; all she wanted was to have fun, and of course, a street guy was not on her list to be her lover.

Under dimmed lights, Aniyah followed Lenvy's lead to a corner in the empty furnished apartment. People danced on the floor— hugged up and freestyle.

"You want me to pour you a drink?" Lenvy hollered in her ear over the music.

"A beer will do," Aniyah hollered back in his ear, bouncing to the music.

Lenvy left and returned. Popping the tab off the can, he handed her the beer. Aniyah tilted the can up to her lips, taking several gulps before she went back to bouncing; giving him the clue she was ready to hit the dance floor.

"Come on, girl, let's see your moves," he said.

Lenvy started dancing with her in the spot they stood. Aniyah held her beer can up in the air as she shook her hips from side to side.

Turning her back to him, she eased her rear up against his crotch. It felt good feeling a man's body part; she wanted it that way, not like in prison where she had no choice.

Moving away from Lenvy, Aniyah turned around and faced the grill in his mouth. She wanted to scream at him, "Please keep your mouth closed." But she did not. If Lenvy thought he was going to score with his new neighbor, he was in for a big letdown.

They steadily danced to the beat of the music until it changed into a slow jam.

Lenvy put his arms around her neck. Once he pulled her close to him, she was quite aware he thought he had her right where he wanted her to be.

Aniyah smiled, as she got a kick out of turning him on, only to later leave him flat in his tracks. She pressed her breasts into his chest.

"Damn, pretty lady, you're hot."

She tickled his ear with her tongue. "I'm sexy."

"That you are." Lenvy moved his hands down to her backside, touching every inch of her.

Aniyah handed her empty beer can to a passerby. Then she followed Lenvy's lead. She eased her hand down to his backside. Attempting to squeeze his buttocks, her hand landed on the right side pocket of his jeans—feeling his wallet was about to fall out.

Without hesitation, she slapped a kiss on his lips, praying he did not cut her with his grill. Her lips stayed glued to his long enough for her to ease the wallet the rest of the way out of his pocket. Plus, if anybody happened to be watching them dance, she wanted all eyes focused on their kiss. She began to rub against his manhood as she continued to kiss him. But with her free hand, she moved quickly, pulling out a few bills. Balling the money in one hand, Aniyah let the wallet fall to the floor. *No way am I going to try to put it back in his pants pocket.*

Aniyah felt his left leg ease up between her thighs.

"Damn, lady, you got my bells jingling." Lenvy grabbed hold of his manhood.

"You need to cool off. Let's go outside."

Aniyah turned away from him, stuffed the money down in her bra. She darted to the door.

"We can go to my place," Lenvy suggested, wiping sweat from his forehead.

The music changed to an upbeat tune. Outside, Aniyah danced faster and faster, twirling around. Lenvy ran after her, trying to keep up with her.

"Who's that lady?" Floyd, the party thrower, asked.

"My new neighbor," Lenvy said.

"She's a hottie."

"Man, don't get any ideas. She's already express delivery to apartment 2D," Lenvy said.

That's what you think. Aniyah became dizzy from twirling around and around, then stopped. "I need another cold beer."

"Got you covered." Lenvy headed back inside.

Aniyah rested against a parked vehicle, pressing down on her chest to flatten any bulges from the money.

Lenvy returned with her beer but held up his wallet. Aniyah played cool to not give herself away.

"I'm glad I went back inside. My damn wallet came out of my pocket. Some broad had it in her hand. Say she noticed it when she stepped on it."

He handed Aniyah the beer, than checked inside the wallet. "Shit, I'm missing some twenties from my paycheck." Angrily, Lenvy snatched the can from her. "I know weave head didn't take my cash."

Aniyah folded her arms. "She'll deny it. And, no one inside is going to admit taking it."

"I know what you're saying. I've copped a few bucks off the floor at parties before."

With a smile on her face, she got off the vehicle. "It's been fun, but I need to get home. I'm tired." She yawned.

Lenvy caught her by the hand. "I make a good blanket."

"I need air, not heat."

"I'll blow cool air on you all night."

"Tell me what kind of work do you do?"

"I fix people's rides," Lenvy said proudly.

"The owner or worker of the business?"

"Worker. Why does it matter?"

"Your paycheck is too weak to handle me."

"Aw...I see...you're a gold digger."

"Call me what you want."

Aniyah strutted to her apartment building. Lenvy walked right behind her, keeping his eyes on her rear. She felt him coming close up on her and spun around to face him.

Giving him a wink of the eye, she rested her hands on her hips. "I'm into men with plenty of money and credit cards."

"Maybe I fit your needs."

"Please." Aniyah laughed. "I bet the only plastic you own is a prepaid one."

"If I do, it's still a credit card."

Aniyah made it to her apartment door. "See you later, neighbor."

"You know, you're wrong." Lenvy scratched his chin.

Aniyah unlocked her door. "I could sleep with you if I choose to for free sex. Play with your mind." Teasing him, she placed another peck on his lips, giving Lenvy the opportunity to pull her into his arms. He pressed his lips against hers. He tried to force his tongue inside her mouth, but that was where Aniyah ended it. She scrambled her way out of his arms. "It's been grand. A lady must get her rest. Be nice and refreshed for the money-man of her dreams."

Lenvy annoyed. "You ain't all that."

"Goodnight, neighbor. Sorry you don't fit my needs," she said, winking her left eye at him. She went inside her apartment, slamming the door in his face.

Aniyah splashed her lips with water, rinsing off any slop from Lenvy's mushy lips. She pulled off her dress and unhooked her bra. As her breasts fell, so did the money.

Her thoughts went to the tips she had learned about pickpocketing from her former cellmate, Katey Walsh, who was serving time for theft. It had paid off. Aniyah counted out sixty bucks.

She stashed the money in her bag. With a growling stomach, Aniyah went into the kitchen, removing the cooled-off TV dinner from the oven. It was warm enough to eat. Sitting at the table, she sat tall, placing a paper towel on her lap. Then she lifted the fork to her mouth and pretended she was eating lobster in a gourmet kitchen.

When she came back to reality, she grumbled, "Where are you, money-man?"

CHAPTER 3

The morning light seeped through the closed blinds. Startled by the sound of a travel-sized alarm clock, Aniyah sat upright in the bed. She fumbled on the nightstand to locate it. *It's Monday morning. Crazy aunt making sure I go look for a damn job.*

The day before while others worshipped, Aniyah had slept a day of comfort from being freed of prison life.

Dragging herself out of bed, she went straight to the shower. Her next move was inside the kitchen. There she prepared a morning breakfast of eggs, bacon, instant grits and juice.

At the table, she closed her eyes and envisioned that she sat on a patio, viewing the soothing waters of Lake Murray. She imagined drinking her orange juice from a crystal glass, with her meal prepared by a chef and served on fine china. She also pretended she was eating with sterling silver flatware.

Aniyah sat upright in her seat as she tasted the flavors of her meal. Once she opened her eyes, she flashed back to reality. Her eyes traveled over to the refrigerator. It had no outside dispenser for water or ice for her convenience. She would have no choice but to defrost the freezer.

The floors were covered with linoleum instead of tile or hardwood floors. *I have to get out of here.* Aniyah got up, tossing her food in the trash. Then she poured the rest of her juice down the sink drain.

From her belongings, she dressed in a sleeveless blouse and blue skirt. It fitted every curve of her body. She smoothed foundation on her face and slapped lipstick on her lips. After sliding her feet into a pair of black pumps, Aniyah tossed a black handbag, compliments of her auntie, on her shoulder.

Peeking out the door, she made sure there was no sign of Lenvy, not wanting to have to deal with her neighbor.

Out on the street, she noticed plenty of the parking spaces were available, since many tenants were off to their jobs. She walked into the direction of Main Street, which was a few blocks away. Down Main Street, she crossed Elmwood Street, where the morning traffic was busy. She continued to walk until she was able view the State Capitol building, straight ahead of her. She also admired the trees along the street, especially the Palmetto Palms.

Aniyah watched as people in their business attire entered office buildings to begin their workday. *Professionals.*

Looking inside the window of a small café, she studied men dressed in dark pants and bleached-clean shirts with ties around their necks. They sat conversing over cups of coffee.

Hot-looking men twirled around in her head and she aimed to get her claws into one of them. Her interview process, she hoped, would start sooner than she thought.

Aniyah's attention turned to a tall building on the other side of the street. She looked up to read the company's name. "Powell Bank," she mumbled, admiring the beautiful glass double-paned doors. Crossing over to be closer to the bank, she watched as the doors swung open repeatedly from bankers going inside.

One day I'll have lots of money to put into a bank.

Instead of going inside, Aniyah went to a vending machine, where she eyed an elderly man walking with a cane. He dropped a few coins into the slot.

"Let me help you." She rushed to his aid, pulling the lever open.

"You're so kind." He brushed the gray whiskers on his chin.

Aniyah reached in and pulled out two Monday's newspapers—she handed one to him and slid the other under her arm.

"Have a good day, Pops." She spotted a nearby bench and took a seat. Unfolding the paper, she read the headline: *"Forecast predicts record summer heat."*

Reading the title made her hot and thirsty. She wanted to go buy a drink, but her plans changed fast when a white limousine drove up in front of the bank. Her eyes blurred from dollar signs that flashed in front of her vision. Aniyah put the paper down on the bench. She waited for the driver to get out. Negative thoughts crept into her mind. She took a deep breath. *What if this is one of the Houstons?* She did not want any contact with her past. She snatched the paper, holding it up to cover her face. She peeked over it.

The driver hopped out and opened the back door. A man who appeared to be in his seventies and dressed in a navy suit got out of the limo. He carried a black briefcase in his right hand. His eyes were puffy from what seemed to her like he did not get much sleep. Wrinkles and wrinkles attacked his face. She did not need another old fart, but the man had to have money, and plenty of it.

"Thanks, Roy. I'll call you when I'm ready to go home," he said. Aniyah listened to his grumpy tone of voice.

"Yes, Mr. Powell." The driver tilted his hat and got back into the limousine.

Her eyes shot straight to the signage on the bank. She wanted to jump to her feet and dance, but instead she sat still, watching Powell, Sr. make his way inside his own bank.

It was time for her to leave. She was anxious to find out everything she could about him, but another limousine drove up.

Aniyah giggled. "What? I'm loving all of this." She kept her eyes on the next mystery person that was chauffeured. She wondered if it was the old man's wife.

The driver opened the door. A younger man holding a briefcase in his left hand stepped out.

Aniyah noticed he did not resemble the first man. The only thing handsome about him to her was the gray tailored suit he wore. She noticed a deep scar on the left side of his face, from his cheekbone to the tip of his lips. It was not the scar that made him unattractive to her; it was his oversized forehead and square head. His belly expanded the suit jacket.

The man never lifted weights in his life.

She saw no bulges coming from his arms much less his pants. But on the other hand he had to have money. *Who is he?* Aniyah wondered. She listened to his conversation with the driver.

"I'll give you a call later. Not sure what time I'm leaving work today."

"No problem, Mr. Powell," the driver said.

"Man, like I've told my drivers in the past. You guys are around the same age as I am. Call me by my first name, Jarvis."

"Yes, Sir." The driver tilted the cap he wore.

"Another Powell. Jarvis Powell. Oh crap. He must be the son," she mumbled.

Aniyah tossed the paper on the bench.

Strutting in front of Jarvis, she buckled to her knees, pretending to fall. Jarvis dropped his briefcase, catching her. She landed on her back into his arms. Her legs stretched long, causing her skirt to rise, exposing her thighs.

"Give me a hand," he called to the driver.

Together they helped Aniyah to a bench.

With his handkerchief, Jarvis fanned her. He studied her beauty while her eyes were closed. He admired the dark eyebrows above her closed eyes. "Call an ambulance."

Aniyah heard the word, *ambulance*. Her eyes popped opened. She acted as if she were in a daze. "Who are you? What happened to me?"

"You fainted," Jarvis said, "and gave me a scare." She eased up, trying to sit up, but Jarvis assisted her. "Take your time."

"I should have eaten before I left home."

"Get her a bottle of water, out of the cooler," Jarvis ordered his driver. "It's too hot to go without food or plenty to drink."

Aniyah smiled at him. "I'm sorry to interrupt your day."

"I love coming to the aid of a stunning woman."

The driver handed Jarvis the drink. Jarvis opened the bottle and placed it to her lips.

Aniyah took sips of the water. "I feel better already."

"Are you certain that you don't need to see a doctor? Or maybe my driver can take you home," he offered.

"I'm good. I'll go and get a bite to eat."

Jarvis turned to his driver. "You can go ahead. See you later."

The driver picked up Jarvis' briefcase, and handed it to him.

Jarvis looked down at his diamond watch, noticing it was ten o'clock. "I have forty-five minutes to spare," he said, gazing at her. "How about I take you across the street and treat you to a meal? I don't want you leaving here falling out again in another man's arms."

Aniyah extended her hand to him. "Then I can't say no."

Jarvis, standing a couple of inches taller then Aniyah, helped her to her feet. He held out his arm. Aniyah locked arms with his. They walked across the street, appearing to be a couple.

Entering the café, Aniyah and Jarvis smelled the aroma of fresh-brewed coffee.

"It's nice and cool in here." He escorted her to an empty table for two at a far-corner window, overlooking a side street with parked vehicles.

When he pulled the chair out for her, Aniyah graciously took her seat. He helped push her chair in closer to the table, covered with a white tablecloth. It was set with Zebra-striped placemats, and a fork and spoon wrapped in white napkins.

"You're such a gentleman," she said, feeling like a princess.

"I try to be." He took a seat across from her. "Now tell me, what's your name?"

"Aniyah Sanchez."

"Hello, Aniyah Sanchez." He held out his hand. "I'm Jarvis Powell."

"Nice to meet you."

They shook hands.

A male waiter handed them menus. Aniyah browsed the menu, but Jarvis knew what he wanted to eat. He had dined at the café numerous times.

"I'll take a cold iced tea. The salmon cakes sandwich with extra mayonnaise is what I'll have." Jarvis handed the menu back to the waiter.

"And for the gorgeous lady," the waiter said, directing his attention to Aniyah.

Jarvis' eyes lit up. "Gorgeous she is," he agreed.

"That's enough." Aniyah blushed. "Give me an order of buttered toast. Iced tea for my drink." Her morning breakfast had her still full.

"You need more than that to eat."

Aniyah chuckled. "One bite at a time."

"So, do tell, do you work around here?" Jarvis was eager to know.

"Looking for a job."

"What kind of professional skills do you have?"

"I...can answer phones. Receptionist," she said, knowing with a lack of office skills that was probably the only job she might get through without getting fired.

"Have you been looking long?"

"First day, and I'm falling apart."

"Are you new to the area or changing jobs?"

"I just moved here from Cancun, Mexico," she lied. *Is this man a detective instead of a banker?* "Hope to find my sperm donor papa."

"So you think he's here in this town. What's his name?"

She paused. "No clue. Black man."

"Whew. That could be any older brother walking around here."

Aniyah put her hands up to her eyes. She pretended that she was about to cry. "It hurt very much when my mama told me she didn't know my papa's name."

Reaching across the table, Jarvis held her hands. He took a deep breath at the softness of her petite hands. The waiter came back with their orders and Jarvis released her hand.

They took bites out of their food.

Jarvis spoke once he stopped chewing. "Maybe I can help you with a job."

"Do you know someone hiring?"

"I'm the vice president of Powell Bank."

"The bank across the street?"

"Family-owned business."

"Sorry for passing out in front of your place of work," Aniyah lied, not making him aware of her devious plans.

He laughed. "My personal assistant, Terry, is going on maternity leave. I'm in the process of reviewing temp applications for her position."

Aniyah took hold of his hand. "Please consider me," she begged.

"The job is temporary. No longer than four months."

"It's a paycheck."

Leaning her head to the side, Aniyah batted her eyes. She watched him take in her sultry look.

"The position is yours." Jarvis figured she would complement his front desk with beauty and brains. It would give him a reason to look forward to going to work, besides business.

Aniyah got up, sat on his lap and pressed her breasts against him. Jarvis sat stiffened in his seat. "I promise you won't regret having me. I'm pretty good at everything I do."

"If you're feeling better, you can come over to the bank with me. Terry will get you started."

Aniyah sat back down in her seat. Her life was changing for the best right in front of her eyes.

"I'm a little rusty, but I do learn fast."

"Nothing major. You'll do fine." Jarvis smiled, knowing she was different than the other women he dated. Her dress nor shoes were of the latest designer wear. Aniyah dressed simple to him. She did not show off a big rock on her finger in hopes of blinding him. Her manners were not of a snob. He felt it was time for him to sample a different kind of woman. He'd had his share of women who lived their lives concerned only about wealth and status.

They resumed eating.

Aniyah took the tip of the napkin and wiped her lips in a sensual way. She caught his attention. He pierced his eyes on her moist lips. *Girl, you still got it going on*, she said in silence. With another napkin, she dabbed her cleavage.

CHAPTER 4

There was plenty of work for Jarvis to review at the bank's main branch in Columbia. He was the vice president, overseeing five Powell Banks, delegated in the position by his father, who thought Jarvis should take his rightful place as his heir. But, after his father's long-time accountant, Mr. Groy, had resigned due to terminal illness, Jarvis was put in charge of his position for the last six months. His father had not yet hired a replacement for the accountant position, so that Jarvis could go back to his regular duties.

Nevertheless, work had to be done. Jarvis sat at his desk, reviewing a printed file of the bank's quarterly budget.

Instead of focusing on the numbers before him, his mind went to Aniyah. *Was she single and could she be the one to fulfill his needs?*

He glanced at the closed mahogany door that separated them. Gripping the pencil that he held tight in his left hand, Jarvis had the urge to get to know her. But after giving Aniyah a job, he realized it was a forbidden rule of his father—she was an employee and too sexy.

Jarvis hopped to his feet. He walked to the door, opening it merely enough to peep out. He eyed Aniyah, leaning over on the desk and conversing with Terry. Viewing her hips, his manly parts reacted. He eased the door closed. Then he shook his leg to relieve his hardness. Once he took his place back at his desk, the phone rang. Jarvis saw the flashing amber light. The call was from his assistant. "Yes, Terry."

"Miss Sanchez doesn't have a contact number to be listed on her application."

"Ask her to come into my office." Jarvis wanted any excuse to see his new employee.

Strutting into his office, Aniyah blurted, "Your girl said you're not going to hire me."

"Take a seat."

Jarvis watched her flop down into one of two brown leather wingchairs facing his desk.

"I don't have a dime much less a phone," she said.

"It's the standard rule of this company that every employee must be able to be reached by telephone."

"I'm out. Thanks for saving me," she said, giving him a wink of the eye. She hopped up ready to leave.

Jarvis got up, running over to her. He caught her by the left wrist. "Slow down. There's always an exception to the rule. Now calm down. Come back and have a seat."

Aniyah flopped back down with her silky Vaselined legs crossed over one another.

Taking his place behind the desk, Jarvis went into a side drawer to reveal a cell phone. "Here, use this until you get squared away."

"You're my kind of…I mean thanks." She swallowed the words she wanted to say and took ahold of the phone.

He scribbled the number down on a sticky pad for her. "Do one thing for me? Don't fill in your number today. Wait until tomorrow. I don't want Terry or anyone else knowing I gave you this cell phone to use."

Aniyah blew him a kiss. "It's our secret." She concluded Jarvis must have had the phone for one of his relationships that went sour. But what did she care; it was a way for her to communicate. Hopefully soon, he would be her main phone contact.

He glued his eyes to the sway in her hips. She swung her arms with the phone he had kept inside the drawer for the past seven months, ever since Carline, his ex-girlfriend, had skipped town on him, in her right hand.

Women always thought of him as a workaholic. Carline had wanted him to be free to escort her around in department stores, like her friends' boyfriends did for them. It broke his heart when she'd left him, but not his father. Jarvis Powell, Sr. had not cared for any of the women he had dated, finding faults in all of them.

Again the phone buzzed. Jarvis was curious as to what else Aniyah was missing on her application.

"Mr. Powell, I want to make sure it's okay for Ms. Sanchez to bring in her contact information tomorrow?" Terry asked.

"That's no problem." He heard Aniyah in the background.

"Girl, what you think, I made it up?"

"I'm doing my job," Terry argued back.

Aniyah opened stacks of incoming mail that the postman had delivered, while Terry handled the many calls that came in.

"I'm tired of opening mail," Aniyah complained. "I feel like I'm working for the post office. What's next to do besides opening mail? This is boring."

"Come here and take my seat." Terry took her time getting out of the chair, weighed down from her huge belly.

"So, whose seed did you swallow?" Aniyah teased.

"My husband's, of course."

Terry stood behind Aniyah, who swiveled around in the leather chair. "I say you don't have kids."

"You got that right. And, no hubby as of yet. Next year, I'll be at least engaged," Aniyah said cheerfully.

"A confident woman."

"I usually get what I want," Aniyah snapped her finger, "any man."

Terry smiled as the phone rang. "Pay attention to how I answer this call."

"Powell Bank, Mr. Jarvis Powell, Jr.'s office. May I help you?"

Aniyah jotted down word for word. She watched Terry screen the call, then connect it to her boss.

"It's that simple. The next incoming call, you'll take it," Terry said nervously.

The phone rang, again. Aniyah followed her instructions, pushing down the flashing amber button to answer the call. She read her script. "Powell Bank, Mr. Jarvis Powell, Jr.'s office. May I help you," she said, but in a sexy voice.

Terry snatched the phone from her. "Hold on, please." She clicked the phone on hold. "Aniyah, this isn't phone sex. This is a business line you're answering. Tone it down." She became annoyed at her new trainee.

Aniyah snatched the phone back and continued with the call. She followed Terry's directions, putting more force in her voice.

"Is that better, teacher?" She swung around to face Terry.

The phone rang three times. "Answer it." Terry cut her eyes at Aniyah.

Their back and forth repeated several times, before Aniyah got the hang of it.

In the middle of a call, Terry let out a loud cry. She grasped her belly. "I'm in labor."

Aniyah witnessed her buckle down on her knees. She panicked. "You better hold that bambino in your stomach until you get to a hospital. I'm not pulling a baby out of your cat hole."

"Ah…!" Terry screamed. She cringed when another sharp pain hit her. Then she began to blow rapidly but stopped for a second and screamed, again. "Forget thinking about your ass. Go get help."

"Girl, labor pains making you curse up in this place of busi… ness."

Aniyah watched her grit her teeth. She realized Terry was in more pain than she thought.

Without warning, Aniyah burst into her boss' office, startling him. He was used to Terry's knocks; his father always came right in whenever he felt like it.

Aniyah yelled, "A baby is about to be dumped out of her cat hole."

Jarvis caught on right away what Aniyah meant. He hurried out of his seat. "Terry is in labor?"

"Yep. And I'm not about to be your nurse, Doc."

Aniyah led the way back into the reception area.

"Call an ambulance," he said frantically, dotting his eyes at Terry, who had rested her bottom on the floor.

Aniyah called 9-1-1, while Jarvis scooped Terry up into his arms, then carried her over to a loveseat, stretching her legs out. But Terry balled up every time a pain struck her below the belly. He stroked her hair, doing his best to keep her calm while Aniyah handled the call.

On the phone, the 9-1-1 operator asked questions Aniyah could not answer. She screamed in the phone, "I don't deliver babies. Hurry here."

"Relax," was all Aniyah heard from the emergency operator.

"I can't. A baby is about to be born right in front of my face." Aniyah held out the phone. "Talk to this woman," she called to Jarvis. "She's nosey as hell."

Jarvis took over the call.

"I'm Jarvis Powell, Jr., vice president of Powell Bank on Main Street. One of my employees, Terry Hagen, is in labor."

Aniyah listened to Jarvis explain to the operator that Terry was eight months' pregnant. He answered other questions with ease, but there was one he needed help with; he directed his attention to Terry. "Did your water break?"

"I believe so." Terry was frightened. She felt the wetness of her undergarment.

Aniyah's eyes shot right to the floor near where Terry lay back on the loveseat. "I see pee from here."

Jarvis took a peek. "Her water broke."

Finished answering the questions, Jarvis traded places with Aniyah, going back to comforting his employee.

Aniyah watched him rub Terry's forehead to console her, while Terry rested between contractions. She stayed on the line until the ambulance arrived, giving her relief to end the conversation.

"I'll ride with you," Jarvis offered Terry, but she refused, only wanting him to contact her husband to meet her at the hospital.

Aniyah did her best to answer the incoming calls. She jotted down most of the numbers for Jarvis to respond to.

Once everything had calmed down, Jarvis confronted her. "I hope you're okay, too," he said.

"Scared the mess out of me."

"Me too. I didn't want to show it and make Terry uncomfortable."

They laughed.

"You did a good job of hiding it. You're nice."

Jarvis smiled, happy to hear her thoughts on him. "I did what I was supposed to do."

The phone interrupted their chat.

"Back to work." Aniyah answered the next call, forwarding it to Jarvis, who had made his way into his office.

A half hour before the end of the day, Jarvis came back to Aniyah's desk. He witnessed her filing her nails. Alarmed by his presence, she dropped the nail file in her lap.

Jarvis didn't bother to scold her. He needed her help. He let out a cough, to clear his throat. "I have a problem. Terry was supposed to stay late today." He needed assistance in preparing for one of his board meetings that was scheduled for the next morning. "Is it possible, you can stay a little late? I'm sorry to ask on such short notice. You'll be paid overtime for it."

Everything was going faster than Aniyah could ever ask for. She put a big grin on her face. "I'm all yours, Mr. Powell, Jr."

"Great. I'll order sandwiches or Chinese food for us to have a bite to eat. I hope that'll satisfy your taste?"

"Food is food."

As he walked away from her, Aniyah glimpsed him licking his lips. It was a sign that he was delighted that he would have the joy of her company.

With her handbag on her shoulder, Aniyah dashed into the bathroom. She brushed her hair to smooth any stray hairs.

Gliding lipstick across her lips, Aniyah turned them juicy red. She pushed up her breasts in the low-cut blouse, exposing more cleavage. To show off her Vaseline-greased thighs, she raised her skirt.

She tossed her handbag over her shoulder. Then she headed back into the reception area, where she came face to face with Jarvis Powell, Sr., president of Powell Bank. He wore a crisp white shirt. The tie around the collar looked as if it choked his neck. Mr. Powell, Sr.'s eyes popped opened when he saw her.

Aniyah spoke before he could get a word in. Twirling her hair around her fingers, she blushed. "You must be Papa Powell."

"That I am," he sternly said, standing tall with his hands in his suit pants pocket. "Where's Terry?" He had noticed the empty chair behind the desk.

"Popping out a baby." She giggled.

"She's not due for another month."

"The pains she was having changed all of that."

Aniyah strutted past him to take her seat in the empty chair. She tossed her handbag back into the bottom drawer.

Powell's eyes widened. He watched the lady dressed like she was at a party instead of a workplace get comfortable in his place of business. He went and rested both hands on the edge of the desk, staring into her eyes. "I know damn well, you're not covering for her."

Aniyah smiled. She reared back in the seat, crossing one leg over another. "I'm your son's new assistant."

Banging his fist against the desk, he angrily said, "Like hell! That boy done lost his peanuts." Powell hurried to the door that led into his son's office.

Aniyah didn't bat an eye. She hollered in laughter. "Get used to me, Papa Powell."

Powell, Sr. startled Jarvis as he entered. He looked up. "Hello, Dad. You're one not to knock."

"Fire that tramp sitting out there," his father demanded, showing authority that he was the backbone of the business that he had inherited from a long line of bankers in his family. And his goal was to make sure the legacy continued.

"Dad, when are you going to start letting me make decisions without you always interfering in them?"

"Jarvis, this building is a bank, not a whorehouse. Get rid of her. She's nothing but a distraction. You've got an empire to run." Powell, Sr. picked up a stack of random papers from his son's desk and fanned them at him.

Since he was a kid, Jarvis had honored his father. Powell, Sr. had been there for him ever since his mother had disappeared from their lives. One way he remembered her every day was by the scar he was told she had left on his face. His father had explained to him that the scar was put there. His mother had hated she had a boy—she had yearned for a baby girl. And, he was told she's run off with another man by the time he was about six years old.

All Jarvis had learned as the man he was today was due to his father. He understood he would have to disappoint Aniyah and let her go. No way would he disobey his father. He owed him that.

"Let me keep her until the end of the week," he begged. "I'll go through the online applications and hire someone else."

"This time, older and ugly," Powell, Sr. ordered.

"Yes, Dad." Jarvis shook his head, submitting to his father's request.

"See you when you get home. My limo is waiting on me." Powell, Sr. turned around and left out, ready to smoke a cigar.

With her left ear to the door, Aniyah listened to their conversation, but rushed back to her seat when she heard Powell, Sr. coming toward the door. She thought Jarvis was the opposite of the old saying; instead of a mama's boy, he was a daddy's boy. This was another obstacle she would have to conquer. She had to react fast. *Old fat head, Papa.*

She rolled her eyes at Powell, Sr. once he came out of the office.

He placed his cigar in his mouth and became distracted by her exposed flesh. "Button up your blouse. Your tits aren't good enough for my son."

Aniyah fastened the top two buttons. She slyly grinned with a bit of sexiness. "He's not my type."

"Hallelujah. I see you got a little bit of brains," Powell, Sr. shouted before he headed out of the office to catch the elevator.

As soon as he disappeared, Aniyah snatched open her blouse. "Your son's money is my type."

CHAPTER 5

No better time than working overtime for Aniyah to put her plans into motion. Luring Jarvis from under his father's spell would be her pleasure.

Aniyah scrambled through the drawer in hopes of finding a bottle of perfume that Terry may have left behind. *Bingo.* She spotted the bottle. She took a sniff and the smell made her gag. *I might as well have been sprayed by a skunk.* Instead of putting the perfume back into the drawer, she tossed it into the trashcan.

Standing to her feet, she checked every vital point of her body. Her breasts were in position, pumped up like a model with implants. Her skirt hung just below her hips. Everything was in place, giving her the okay to proceed into his office.

She opened the door and Jarvis looked up at her. The girl he had rescued had changed her dress code. The skirt that hit almost to her knees had risen to show off her silky legs. But, he drooled over her breasts popped out of her top—begging him to taste one. His head thumped from the thought that at the end of the week, it might be the last time he feasted his eyes on this luscious woman. Loosening his tie, he felt breathless. Aniyah may not have been a keeper in his father's eyes, but she was a winner from his 20/20 vision.

"Take a seat; I'll be right with you," he said, trying to keep his focus on the last paragraph of a memo on his desk.

Aniyah sat and glanced to see what he was reading. "Something real important?" she asked curiously.

"No. The same old, same old. Things my dad expects from me."

"He sure doesn't like me."

Jarvis laughed. "My dad only loves two things: the bank and me." He went back to finish reading the memo. "All done." He looked straight at her legs, spread somewhat apart. The memo dropped out of his hands. His eyes took the place of his hands, mentally touching the silkiness of her legs.

Aniyah stared at the pencil can on his desk, not letting on that she realized she had captured his attention.

Moving his eyes away from her inner thighs and looking at her beautiful face, Jarvis got back to business. "Before we began, I do have something to tell you."

Aniyah was aware that she was about to be fired on the same day she was hired.

"My dad's got a thing about certain type of women working in his banks."

"And, I'm not the type your papa likes?"

"Dad thinks you're too beautiful. His rules. I promised you this job until Terry comes back. But to be honest...I can only keep you for one week."

Aniyah placed her right hand on her cleavage. She gently stroked herself, tilted her head and in a soft tone, she said, "I can't believe I'm getting kicked to the curb. I need this job. No money means no place to live. I'll starve."

"I'm so sorry." Feeling bad telling her she had to leave, Jarvis stood and walked toward her. He also wanted any excuse to get closer. He placed his hand on her shoulder, while all the time he feasted his eyes on her cleavage.

Aniyah rose, falling into his arms. "Please. I need the job." She wept.

"Maybe I can help you find another one somewhere else. Let me try to do that for you, since I promised you a job here."

"You're so caring."

With his tie, Aniyah wiped her fake tears. Jarvis delighted to have her scent on him. He was eager to make an advance at her, but held his cool. Aniyah sensed his attraction to her, more and more.

Jarvis eased away from her. "Let's head down to the conference room." He led the way.

Aniyah followed him to a room, set up with a rectangular mahogany desk, surrounded by twelve chairs. On the table were company logo ink pens, empty water glasses, notepads and black binders filled with documents.

Jarvis instructed her on how to arrange the rectangle table for a meeting. Then he left her alone.

Stuffed in a room was not where Aniyah wanted to be. In front of the seating for twelve, she tossed a binder on the table. Then she continued to complete the rest of her task as instructed.

Once finished, she turned the light off and dashed out.

"Done deal," she said, entering his office. She saw that Jarvis had cleared the desk enough to turn it into a table—set with sandwiches and drinks.

"You should be hungry."

"Yeah, I am."

Aniyah sat down, moving the chair closer to the desk.

"Chicken salad or turkey."

"I'll have the chicken salad."

"I'll check my contacts for you a job." Jarvis watched her eat her sandwich. With each bite she took, he studied the movement of her sultry lips.

"I like working here," she lied. "You can't change your papa's mind."

"He's stern to his word when it comes down to this bank."

Putting the sandwich down, Aniyah picked up a napkin. She covered her eyes. Thinking of her deceased mother, she went into her tearful mode.

"Don't cry." Jarvis stopped eating. He reached for a napkin off the desk. Hurrying over to her, he gently wiped her flowing tears.

Aniyah decided to take a chance, getting up, she threw her arms around his neck, holding him tight. She rested her head on his shoulder.

Jarvis locked his arms around her waist to comfort her. "I hate you feel so bad, but it's not my doing; it's my dad's decision."

Aniyah placed several kisses on the side of his face. She changed the subject over to his scarred face, placing her hand on it. "How did you hurt yourself?"

Jarvis explained in detail of his injury. He was moved by her gesture. No woman he had ever dealt with ever gave his scar so much attention.

"So sad," Aniyah said sympathetically. Then she placed a passionate kiss on his lips. She did not stop there; she forced her tongue inside his mouth.

Jarvis took in her sultry lips against his. He, in return, kissed her back. It seemed like forever to him. He felt his manhood grow and eased his left hand up her skirt, to discover her hidden jewels.

Aniyah felt moisture build up between her legs from the touch of his hand on her flesh. *This is not the time for me to get caught up in how great of a lover he might be—one step at a time.* Right away, she pushed him away. "See you tomorrow." She exited his office. As much as she wanted to continue, things had to go as planned— by the end of the week, he would crave for her and she would not have any need to be an employee of Powell Bank.

CHAPTER 6

In the backseat of the limousine, Jarvis glanced down at his crotch, making sure he no longer had a bulge in his pants. He licked his lower lip, still feeling Aniyah's luscious lips against his.

Loosening his belt hidden under his stomach, he mumbled, "Time to hit the gym again." No way was Aniyah going to leave his life without him having a sample of what she was like in bed. "Good night," he said to the driver. Then he hopped out of the limousine.

Entering the foyer of the family home, he flicked on the light switch. The chandelier hanging above his head sparkled.

Jarvis set his briefcase down on the hardwood floors. The stale odor of his father's cigar tickled his nose.

From the upper level, Powell, Sr., dressed in his cigar robe, came down the flight of stairs. He puffed his Cuban cigar that hung from the side of his mouth. "You're just getting home?" he fussed.

"I stayed behind to get things ready for the morning board meeting."

"I guess you kept that tramp behind to help you."

"Yes I did, Dad." Jarvis loosened his tie. "I needed the help."

"How can you be so damn dumb to hire a tramp? You saw the way she dressed and looked."

"She needed a job," Jarvis said, hoping his father would have a change of mind about Aniyah. "I feel like she needs a chance."

"The hell with her," his father roared. "Put her back on the streets. She can handle that better."

"You don't even know her. You're outright being cruel."

Jarvis attempted to walk past his father, but Powell, Sr. caught him by his shirt. He blew smoke, fogging Jarvis' face.

"I'm not letting anything I've built be messed up because you feel pity for a pretty face. You saw what happened with my old friend, Rupert Houston. I let you read the articles about him."

"Dad, that was sometime ago. You can't blame Aniyah for what that other woman did to him. Every person is different."

"Damn you, Jarvis, stop being blind. Women like her use their body goods to draw in powerful men like us. Rupert got caught up with a tramp and got him nothing but a heart attack. And problems for his daughters."

"Okay, Dad, I understand," Jarvis said, not wanting to hear more of what his father had to say. He jerked away from him and went straight upstairs to his room, one of seven master suites that had been through many design changes since he was a kid.

An all-natural mahogany, king-size bed rested up against the soft taupe, faux-finished wall. The bed was covered in a duvet with touches of taupe, burgundy and green tones. Artwork of jazz musicians in mahogany frames hung throughout the room. A marble-trimmed gas fireplace was only for cold nights, not for romantic evenings. His father never allowed him to bring women into the home.

Jarvis kept any type of involvement with women private as long as he could. Aniyah would be no different. The enjoyment of her soft lips and her body close to his made him realize that he would not let her out of his life yet. He would cover his tracks to keep his father clear of his relationship with her.

On the nightstand, Jarvis clicked the switch of a crystal lamp to turn it on. He went under his mattress, picking up a photo of his mother holding him as a newborn.

As a teen, meddling in his father's shoe closet, he'd discovered the photo, buried in an envelope. Powell, Sr. would no doubt throw it away if he learned he had taken possession of it. It would be *trash* exactly like his mother, so his father would say.

Studying the photo, her smile made him feel welcome, but her actions to leave him when he was small made him feel alone. The glow in her eyes gave him a sense that she was a kind woman. Nothing read on her face that she would abandon her child. His father painted his mother as a deceitful woman, only caring about her needs, not his or her child's.

The clock read eight o'clock. Jarvis wondered what Aniyah was doing. He thought of how she might be soaking her body in a warm tub of water. He wished he were with her to bathe her back, and place kisses on her neck.

Removing his white shirt, Jarvis heard one bang on his room door. He hurried, tossing the photo back under the mattress.

Powell, Sr. entered without him giving the okay to come in.

Jarvis sat on the bed. "Yes, Dad."

Powell, Sr. walked over to him still puffing on his cigar. "I decided I would do the hiring for you."

"Dad, it's my office."

"You don't seem to do a damn good job at hiring."

"The person will be working for me. It should be my call."

Enraged, Powell shouted, "Until I take my last breath, I own Powell Banks. You have no say-so in this matter." He poked Jarvis in the chest. "Deal with it."

Swallowing every bit of his anger, Jarvis watched as his father choked on his cigar, turned around and walked out. The cough did not faze Jarvis; it was a part of his father's smoking habit.

Furious, Jarvis threw his shirt across the room, then kicked off his shoes. He mumbled, "I'm nothing but his puppet. The hell with him."

Jarvis echoed the words he had said many times, but he always winded up right back submitting to his father's requests. This time he was convinced he would do what he wanted to do.

Lying in the darkness of his bedroom, and in the quietness of the house, Jarvis felt there was no life to the family home. Holidays were spent with he and his father sitting across a dining table, seated for twelve. No real conversation, except talk about business at the bank. There were no home-cooked meals from a woman of the house, only servants.

Throughout his childhood, he was groomed for banking. Powell, Sr. had him counting money ever since he could remember.

Then came his schooling; as a kid he dreamt of becoming a criminal justice lawyer, but he was reminded by his father, that he was to continue the legacy of bankers in the family. Jarvis graduated with degrees in accounting and marketing.

Turning on his side, he reached over and felt the other side of the bed. The sheets were cold from never having a warm female body to heat them up. If it was up to him, he would have a woman by his side, but the rule of the home was that none of his dates were allowed in the Powells' home. Jarvis figured his father was afraid that a woman would come and plant her feet in the home— rob the Powells of their assets.

All his relationships started out strong, but somehow everything went sour when he introduced them to his father. No one Jarvis dated ever lived up to his standards.

He decided from here on out, he would make it his business not to date snobby uppity women that only cared about diamonds, spa appointments, yachts and country clubs, and going on shopping sprees to spend money because it was at their access. Self-centered was all they were. He believed Aniyah was not that way. He presumed from the way she dressed she did not have those issues.

CHAPTER 7

By the end of the previous day, Aniyah was tired from learning how to work phones and Jarvis. But this sunny day, she was refreshed from a good night's sleep.

She knocked on her neighbor's door.

"Morning, Foxy," Lenvy said, eyeing her red-hot dress, with a neckline that scooped low enough to give him an eye full. "You ready to join me in bed," he teased.

"Hell no! Boy, I need your phone number in case something comes up around here."

He hit her with his digits and in return, Aniyah gave him hers.

"Bye." She strutted, giving him a moment to feast his eyes on her swinging hips and legs, moisturized in Vaseline infused with shea butter.

Employees dashed through the revolving doors of Powell Bank. Aniyah was among them.

She took her time walking on four-inch, high-heeled, open-toe black shoes. The dress she wore hit nowhere near her knees. Her face was padded with a little extra makeup. Black eyeliner darkened her already black eyelashes. The lipstick she wore looked as if she had finished drinking pomegranate juice.

As women entered the bank, Aniyah eyed them. They did not

have a thing on her. Most of them wore flowing skirts down to their knees or short summer dresses. The attention was all about her. She was on her mission to win the next-in-line top man of the bank or else she would be back on the streets to search for another wealthy man.

Businessmen kept their eyes on her, but whispers and giggles came from the women. *They're jealous.*

She caught a glimpse of herself in a wall-to-wall mirror, painted with Palmetto Palm trees. Aniyah struck a pose, and then headed to the elevator.

The doors opened and she, right along with other employees, got on the elevator. She stood against the back silver paneled wall until it was her turn to get off on the sixth floor.

Her heels sank into the blue carpet in the receptionist area. She went straight to her desk and took a seat. Opening her handbag, Aniyah pulled out a box of condoms that she had purchased at the pharmacy the previous day. She had fooled around long enough in the sack without catching a disease, and she wasn't about to become someone's mama anytime soon. She slipped a condom in her bra, and then she tossed her bag into the bottom drawer.

As she darted her eyes at the closed door to her boss' office, the phone rang, startling her. She lifted the handle off of the receiver. "Here I go," she mumbled. She could not wait to leave the job for good. "What's up?" What she'd learned about answering the phone the previous day from Terry had totally slipped her mind.

"That's no way to answer a damn call," Powell, Sr. scolded her. "My bank is a place of business, not a hip-hop club."

"Oops, I mean, Powell Bank."

"I see right now you're not going to last to the end of this day, much less a week," he complained.

"Excuse me." Aniyah crossed her legs. "I'm not that awful."

"Let's say, you're not winning points with me. Get my son on the line."

"I was going to see if he's in yet." She put him on hold. She clicked another button, connecting with her boss.

"Good morning, Aniyah," Jarvis said, delighted to hear her voice.

She answered in her sexiest voice. "Yes, it's good, now that I hear your voice, Mr. Powell."

After a long miserable night of loneliness, Jarvis was happy to hear a pleasant voice. He smiled. "Come into my office when you get settle."

"I aim to please, but your nasty papa wants to talk to you."

"I'll handle Dad."

Aniyah connected them. She ran into the bathroom, giving herself a once-over. Then she hurried out and went straight to her boss' office, anxious to go fishing and reel her man in. She knocked on the door.

"You may come in," Jarvis called.

Aniyah stepped inside.

Jarvis, who was about to take a sip of his black coffee, spilled it on his white shirt when he eyed her curves in the dress. A strand of her flowing hair lay on her opened collar. He prayed his father would not come down to his office and fire Aniyah on the spot before he could hire someone else to replace her. "Good morning," he said, placing the cup on the desk. Jarvis pulled his handkerchief out of his lapel pocket. He dabbed the spill on his shirt.

"A hottie morning to you." He knew this was her cue to get closer to him. She took the handkerchief out of his hand, wiping his shirt, but a stain had been made. "Take it off. I'll wash it for you," she suggested.

"That won't be necessary; I keep extra clothing around here," he said, with fumbling fingers. He felt the softness of her hands as he took the handkerchief from her, but his eyes were radar on her cleavage as she leaned over.

Aniyah did not hesitate to take advantage of the moment; she sensed his attraction for her. Pushing her way onto his lap, she smothered his lips with a kiss.

Jarvis, weakened from her touch, threw his arms around the middle of her back. They realized that passionate sex was long overdue for the two of them. The phone rang and Jarvis came up for air.

"We have to answer that. It may be my dad, again," he said.

"Forget him." Aniyah loosened his tie.

"I can't do that. My dad would be down here in a heartbeat. He would think right away there is something going on between us. I don't need him on my back." He snatched the phone off the receiver. "Jarvis Powell, Jr."

"Teach the tramp to answer the phones immediately when it rings," his father complained.

"She's in the restroom," Jarvis lied, loving the kisses Aniyah placed on his neck. "What's wrong, Dad?"

"What time is your board meeting?"

"It was eight o'clock this morning. It's over with."

"Email me a copy of the minutes. And tell that damn tramp, I don't want to see a bunch of errors on it."

Jarvis looked up at Aniyah, aware she had heard his father's loud voice. "Dad, her name is Aniyah."

"Tramp," Powell ranted before he silenced their conversation.

While Jarvis eased the phone back on the hook, Aniyah tickled his right earlobe with her tongue. "I know your papa doesn't like me. But you have the hots for me."

"You're tempting."

Aniyah kissed his lips. "Take me home with you tonight."

"I live in the family home. My dad would run you and me out."

"Sneak me in." She eased her hands down to his lap. "I'll become a reality for you."

His male parts had begun to react. He was not about to let a cold shower do the job, when in front of him was the woman he desired. "The…penthouse. We can go there," he disclosed. It was his getaway spot.

"Sounds like fun." Aniyah closed her eyes. She laid a succulent kiss once again on his lips while she touched the only solid muscle on his body.

Jarvis tried to pull down her lace panties, but Aniyah moved his hands. She jumped up off of his lap. "More, later."

After she straightened her dress, she blew kisses at him. Then she winked at him, deciding not to reveal her condom packet.

Overheated, Jarvis wiped the sweat off of his forehead. He had never dealt with women that made him chase behind them. Most women gave in easier. "We'd better get back to work." He recalled the minutes from his morning meeting. "Before you go, please type into the computer these minutes. My father's assistant, Suzy, handwrote them. Her tablet crashed once the meeting got started."

Being an employee for one day, Jarvis did not trust Aniyah to handle his meeting.

She took possession of the minutes. Then she put motion in her stride, letting his roaming eyes capture her curvy hips.

Out at her desk, Aniyah called her neighbor on her cell phone. "Hello, Lenvy."

"Hey, sexy, what's up, Baby?" Lenvy said.

Aniyah teased him. "I got a bedtime date with my man."

"That's too much info. I'm not getting the goodies."

"Whatever."

Aniyah looked up to see Powell, Sr. standing in front of her. "Got to go, Lenvy." She clicked the end button.

"No cell phones or personal calls. Wait for your break," he said. His eyes flashed to her clothes. "There's a dress code around here. You'd better find out quick what it is."

"That cigar stinks." Aniyah held her nose. "I look good." She modeled in front of him.

"Not good enough to be prancing around my son." Powell, Sr. came closer to her, pointing his finger in her face. "I'm familiar with your kind. You want to get in his pants to get to his pockets."

"You see this." Aniyah swung around. "I don't have to do anything. A man and his money will come on its own to me."

Powell, Sr. stared into her face. Aniyah felt uneasy, thinking he might recognize her from previous news articles.

"You make sure by Friday, you're gone. Back on the streets, where you belong," he said and marched to the elevator.

"Asshole," she grumbled, but let out a sigh of relief that Powell did not recognize her.

Powell, Sr. went straight into his son's office, but it was something about Aniyah that was familiar to him. He couldn't pinpoint it. "I'm telling you, that tramp out there is nothing but trash, if I ever saw it," he said, annoyed at Aniyah.

"Dad, please stop complaining about her. She'll work to the end of the week and be gone."

"I've already hired someone to replace her on Monday."

"Dad, let me hire my new assistant."

Jarvis made his way over to a file cabinet, searching for a folder.

"You call that tramp decent hiring," his father argued. "A stripper, that's what I see in her."

"Come on; that's pretty low."

"I call it as I see it," Powell, Sr. complained.

Jarvis removed the file he wanted and faced his father. "Dad, stop being so difficult."

Powell, Sr.'s eyes went right to the spot on Jarvis' lips where Aniyah had left her lipstick mark. "I don't believe you." He gritted his teeth, taking his white handkerchief from the inside pocket of his gray suit. And as if Jarvis was a kid, he wiped his lips. The lipstick spotted the handkerchief. "You've been with her."

Jarvis wiped his lips of any unfound lipstick. "Dad, my personal life has nothing to do with you."

"I want her gone!" Powell demanded, poking Jarvis in the chest. "Your life belongs to me. You'll see who is really in charge. Let me catch you with that tramp. Don't play with me. Remember, you're Jarvis Powell, Jr. The end of this day…ditch her."

"Come on, you said Friday," Jarvis argued furiously. He took every poke his father gave him.

"Today," his father shouted, pounding his fist on the cabinet. Powell, Sr. took several puffs of his cigar. "I want her gone." Being the top man, he did not follow the non-smoking rule of the bank nor the city code.

The door slammed. Jarvis was left to give Aniyah the bad news.

Inside the receptionist area, Aniyah pecked away on the computer. She turned toward the sound of Powell, Sr.'s harsh voice.

"Keep your damn lips off my son."

Aniyah smirked. "Jarvis, lips are delicious."

"You're jobless," he roared, pointing to the exit sign. "Get your stuff and let the door hit you in your rear end."

"You old mean pig."

Before Powell headed out, he shot back. "Just get the hell out."

She did not wait for the elevator doors to close behind him. She ran into the office.

"The old grouch says I'm fired," she whined.

"I'm sorry, Aniyah."

It did not faze Jarvis that Aniyah called his father out of his name.

She began to cry. "I really need this job to keep up with my rent."

Jarvis consoled her. "This situation is my fault. I thought that I'd wiped away your lipstick. I'll cover two months of whatever your rent is."

"You'll do that for me?" Aniyah wept and rested in his arms.

"It's the least I can do for you." Jarvis held onto her tightly. The warm touch of a woman's body made him ready to get away from his boring life. He was convinced she had to be a part of his world. Caught off guard, Aniyah kissed him again. He took in her sultry lips before he came up for air, hoping their evening plans were not called off. "It's still on with us tonight."

"Hell yeah. I need a shoulder to cry on."

Jarvis wiped her tears. "Please work to the end of the day."

Aniyah was not about to leave yet. "I'll stay and finish your minutes." She touched his lips before she sashayed away.

By the end of the workday, Aniyah pecked on the computer the last line of the minutes. Jarvis had to come and correct several of her typos before the minutes were emailed to his father.

Aniyah was relieved that she would no longer have to be bothered with office work. It was not her thing. She gathered her belongings ready to leave to start her new line of work.

"Give me five minutes," Jarvis said, peeping out his office door.

But five minutes turned into another twenty minutes. Impatient,

Aniyah found her way into his space. Jarvis held the phone to his ear. She could tell he was in a deep conversation. He put his index finger on his lips when he noticed her. She presumed immediately that he was speaking with his father.

Pushing aside a stack of papers, Aniyah hopped on top of his desk. She leaned back on her elbows, stretching her legs out in front of him.

Glowing like a solar light, Jarvis watched her kick off her shoes. While he continued his conversation with his father, he massaged her right foot. "Dad, I see what you're saying. I apologize. See you at home." He hung up the phone.

"Getting on Papa's good side," Aniyah teased.

"I want to keep him away from my personal life."

"You mean me, the tramp he thinks is not good enough for his son."

"Dad thinks no lady is worth me. But, I say you and I can be perfect for each other."

Jarvis leaned forward and placed a kiss on her lips.

"Time will tell."

"I have to stay a little bit longer—about fifteen more minutes. Dad wants me to finish going over some figures that are not balancing in today's tally."

"I'll wait outside for you."

"No. I don't want to bring any attention to us. Meet me around the corner. I'll be in the limo. What are you driving?"

Aniyah lifted her dress. She extended her legs and pointed to her feet.

"Getting around on these," she said.

He laughed.

After jumping off the desk, Aniyah put back on her shoes, leaving Jarvis to finish his duties.

It showered on the streets. The curbs were full of puddles. Aniyah had no umbrella to keep her from getting wet. She decided to stand in the doorway hoping the rain would stop.

"You're still here?" Powell, Sr. questioned, sneaking up behind her. He carried an umbrella in his left hand and a briefcase in the other.

"I'm waiting on a friend who works here," Aniyah lied.

"I should fire her ass, also."

"Maybe it's a male." Aniyah smirked.

"As long as it isn't Jarvis Powell, Jr."

"I have no interest in your son," she fibbed.

The rain steadily poured.

"You should invest in an umbrella, instead of slut dresses."

"Go choke on your cigar. Leave me the hell alone."

"Good riddance." Powell, Sr. laughed, pushing her out into the rain. Then he snapped open his umbrella. He made his way to his limo parked out front.

Tripping on her heel, Aniyah fell right into a puddle of water. She scuffled to her feet. Her dress soaked and clung to her body. Her makeup washed away to show off her natural beauty.

She ran over to the limo, banging on the window until the driver pulled off with Powell, Sr. in a burst of laughter.

"Payback will be a blast," she bellowed.

Aniyah ran around the corner with her hair laying flat to her head. She found shelter under a store awning.

Before long, Jarvis arrived in his limo. He hurried with an umbrella to protect her but noticed she was drenched. "What happened?"

"Your papa pushed me down."

"I apologize for my dad's stupidity." Jarvis held the umbrella above her head, walking her to the limo. He opened the door and Aniyah got in. Running to the other side, he joined her. He instructed the driver to take him to the penthouse.

Aniyah squeezed water out of her hair, which dripped on the beige leather seats.

It was not long before the limo parked in front of a tall building. Jarvis directed his attention to the driver. He handed him a roll of money. "You drove me to the movies."

"My lips are sealed," the driver said.

The rain continued to pour down as Jarvis led Aniyah out of the limo, holding the umbrella above their heads.

They walked inside a lobby full of an array of flowers throughout. It made Aniyah think of springtime. She shivered while she walked with Jarvis to the security desk.

The security guard, wearing a black suit, recognized Jarvis right away. "Good to see you, Mr. Powell. It's not football season."

During game time was when Jarvis frequently visited the penthouse.

"I thought I would come by. This here is Aniyah, my guest," Jarvis announced.

"Nice meeting you, Ma'am," the guard said as Jarvis noticed his eyes popped wide open at the wet dress that clung to her body. A wave of the hand was all Aniyah gave him.

"Here you go." Jarvis pulled out of his pocket a hundred-dollar bill, handing it to the guard. "You never saw us."

"I got you covered." The guard took off his glasses. He chuckled. "I'm blind without these bifocals."

Jarvis put his arms around his date, and led her to the elevator. A quick second and the elevator doors opened.

Jarvis slipped a private keycard into a slot and the elevator doors closed. He pushed Aniyah up against the wall, smothering her lips until the doors opened to a luxurious penthouse apartment on the eleventh floor.

Aniyah kicked off her shoes right away. Her feet sunk into the plush white carpet. The open floor plan of the living room made her think her whole apartment could fit in it. She saw Jarvis was a true football fan. On the wall, in the living area, behind the black leather sectional sofa set was a large framed photo of the South Carolina football team.

She walked in and admired the kitchen, painted white, the same as the living room. The appliances were made out of stainless steel and the countertops were black granite, which displayed a canister set made in the shape of a football.

The chill from the air conditioner made Aniyah fold her arms. "I need to take off these wet clothes."

Once she pulled her dress over her head, Jarvis saw underneath her garments was wet as well. If he did not know any better, he would have thought it was Valentine's Day.

"Follow me, I'll show you to the bedroom. I have a robe you can put on until we get your clothes dry."

Jarvis led the way to the right side of the home. Aniyah tiptoed behind him down a hallway where more football pictures decorated the walls. She entered his master suite. Her eyes lit up when she saw the cherrywood, king-sized bed, made up in a champagne lightweight quilt set. Over the bed was another framed art piece of a football stadium. "You love football."

"Yes, it's my passion," Jarvis stated. He had made his way into the master bath and gotten a Ralph Lauren towel off a rack. Returning, he handed it to her to dry off.

Aniyah slipped out of her undergarments while he headed inside his walk-in closet to get her a robe. She dried her body off, then let the towel fall at her feet.

When Jarvis came out of the closet, his eyes jumped back and forth from the fullness of her shapely breasts to her inner thighs.

With her arm stretched long, he attempted to hand Aniyah the robe, but she snatched her hand back, letting it fall to the floor on top of the towel.

She kicked the towel and robe to the side. Then she loosened his tie, removing it from around his neck. She playfully used it to dance with.

Jarvis removed his suit jacket, concentrating on how fast he could get out of the rest of his clothing. He did not want to delay the action that would turn his master suite into a love nest.

Aniyah got on the bed. She shook her breasts. "Come, tackle me."

"I love a touchdown," he said, finally free of his pants and boxers. He gave Aniyah a view of his manhood.

She was surprised he was not a part of the weenie club. His thick prime meat was hidden under his baggy suit pants. She disregarded his other faults, jumping straight into his arms. As if she were a football, he caught her.

He lay her back on the bed, leaping on top of her. They kissed.

Aniyah was well prepared, handing him a condom for his manhood.

Jarvis eased inside her. As he stroked her with force, he smothered her lips, and gave her a juicy kiss, followed by taking one of her breasts for his delight.

She worked her body right along with his. So caught up in how good of a lover he was, she forgot she was the one that was to get him to hunger her. Before she knew it, she let out a loud scream; with Jarvis exploding like he had popped open a bottle of champagne for New Year's Eve, but instead it was summertime.

With sweat dripping down his chest, he rolled off of her. The rapid beat of his heart felt like he had finished doing a set of pushups. "I wish I could hold you in my arms all night." He placed a kiss on her forehead.

"I'm not going anywhere."

"I have to go home. My dad will be wondering where I am."

"He'll probably guess you're with me."

Jarvis laughed. "He'll be right."

The softness of the pillow-top mattress felt so comfortable to her. Aniyah was not about to leave without making this her new place of residence. She turned on her side. "It's so nice here," she whined.

Jarvis pulled her back over on her back. "We'll have plenty of time to come here to be with each other. I promise."

"This bed is like cotton. Sleeping on my friend's couch is miserable. Her four kids use the beds. I have no money."

Jarvis was puzzled. "I assumed you lived alone and handled your own rent."

She realized she had added more lies about her living arrangements. Her scheming was a little rusty, but she hurried, getting back on track. "Six hundred dollars a month I pay to sleep on a couch," she said quickly. Aniyah placed her hands on her spine and moved from side to side, pretending her back was in pain.

Without any thought, he belted, "Stay here tonight. Sleep comfortable."

"What if your mean papa shows up during the night?"

"He knows nothing of this place." It was his secret place that his father had no clue about.

"This can be our love nest." Right away, she forgot about her problems. Aniyah began to play the game of getting him permanently trapped into her web, but at the same time, she would enjoy the great sex he knew how to give. She pampered his body with her tongue from his head down to his toes, absorbing the taste of his flesh.

Before he could get a chance to cover up his manhood to reenter her passage, Jarvis exploded.

Not complaining, Aniyah was disappointed; she had wanted him to hump her one more time.

It was getting late, and Jarvis did not want his father snooping around in his personal life. "I have to go." Jarvis slipped his clothes back on.

"See you tomorrow." She passionately kissed him goodnight.

Jarvis pulled out a couple of twenties. "Here, take this as a bonus for your hard work."

"What? I'm not a hooker."

"I didn't mean it that way. It's for your hard work at Powell Bank."

"Then I accept. Thanks, honey." *And I accept my new place to stay.*

Aniyah jumped into her clothes. She walked a distance in the rain to her apartment. She grabbed her clothes, tossing them into a large trash bag.

Aniyah set the key to her apartment on the desk, leaving a nasty note beside it for her Aunt Tessa. She did not bother to knock on the neighbor's door to inform him she was moving, not wanting to explain her life to him at that moment.

Making her way down the street, with the trash bag in her arms, she headed back to her new home. Joyfully, she sang, "I'm in the money and the honey."

Jarvis was the full package—money, a great bed partner and a nice guy.

Back at the penthouse, she decided to get in contact with her neighbor.

"Hello." Lenvy yawned.

"Wake up. I called to let you know I've moved. I'm living big-time now."

"You don't play, do you?"

She giggled. "Sometimes you gotta do what you gotta do."

"Don't act like you don't know me when you see me."

Aniyah laughed as she hung up. "You're history, Lenvy." She deleted his number from her contact list.

CHAPTER 8

Resting in the backseat of the limo, with his eyes closed, all Jarvis thought of was in less than forty-eight hours was that he'd rescued a beautiful woman, given her a job, fired and bedded her, and now he had given her full access to his penthouse.

"Damn, man, you're smarter than that," he yelled to himself.

The driver looked back at him, "Is there something wrong, Sir?"

Jarvis waved his hand at him to give him the okay that he was fine. "Thinking out loud." He calmed down.

All he saw with his eyes closed was the vision of Aniyah's plump breasts. He was tempted to order the driver to turn back around and take him to her. But he decided to go home.

His gut feelings told him that she was the woman in his life. Like his penthouse, she would be his secret as well.

Morning couldn't come fast enough. Jarvis stopped at the penthouse before he went into the office. He entered into a quiet place. Aniyah slept, snuggled under the covers.

Removing his clothing, he crept into the bed. Aniyah awakened once he swallowed her into his arms.

"Good morning." She hopped up, running into the bathroom. "Sorry, I have to pee."

He laughed. "Did you sleep well?"

"The best in a long time."

Aniyah finally came back to bed. He kissed her, smelling the odor of toothpaste, while he glided his fingers through her hair. "I love messy morning hair."

"I love a naked man in bed."

Jarvis felt the touch of her left foot, easing up his right leg. She stroked his manhood until it hardened. He moaned.

He locked eyes with her, watching her rip open one of the condoms. She covered his manhood. Then she slid it inside her. She rode him like she was a trained jockey.

Jarvis flipped her over and took control. He stroked her with force, sweating to the point he was like a leaky faucet.

Together they climaxed. Jarvis fell back onto the bed, breathing like he'd had a panic attack.

"I want you in my life," he admitted.

She whispered in his ear, "That means you want me to stay here."

Before Jarvis could answer, her tongue got lost in his mouth. Again, they reached another climax.

Checking his watch, Jarvis saw that he was an hour late for work. He hurried and got dressed, while Aniyah, nude, walked him to the elevator.

"Thanks for letting me stay the night." Aniyah placed a peck on his lips.

Jarvis pulled her into his arms. He gave her a sultry kiss. "You're not going anywhere." He reached into his pocket, handing her a spare key.

Aniyah tossed the key in the air, catching it several times. She went from room to room, admiring her new living quarters.

CHAPTER 9

After spending most of her life taking care of bigger homes for the wealthy, it was light stuff for Tessa to clean the 3,000-square-foot home that she shared with her husband. Baron Chavis insisted on her hiring help, but she would not hear of it. She felt it was her duty to keep their home spotless.

The cheesy smell of her chicken enchiladas baking in the oven reminded her that it needed to be checked. She turned the vacuum cleaner off, making her way into the kitchen.

Tessa washed her hands in the stainless steel basin. Beneath the sink, inside the cabinet door, she pulled off a sheet of paper towel from the towel holder. Then she dried her hands.

Opening the oven, the aroma of seasoned chicken went up her nostrils. She removed the Temp-tations ovenware, placing it on top of the smooth countertop stove.

Her pots of black beans and rice had finished cooking ten minutes earlier. She decided to eat a little before dinner. Scooping the beans and rice onto the plate, Tessa laid an enchilada on top. She grabbed ahold of a wooden handled fork.

Instead of eating at the table, she took a seat at the kitchen island, surrounded with barstools.

Steam seeped from the chicken. She blew on her food until she was able to eat it. "Yummy," she said, tasting the spices of the dish.

Once finished, she cleaned the soiled dishes. She took off the apron she wore over her floral blouse and mid-length skirt, then folded it and placed it in a drawer.

She surveyed the kitchen. The counters were clear of any kind of kitchen gadgets. The appliances were hidden behind the numerous cabinets. She headed into her husband's study, got the vacuum cleaner and put it inside a hall closet that housed the cleaning goods.

The grandfather clock in the foyer chimed. One…two…three chimes, she heard, informing her that it was three o'clock in the day.

Tessa went into the master bedroom, ready to slip on her shoes but felt her up-do hairstyle was about to fall down. Instead of putting on her shoes first, she twisted her hair back up, securing it with bobby pins. She stepped her feet into a pair of yellow flats. Then she tossed a multicolored straw bag on her arm.

Inside the garage, Tessa got into her car. One flick of the remote, and the doors slowly opened. She eased out of the driveway. Her destination was to visit Aniyah. She did not look forward to seeing her wild niece. It made her angry that Aniyah was stubborn and headstrong.

It took Tessa thirty-minutes to arrive at the apartments. Her bag swung as she moved her arm. She rang the doorbell and waited, but there was no answer. After pounding on the door, there still was no answer.

Her last resource was to call her niece's name. "Aniyah, are you in there? Answer the door."

After another call to her niece, Tessa was convinced she was not at home.

Lenvy heard her. He opened his door. "You're wasting your time," he called. "Home girl don't live there anymore."

"She moved?" Tessa asked, turning to see Lenvy in the doorway dressed in a pair of shorts.

"She's like the stock market; she's moved to the top for now."

"Where to?"

"You got to take that up with her. Not my business to keep a check on a pretty lady."

Tessa, scared for her niece, assumed the money she had given to Aniyah was long gone. "I smell trouble," Tessa said with tears almost in her eyes.

"Maybe she'll call you."

"I doubt that. You don't know my niece." Tessa fumbled in her bag, locating the spare key. She dangled it.

"Lady, you're fussing and got a key?"

"I didn't want to barge in on her. I got this place for my niece for three months."

"Too much info for me. Got to go." Lenvy closed his door.

Tessa unlocked the apartment. Inside, she noticed a note left on the table.

"Dear Auntie: I'm out of here. You put me in this raggedy place, while you live in your high-class home. This is a jail cell. I have a better place to live, no thanks to you. Don't look for me. Mama is dead and so are you. You have your life. I'll go on and live mine. I'm my own family. Aniyah."

Tears rolled down Tessa's cheeks. She brushed away the wetness on her face and locked the apartment door.

No faster than he clicked the lock on the door, Lenvy was on his cell phone. Two rings and Aniyah answered on the other end.

"Hey, Hollywood," he said.

"You must have the wrong number," Aniyah said. A male voice was all she could detect.

"Oh, too high and mighty to remember your old neighbor."

"Lenvy?" Aniyah thought he had written her off as well.

"Glad to hear your memory still works."

"What the hell do you want?" she asked, before she decided to give him the final goodbye.

"Your peeps came by here looking for you."

Lenvy snapped open a can of beer. He took a deep swallow out of it.

"Aunt Tessa?" Aniyah realized that would be the only person who could be looking for her.

"Drives a nice Benz," Lenvy admitted.

"Whatever. No big thing. I got a limo driver."

"Work it, Baby. Come pick me up for a spin."

"Lenvy, go take a ride on a bus." She'd had enough of his conversation.

"Oh, you dissing me after I call you to give you the four-one-one."

"Delete my number. I only take calls from my man."

"So it's like that," Lenvy said, aggravated with her. "See you next to the garbage when your warranty wears out with him."

She wiped her forehead. "Jerk!"

Lenvy hit the END button. Aniyah was left with a dial tone.

Back at home, Tessa walked inside to run into her husband.

Aware of her niece's history, Baron understood his wife's tearful face. He empathized with her. "What has Aniyah done?"

Tessa showed him the letter. After reading it, Baron tossed it into a nearby trashcan. He threw up his muscular arms from weight lifting around her.

"It's for the best she's gone. The Houston sisters won't have to ever know she's free."

"She's my sister's child." Tessa pulled away from him. "I don't need you to be cruel to me like Rosie Aniyah."

"I love you." He pulled her back in his arms. "Your niece doesn't. I told you, she'd hurt you." Baron held Tessa tightly not let her pull away from him again. "Your niece lives in a fancy world."

"I thought she was better. She had lots of psychiatric help in jail."

"It doesn't help everyone."

"I pray she doesn't wind up back in jail," Tessa cried.

"No more tears. Wherever she's at, she's where she wants to be."

Baron loosened the bun in his wife's hair to let the bobby pins fall to the floor, and her hair fell freely. He placed kisses on her tearful eyes.

Lifting her face with his right hand, he kissed her on the lips. He eased his left hand under her dress, sliding her panties down to her ankles.

He scrambled his pants opened to fall. With her body flushed to the front door, Tessa moaned when he entered his hardened manhood inside her.

Aniyah's worries were no longer a concern to her. It faded away with every tingling sensation and movement of passionate sex her hubby gave her.

CHAPTER 10

With clothes scattered on the bed, Aniyah debated what to wear. Dress relaxed was what she had remembered Jarvis telling her during their morning conversation. Her hands went straight to the denim capris and a tank top. Slipping them on, she slid her feet into the flat sandals, exposing her freshly painted toes.

"Is my date ready to go?" Jarvis stepped off the elevator into the penthouse.

"Putting on lipstick." Aniyah smacked her lips, dropping the tube in her handbag.

She placed the bag handle on her shoulder. Then she walked into the living area.

She was happy Jarvis had begun hitting the gym. She admired his body, for the inches he had begun to lose around his waist-line. Patting him on his stomach, she complimented him. "My man is getting fit."

"Got a few more pounds to go."

Aniyah pulled on his blue khaki tie. "This is not relaxed." She loosened it.

"I always wear a tie."

"Not today." Aniyah took the tie from around his neck. She went on to remove his khaki jacket.

"You're undressing me." Jarvis' scar disappeared as he smiled.

Aniyah giggled. "Not all the way. We wouldn't get out of here." She unbuttoned two of the buttons on his three-quarter-sleeved shirt, exposing some of his chest. "Sexy." She kissed him on the chest.

Jarvis saw that Aniyah was not letting up on her flirtation. In return, he teased her back, sucking the lipstick off her lips.

Aniyah tried to unbutton more buttons on his shirt, but he stopped her.

"Can't spoil the date I've planned."

Aniyah eased away from him, licking her lips. She replenished her lips with lipstick. "You haven't told me yet where we're going."

"Lake Murray. You may want to carry a sweater around the water."

"You're taking me to your papa's house?" Aniyah's eyebrows rose. She was anxious to get a tour of her future place of residence, hopefully.

Jarvis shook his head. His answer was not what she wanted to hear. It was going to take baby steps for her to get into the Powells' home.

"We're going to dine on seafood. You do like seafood?" he asked, knowing he loved the fresh fish caught from the lake.

"Of course. Any fish stuffed with crabmeat."

"Whatever your taste bud desires."

Aniyah didn't bother to get a sweater. She pushed the elevator button for them to leave.

Outside, she looked for a parked limo. Jarvis walked over to a two-seater, royal-blue convertible Mercedes-Benz. "I'm your personal chauffeur." He opened the door.

Aniyah eased into the ride. Her butt sank into the leather royal-blue seat, giving her the feeling she was sitting on the ground.

Jarvis hopped in, throwing his jacket across the backseat. With a click of a button inside a panel between the seats, the rooftop rolled back. He sped off with Aniyah's hair blowing in the breeze.

They drove for a while until they came to a bridge to cross. Aniyah stared at the body of water. She marveled over the view. She had found her passage back into Lake Murray.

"I love it here. And, you will, too," he said.

If you only knew. She dismissed her thoughts and sat back while he drove her to the marina, where they would dine.

Boats were docked on the side of the restaurant. Aniyah heard loud beach music playing but could not see where it was coming from. She walked with Jarvis along the graveled walkway.

They held hands while they climbed the stairs to enter the full operating restaurant, where people dined, and on the other side, had drinks at a covered-top deck bar.

Right at the top of the staircase, Aniyah came to a halt. Her eyes shot right at her Aunt Tessa and hubby, clinging champagne glasses. She eased behind Jarvis. With sweaty palms, she pulled her hand away from his. Aniyah recalled noticing the bathroom was on the lower level of the double-deck staircase. "I need to use the toilet," she said, panicking, and dashed out of sight.

Jarvis stood with his hands in his pants pockets. He immediately noticed Tessa's hands waving for him to come over to the table, where she dined with her husband.

He took one last look to see if Aniyah would reappear from the bathroom. Then he hurried over to say hello to the Chavises before she would return.

"Hello, Jarvis." Tessa smiled. "Good to see you."

Jarvis gave her a peck on the back of her hand. "It's good to see you, Mrs. Chavis."

"Good to see you, man. You're here with your father?" Baron asked. He stood and gripped Jarvis' hand to give him a handshake.

Jarvis looked back to see if Aniyah was coming, not wanting to be seen with her by his father's business associates.

"I'm enjoying the fresh air. Might get a bite to take home with me."

"You're welcome to join us," Tessa suggested, pointing to an empty chair at the table for four.

Jarvis noticed a bottle of champagne on ice. "No, Ma'am. Looks like you're celebrating a special occasion."

Baron smiled. "My love for my wife." He rested his hands on top of hers. "You'll be doing this soon once you find the right lady."

"I hope, Mr. Chavis, she's as beautiful as the woman on your arm."

Jarvis patted Tessa on the shoulder. He noticed that Tessa had dark brown eyes and recalled in her younger days, her hair was once fully black like Aniyah's.

"That's sweet of you to say." Tessa blushed.

Jarvis looked back again for his date. "I should be going. Good to see you, Mr. and Mrs. Chavis. Enjoy your meal." He shook hands with Baron one last time. *How am I going to detour Aniyah?* He had no idea.

Inside the bathroom, Aniyah closed the stall door. Then she took a deep breath. Her appetite had vanished. She scratched her hair. "I can't stay in here forever," she muttered.

Thanks to two women speaking of taking a boat ride, she decided that would be her excuse.

Outside the bathroom, she saw that Jarvis awaited her.

"I'm not geared up yet for eating," he said.

Aniyah was relieved. "Let's rent a boat. You do know how to drive one?"

"Of course I do. That was my plan for us, after we ate."

"Food can wait. Take me out on the water."

Aniyah pulled him by the hand toward the exit. Jarvis moved as fast as she did. They made their way out of the restaurant area.

He put his arms around her waist, leading her over to a pontoon boat. It was inscribed with his name on it.

Aniyah raised her eyebrows. "This is your personal boat."

"Last year's birthday gift from Dad."

Jarvis held her by the arm, helping her inside.

She sat right across from him. He started the engine. Her hands sweated more once she eyed the body of water. She did not have a clue how to swim.

"Can I have a life jacket?"

He laughed. "The boat comes equipped with them. But it's not necessary. You're safe."

Jarvis eased out from the dock.

Aniyah settled back in the seat, taking several deep breaths while he drove onto the lake. She watched other boaters race by them. Not far away, she admired the luxury homes.

"Out here is where you leave your worries." Jarvis admired the waves of the water.

"You come here often?"

"Not as often as I would like to. But now I have you to share it with."

Jarvis stopped in the middle of the lake and parked.

Aniyah panicked. "Oh hell, no, don't tell me this boat has broken down?" She fanned herself.

"There's no problem," he assured her. He came to her and stroked her hair. Then he placed kisses on her neck.

Aniyah placed her arms around his waist, turning his face to hers to connect with his lips.

The horn of a boater blew once their kissing became an attraction.

"Way to go, man," a boater bellowed.

Aniyah waved her hand at the boater.

Jarvis went back to his seat. Annoyed, he roared up the engine. "Nosey folks."

He drove to the dock of a place of residence.

The sun disappeared under the moon. Aniyah eyed the back of the house. "That's a mansion. Who lives there?" she asked, pointing.

Jarvis chuckled. "I do. This is part of the Powell Estate."

"You're not scare your papa might see me?"

"We're on the ballroom end of the estate."

Jarvis cut the engine off. He no longer worried about ongoing boaters. Hurrying over to Aniyah, he locked lips with hers. She, in return, unbuttoned his shirt and he took it off the rest of the way to expose his chest.

She tossed her tank top and bra on the seat. The coolness of the evening air tickled her nipples.

They kicked off their shoes. Pants went flying. They were free of being hostages of clothing.

Jarvis laid her on the floor and rested her head on an inflatable pillow.

Aniyah pulled him down on top of her, connecting her lips to his once again. She held a strong grip around his neck.

Jarvis eased his hand up her right leg to reach between her legs, entering his middle finger inside her. He played with her until her juices wet his finger.

"You're delicious," he whispered, licking her earlobe.

Aniyah, with her legs spread far apart, felt Jarvis about to ease his manhood inside her. She stopped him. "Baby, you got to cover your goods." She pointed to her handbag and he dashed for it.

He watched her remove a condom from the box, turning it over to him. Once covered, he entered her. It did not take long before they belted a loud scream. They relieved themselves of any tension in their bodies.

Jarvis rested on the floor near her. He focused his attention on the sky and pointed. "See those two stars close together."

Aniyah looked up. "I do."

"That's us. Two lucky stars."

Aniyah rolled over on top of him. "One more round before we leave," she whispered. Aniyah took charge, using her tongue once again to explode every part of his bronze body. But Jarvis did not let her stay in charge for long; he tossed her on her back, entered her, and together they moved to one beat. Aniyah cried out, not wanting him to ever stop.

Jarvis kept riding her as long as he could before he exploded.

They lay flat on their backs, taking a break before they got dressed.

Overworked from passion, they had built up an appetite. Jarvis drove the boat back to the marina. Aniyah had no doubt her aunt and hubby were long gone.

The sound of the band playing on the platform from the bar caught her attention. They headed there. She patted her feet as she dined on crabmeat-stuffed flounder, while Jarvis tackled the Coastal Seafood Bow-Tie Pasta, topped with shrimp, mussels, lobster and scallops in white garlic butter sauce. They drank two glasses of white wine. Jarvis sipped on his while Aniyah gulped hers down.

"You care for another one:" he offered.

Aniyah browsed the cocktail menu.

"I want a Margarita."

She was served three drinks, gulping down each one. Attempting to stand up, her head twirled and her body wobbled like a floater on the lake.

Almost falling back into the seat, Jarvis caught her around the waist. He led the way out.

"He's my man," Aniyah bragged to a female bypasser, presuming she was eyeing Jarvis.

"I'm yours," Jarvis agreed. "I'm sorry," he whispered to the woman. Then he rushed Aniyah to his vehicle.

She steadily tried to kiss on him as he helped her inside. Jarvis slammed the door and got in himself. Aniyah did not give him a chance to start the engine. She reached over and tried to remove his shirt.

"Baby, you're drunk. Sit back. Let me drive," he argued, pushing her hands away.

"I feel good." Aniyah flung her hands behind her neck. "And, I'm hot."

Jarvis drove off.

To his surprise, Aniyah scooped off her tank top, removing her bra. She tried to undo his clothing, but he fought her off. To avoid an accident on the highway, he pulled off the road and stopped.

Jarvis grabbed her bra.

"Here, put it back on, now. This is not ladylike," he scolded.

She snatched the bra from him. "But I'm hot." She turned her lips down into a pout.

"Put it back on, Aniyah!" he demanded.

Aniyah bent over and let her breasts fall into the bra cups, snapping one hook to fasten it. Jarvis helped her slip back on the top.

"You mad at me?" Aniyah continued to pout.

"Next time you drink only what I drink."

About the time they reached the penthouse, Aniyah had fallen asleep. He carried her inside his place. Then he undressed her, putting her to bed.

His attraction for her was strong, but he wondered if she would fit into his lifestyle. Only time would tell, he thought. But her behavior tonight was not something he would accept.

A few hours later, Aniyah awakened with a headache. She realized she was in bed, but Jarvis was not by her side. She picked up the phone and contacted him.

"You're back to reality," he said.

"I have no clue how I got home. The drinks got to me."

"I'd say they did. You yelled at people. You took your clothes off in the car."

"I was that bad?" Aniyah played along with him. What was Jarvis thinking? They were on the town having a good time. What did he expect? she questioned herself.

"I don't like that side of you. It's not becoming of a lady."

"No more drinks."

"Only two."

This was one mistake she would not make with him again. The date could have caused her to be booted from the little security she was trying to hold on to.

The next few days, Aniyah called and texted Jarvis but got no answer. Chewing on corn chips, she paced the living room floor until the bag of chips was empty.

The elevator doors opened. Suited down, Jarvis entered the penthouse.

Dropping the bag at her feet, she ran into his arms, smacking kisses on his face. "I'm so sorry about getting drunk."

"That's the past. I admit I was angry. But, I decided I won't hold it against you."

"You're my kind of man." Aniyah loosened his tie, pulling it from around his neck.

"I have to get back to work. I'm between meetings." Jarvis took control of his tie.

Aniyah ignored what he said, pulling him by the arm over to the sofa. She pushed him down in the seat. Then she squatted her butt on his lap.

Scrambling with his clothing, she removed his jacket and unfastened the buttons on his shirt. She eased her hand down to the crotch of his pants. Jarvis' manhood grew in an instant.

Aniyah did not stop there. On her feet, she dropped the robe that she pranced around in, letting it fall to the floor, followed by the gown that was hidden underneath.

Again, she sat on his lap, pushing him until he rested on his back. She unfastened his pants, and slid them off, including his boxers. *Whatever clients are waiting on you, darling, will just have to wait.*

Aniyah reached between the cushions of the sofa and pulled out a safety packet. With honors, she covered his hardened manhood with a condom. As she eased it inside her, between her legs she felt a tingling sensation. She yearned for his body as much as he yearned for hers.

"You're too much," Jarvis barely said, while he held on to her jiggling breasts. She rode him like she was in a rodeo.

Sweat built up on their bodies. Once they exploded, Aniyah fell down on his chest. She hated that which felt so good ended too quick.

They rested for a moment, before Jarvis gave her a kiss. "I got to get back before Dad starts looking for me." He got up and grabbed his clothes, slipping them back on. There was no time for him to jump into the shower. The scent of Aniyah's body would have to stay with him.

"I wish you didn't have to go." She lay naked.

He landed one last kiss on her forehead. "Got to go. I'll give you a call."

Once Jarvis was gone, Aniyah ran into the bathroom, where she showered.

How am I going to keep from falling for this man that makes me feel alive? She let out a loud scream. "I can't. The bankroll is all I need. Cha-ching!"

CHAPTER 11

*I*t was a typical end of a weekday at Powell Bank. Tellers waited on customers who cashed paychecks, made deposits or withdrew funds from their accounts.

In the service department, five club chairs in the waiting area were occupied with others that needed to handle their financial business.

On the sixth floor, Jarvis sat behind his desk reviewing financial documents. But on the eighth floor, Powell, Sr. lay back in his office chair.

One flick of the lighter, and his cigar was lit. He took a few puffs on the cigar, leaving it dangling on the side of his mouth. He sat upright in his seat. The first of the month had slipped by and he had catching up to do. He removed a stack of bills from a brown cardboard file, which had nothing to do with business. He took his time writing checks for his home mortgage payment to his American Express bill. There was one last bill he needed to pay.

He stood and walked to a wall safe, stored behind a self-portrait. Unlocking it, Powell, Sr. pulled out an envelope. Leaving the safe unlocked, he made his way back to his desk.

Inside the envelope, he pulled out a photo of the person he was happy to issue a check to. He'd been making the payments for years, but it was worth what he received in return.

Once the check was written, and he was ready to address the

envelope, he was interrupted by the buzzer on his desk phone.

"Yes," he answered to his receptionist, who was much younger than the receptionist he had hired for Jarvis.

"There's a man here to see you. He won't give me his name. He says you know who he is."

"Send him in."

Powell, Sr. rushed to the safe, giving it a push to close it. When he hung up the portrait to cover it, his visitor, whom he had been waiting to hear from for weeks, entered.

He eyed the young man with dusty-blond hair, dressed in dark blue jeans, and fitted white tee shirt, with a black cap, turned backward on his head. A pencil rested on his right earlobe and a diamond post glittered on his left lobe. In his hands, the young man carried large manila envelopes.

"It's about time you come up with something. You're the slowest private eye I've ever met."

Powell, Sr. sat back down at his desk. He tossed papers on top of a photo and flipped the check on the blank side.

"Highest payer gets worked on first," the private investigator uttered.

"Don't give me that crap," he argued. He flagged the investigator to reveal what he had for him. "Show me what you came up with. And it better be worth my money."

"Cash, please," the private investigator said, holding out his right hand.

Powell, Sr. went into his drawer, taking out a white letter-sized envelope. "Here you go. Now give me what I ask for." It did not take long before he obtained the envelope. He pulled out the first photo. "Where is this place?" He studied the photo of Jarvis going into the upscale apartments.

"Address is on the back. It belongs to your son."

"He owns nothing."

"Oh, he does. That penthouse crib is paid in full."

"He'll have some explaining to do." Powell studied the rest of the photos. He looked at the next one. It was a photo of the back of Jarvis, but he did not recognize immediately the woman next to him. "Who's the broad?"

"Aniyah Sanchez."

Powell, Sr. crushed his cigar into an ashtray. "The tramp I had him to fire. How stupid can Jarvis be?"

The investigator chuckled. "Keep looking, there's more." He got a kick out of his clients when they witnessed the dirt he unfolded of their loved ones.

Powell, Sr. went to the next photo. His eyes widened. He stared at Jarvis' and Aniyah's lips glued to each other. Other photos showed them out on the town, Jarvis leaving late at night from the penthouse, and him holding his wallet in front of the security guard.

"Explain this one." He pointed to one of the photos.

"Your son is paying off the guard to keep quiet about the chick and his crib. She's living there, full time."

Powell, Sr. snatched another cigar from his cigar box. He lit it and took a puff. Wrinkles crushed together in his forehead. "Jarvis will pay for this. I'll handle her. I'll fan a few bucks in the tramp's face. She'll be gone."

"All you have to do is say the word. I'll get the rundown on her."

"I want good stuff to get her far away from the Powell fortune."

"Two thousand…dollars." The investigator shook the loose change in his pocket.

"Get the information."

"Is it a deal?"

"Deal. Get going. Get to work."

"I aim to deliver." The investigator smiled. He dropped the next envelope on the table. "There you go. All the info you need on her."

"You con artist." Powell, Sr. chuckled. "But I like your style."

The envelope unveiled Aniyah's history, which included several articles written about her before she went to prison.

"I'll be...damned. I thought she looked familiar. She tried to get over on my buddy, Rupert Houston's family. Now she's going for blood. My family fortune." He fumbled through the photos and located the one with the address of the penthouse written on the back. "The tramp has met her match," he said angrily and jumped out of his seat. He crushed another cigar into the ashtray although he had paid good money for them.

Powell, Sr. rushed past the investigator.

"Hey, what about my cash?" The investigator watched him exit the office.

"Bill me," he yelled back at him.

"I want cash." No pay, no photos was his motto. He gathered up the rest of the photos left on the desk. Then he dropped them in their rightful folder. His eyes brightened when he lifted the articles up, discovering a photo and check left on the desk. He peeked to see whom it was written out to. "Jackpot," the investigator rejoiced, matching the check to the full name on back of the photo. More curious, he looked inside the envelope and got more information about the person Powell, Sr. was dishing big bucks to. He made his way over to a copy machine, and printed his newfound information—more ammunition to add to his findings. He placed the items back on the desk in their same position and decided to dump his envelope of photos, scattering them on top.

Outside the penthouse, the private investigator parked a few car lengths from where Powell, Sr.'s limo driver was parked. He turned his cap forward on his head, pulling it down on his face. He looked inside to see Powell speaking to the security guard.

With his camera in his hands, the investigator snapped photos of them exchanging words, while nibbling on an apple.

The investigator decided he needed to get closer. He switched shirts, tossing a yellow tee shirt over his head. Inside the glove compartment, he removed a pair of dark shades and a fake mustache. He disguised himself.

Entering into the lobby, the investigator took a seat in the lounge area, near an unlit fireplace.

He picked up a magazine off of a table, then held it up to his face, pretending to read it. He listened to Powell's roaring voice.

"I'm not here to negotiate with you. I'm Jarvis Powell, Sr."

"I'm sorry, but I can't let you up, unless the owner gives me the okay. I'll give him a call," the guard said, picking up the phone to contact Jarvis.

Powell, Sr. reached over, snatching it out of his hand. He clicked the button to the OFF mode. "This is between you and me. Trust me," he said to the guard, "by tomorrow you'll be bagging groceries at someone's supermarket. I'll personally buy this place."

The guard saw that he had gone a bit too far. He was speaking to a man that had power to make him lose his good pay. He submitted. "You win. But you better cover my back if I wind up losing my job."

"If that happens, I'll make you one of my security people." Powell, Sr. chuckled. He felt grand that his power had overruled. He shoved a hundred-dollar bill in the guard's hand. "Buy yourself something." Powell, Sr. patted him on the back. "Good fellow." He chuckled again.

In the corner, the investigator snapped more photos until Powell, Sr. disappeared into the elevator.

CHAPTER 12

In three months, living at the penthouse, Aniyah had turned the master walk-in closet into her personal store. Handbags took over the top shelf. Rows of designer garments hung on hangers and boxes of shoes were stacked on the floor.

She marveled over the drawers of lingerie Jarvis had purchased for her. Every intimate moment they spent together, she wore the sexy pieces, being his private lingerie model.

After one of their nights of passion, he'd placed a diamond necklace around her neck and latched a diamond tennis bracelet around her wrist. He wasn't a man with looks, but his devotion to her began to make her see men in a different light. As much as she wanted to fully open her heart to let him in, she had to keep her heart closed to not get hurt.

Out of the drawer, Aniyah took out a white sheer gown that was neatly folded on top. Her weight had gone down some, but her curves were still in the right places.

Slipping the gown on, she pranced in front of a free-standing, floor-length mirror. She marveled over her jewelry. She stared at her breasts through the gown. It was Jarvis' tongue she needed to pamper the firmness of her nipples. Aniyah decided to invite him for a delightful lunch treat.

Returning into the master bedroom to call him, she sniffed the odor of tobacco, which led her to go into the living room to see where the aroma was coming from.

The white around her pupils showed, when she noticed Powell, Sr. comfortably sitting on the sofa. She propped her hands on her hips. "Who let you in here? Leave."

Her eyes beamed on the elevator door, but Powell, Sr. stayed put.

"Go put some clothes on," he fussed.

"Leave," she repeated, turning away. She headed back into the bedroom.

Powell, Sr. followed after her.

Aniyah grabbed a pair of pants, but before she could put them on, he snatched them from her. He shoved his cigar into the leg of the pants, burning a hole in it.

"That's a good pair of jeans," she argued.

Powell, Sr. gripped her by the wrist, turning her to face him. He snatched off her sparkling necklace, leaving a nasty mark. He snatched off the bracelet and everything went into his pocket.

"You crazy jerk, give me back my jewelry," she said hysterically. She tried to reach for his pocket, but he slapped her across the face. She felt a burning sensation on her cheek. Stubborn, she did not shed a tear.

He pushed her onto the bed. "You played over my friends, the Houstons, and now you think you're going to embezzle money from the Powells."

Tears rolled down her face from the words he spoke about her, even though she had to admit to herself that what he said was true. She eased her way to the top of the bed, unaware of what to expect next.

From the rage in his eyes, Aniyah prayed Powell, Sr. did not try to kill her. It was like he was after her for all the wrong she had ever done in her life.

"I want you out of my son's life. You hear me?" he scolded. He made his way to the top of the bed, attempting to grab her again, but Aniyah dashed out of the room.

"Jarvis...wants me." She tried to make her way to the elevator.

Before the doors could open, Powell, Sr., with a ball of her hair in his hands, dragged her back toward the sofa.

Aniyah felt a sharp pain in her scalp. She cried, "I'll leave. Now let me loose."

Her long locks fell from his hands.

"I have a lot invested in Jarvis, and you're not about to mess things up."

She wept. "I need to say goodbye to him."

"Not in this life. Get dressed and get lost." Powell, Sr. pointed in the direction for her to leave.

"Pay me," she said bravely, hoping her words would not cause her harm. "I've been your son's lover. I say I need to be paid for the time I wasted with him."

She watched, as he did not flinch. Powell, Sr. removed his checkbook from his inside suit pocket and scribbled a check. It had to be enough to hold her over until she found another man.

He held his hand out and she took possession of the check, staring at the unbelievable amount. Her eyes brightened like a flashlight. "One dollar?"

"That's what you're worth."

She tore the check up into bitty pieces, tossing them at him. "At least give me back my daggone jewelry."

"It was bought with Powell money. Go work the streets. Buy your own. Be gone or I'll tell Jarvis about you. I'll even give a call to your Aunt Tessa and tell her I'm calling the police on your sorry ass," Powell, Sr. shouted, while he walked over to press the button for the elevator.

With her aunt married to an attorney, Aniyah was not surprised he was her acquaintance.

She moved her body, coming on to him. "You want me all for yourself?"

Powell, Sr. chuckled. He pulled out a hundred-dollar bill, dangling it. "Money is the only thing that turns me on. Get the hell away from our lives." He stepped into the elevator and disappeared.

Aniyah screamed, "I hate you, old fart."

Her plans to invite Jarvis for lunch were shattered.

She trashed the burned pair of jeans, slipping on another pair. Her head hurt from the thought of having to leave the life she felt secure in. But she was happy she had kept most of her heart in check. A piece of it was going to miss Jarvis; for the good person he was, nothing like his father.

She collected what was most important to her to pack into one of the gifts from Jarvis, her Gucci luggage. She decided to leave the row of lingerie he loved to see her in. She sprayed spritzes of perfume on several pieces, leaving the scent to be his memory of her.

Tears flowed down her face as she rolled the luggage to the elevator. The doors opened, with her almost peeing in her pants.

"Going on a trip," the private investigator said, turning his cap backward on his head.

Aniyah stepped back, fearful that the investigator was there on Powell, Sr.'s behalf. She trembled. "I told fat head I was leaving. Please don't hurt me."

"Gorgeous, I'm not a hit man. I get dirt on people."

"You work for old fart, Powell?"

"Got the goods on you for him."

"You nosey creep," Aniyah fussed.

Losing control, she beat on him with her handbag.

"Chick, get off me," the investigator dodged her blows, "I'm here to save you from leaving his son."

Aniyah stopped swinging. She took a deep breath. "Talk fast."

"The banker likes pushing people around with his cash."

"'I Spy,' he wants me out of here. So I'm leaving. I'm not going back to jail."

"Forget about the slammer. All you have to do is get three thousand dollars from the banker for me...you won't have to leave."

Aniyah placed her hands on her hips. "He gave me a check for a dollar. And you think he's going to up and give me three thousand. You're giving me a migraine." She placed the palm of her hand on her head and took a seat on top of her luggage.

He waved the envelope in his hand.

"What you got there?" Aniyah jumped up to snatch the envelope from him, but the investigator held his arm up over his head. She tried to grab it but could not reach high enough.

"The goods on the banker are going to cost you three thousand dollars. Get it out of him, unless you got cash."

"I have nothing. Let me see what you got."

"Are we in this together?" he asked, still waving the envelope.

"Of course."

He lowered his hand. Aniyah grabbed the envelope, opening it.

"You turn on me. It's hell, Gorgeous."

"I won't. I promise." Aniyah examined the goods. She studied the woman in the photo. "This freakin' can't be."

"Turn the picture on backside."

She read. "Sina Cole. Is this Jarvis' mama?"

"There's more." Out of the envelope, he showed her the copy of the handwritten check. Aniyah saw that it was written to the woman. She became suspicious. "I thought Jarvis' mama ran away and left them."

"Rich men love writing their exes off with money. He's been paying her every month for years."

"That creep," she said but did not understand why Powell, Sr. was paying her monthly payments. "I wouldn't give money to someone who left me. Where is she?"

"I need to get paid for this information before I dish out any more."

"This will do for now," Aniyah said excitedly, flipping her hair around her finger.

"You tell banker man you know about her, he'll negotiate a fee for you."

"I won't have to leave." She grinned. Her headache vanished. "I can stay right here. Take me to Powell Bank." Aniyah began to get back her ruthless ways.

"Three thousand dollars for me. Cash only," he said.

"Wait for me downstairs. I'll be right down."

The investigator took a seat on the sofa. "I'll wait right here." He was not about to let Aniyah pull any fast trips on him.

The floors became a dance floor. Aniyah bounced around. She unpacked her luggage to not let Jarvis get suspicious in case he stopped by while she was on her errand.

All the clothes went back into the closet. Out of breath, she spoke, "Let's go do this."

The investigator pointed his finger at her. "Don't try to pull a fast one over on me. Or else," he warned.

"I'm so scared. I'm shaking." She wiggled her fingers in his face.

With the investigator on her heels, Aniyah turned around and headed for the elevator.

The investigator beamed. "You're not as weak, Gorgeous, as you tried to make me think you were. But you still better pay me my cash."

The floor to Powell, Sr.'s office came soon enough for Aniyah. She stepped off the elevator, heading straight into the reception area.

She strutted up to the desk. "I'm here to see old fart, Mr. Powell."

The receptionist peeked over her box-shaped frames propped on her nose. "Ma'am, is everything okay with you?"

Aniyah did not think much of what the receptionist asked of her. "I want to see the old fart," Aniyah demanded, raising her eyebrows.

"He's informed me that he doesn't want to see anyone."

"I'm Aniyah Powell," she responded.

The receptionist wondered what family member was Aniyah. She called her boss, introducing Aniyah exactly as Aniyah requested.

His voice escalated through the intercom. "That tramp isn't a Powell. Tell her to leave. This is not a strip club."

"I don't think so." Aniyah marched into his office.

"Get out," he yelled. "I warned you." He picked up the telephone.

Aniyah ran over, and using her index finger, she pushed down on the receiver.

"You had your way with me at my house. Now it's my time to call the shots."

"You don't give up. Do you? Let's call my son to come join in our conversation."

"Go right ahead and call him. We can talk about his mama, Sina Cole. The one you're been paying off to stay away."

"Nonsense." He loosened his tie. He lifted open his cigar box and lit one. "I know no broad by that name."

"Yes you do," Aniyah said, as she was about to make up a partial lie. "You see, the same way you can get things on me, I got former prison friends that can get information for me in a snappy. I've got a copy of the check to show Jarvis that his papa is still in contact with his mama. He'll want nothing else to do with you either."

Aniyah watched him wiped sweat from around his forehead and neck. She enjoyed seeing him squirm. "Having hot flashes?"

"You're trash," he roared.

"Recycled into a treasure for your son," she said, holding her hand out. "Give me back my necklace and bracelet."

Powell, Sr. did not procrastinate. He took the jewelry out of his pocket, throwing it at her.

Aniyah picked the broken pieces up off the floor.

His main concern was to get her off the subject. He did not want the rest of what he was hiding to be investigated. "It's about money to tramps. How much do you want?" he asked, scratching his forehead.

"It's sure not a damn dollar." Aniyah rolled her eyes and head. "Six thousand dollars. I have things to do."

Everything was going smooth for her. Powell, Sr. was not as tough as she thought he was when pushed into a corner.

He did not flinch. He pulled out his checkbook. Check number 3200 was written to her. "It's worth every penny to get you off my back." He flung the check at her.

Graciously, Aniyah snatched it off of his desk. Her eyes went straight to the amount. "That's better."

"Now be gone!"

"I'll leave when I'm good and ready. The penthouse is where I'll stay as long as Jarvis wants me there."

"It won't last long. He'll learn the truth on his own about you."

"He'll be hurt twice in one day. 'Cause I'll sure give him the lowdown on how his papa knows where his mama is."

"Ridiculous."

Aniyah got closer to him, yanking the cigar from his mouth. She broke it in half.

"That's a damn good cigar. You know how much one costs?" he roared.

"Less than my diamonds you broke."

She reached for the wooden box that stored his cigars. Powell, Sr. scrambled to take the box from her, but she got a grip on it. She grabbed a handful of cigars, crumbling them like she was mixing ground beef. Aniyah laughed. She sprinkled the pieces on his desk. "Stay out of Jarvis' and my way. He's not your possession. He's my man." She dropped the cigar box on the desk.

"You'll pay for this," he bawled.

"Love you, too, future father-in-law."

"Like hell. You won't carry my family's name."

On the first floor of the bank, Aniyah went straight to the teller, who was surprised to see the amount written out to her.

"I'll have to get the check approved."

"Do what you gotta do? Hurry up." Aniyah was annoyed.

The teller kept her eyes on Aniyah while she got Powell, Sr. on the line. Without question, he approved the release of the funds. Aniyah took it in big bills, placing three thousand of the money in a separate envelope.

Outside she got into the investigator's vehicle and handed him the envelope. Catching her off guard, the investigator took her by the chin. "That's a beauty you got on your neck. And your cheeks are rosy."

She brushed his hand away, then pulled down the mirror over the dashboard. "That piece of lard will pay for this," she said, wondering how she was going to explain her bruises to Jarvis.

"I'm proud of you." The investigator opened the envelope making sure he was not double-crossed.

"You saved me from having to leave."

"Take my card. You might need me again."

"I probably will need to locate Jarvis' mama soon."

Aniyah placed the card in her bosom. Opening the car door, she stepped out.

"I'll give you a ride back home," he offered.

"Our business ends here."

Aniyah waited for him to drive off before she ran across the street to deposit her money in another bank for safekeeping.

But little did she know, the investigator had circled the block and returned. He looked to see where she went, but he saw no sign of her.

The day had been turmoil for Powell, Sr. He would find another way to get rid of Aniyah. He put his thoughts to work. It would be his son he needed to get to in order to get rid of her.

Up from his desk, he was about to head down to Jarvis' office when the investigator stormed into his office.

"My receptionist is not doing her job." Powell, Sr. was aggravated.

"She must be on a potty break."

"What are you doing back here?"

"My money you owe me."

The investigator no longer wore the mustache or glasses. He had changed back into his original clothing.

"I told you to bill me. I got things to take care of," Powell, Sr. insisted.

"I work in cash only. This is my off-the-record job."

"I'll give you your money. Wait outside my office."

"No funny business." The investigator left out,

On a wall behind a picture of golfers was another hideaway safe. Powell, Sr. used the same key as he used for his other safe to unlock it.

But outside the office, the investigator saw that the receptionist had not returned, giving him time to snoop. Through a crack in the door, he watched the banker remove large bills, but at the same time, he steadily looked behind, making sure the receptionist did not catch him. He watched him lock back the safe, hanging the picture over it.

Powell, Sr. tossed the key in his desktop drawer. He hurried out of the door to catch the investigator, who had parked in a seat, as if he had never snooped.

The receptionist still had not returned.

"Get lost." Powell, Sr. handed over the funds. He was worn-out from confusion.

Heading to his vehicle, the investigator snickered. His day of earning was productive. He had made enough to take a vacation.

CHAPTER 13

With two Advils thrown to the back of his throat, Powell, Sr. swallowed the pills with a glass of water. His head throbbed from his wrongdoing.

He closed his eyes, thinking of the sacrifices he had made to keep a grip on Jarvis. It took a woman for him to bring downfall to the success of a businessman. One day, a man could be on top of the world, and as soon as a woman lured him into marriage, then divorced him, the courts rolled his fortunes over to her. All the man was left with were his clothes, a room and his pride. Business suits were traded for rugged shirts and jeans.

The more he contemplated of how Aniyah was on the move to put his son in that position, the more his head throbbed. He craved for a cigar to smoke, but on his desk were the crumbled cigars, thanks to Aniyah.

Browsing through papers that needed his review and signature, Powell, Sr. was not in a work frame of mind. He got up, reached for his briefcase and strolled out of his office to the receptionist's desk.

"Hold all calls for the rest of the day."

"Is there a problem, Mr. Powell?" The receptionist noticed his flushed skin.

"I have a lot going on. See you tomorrow."

Outside, the limo awaited him. The driver opened the door and he got in.

"Take me home," he grumbled.

"Will do, Mr. Powell." The driver saw that he did not have his usual smoke stuck in his mouth. "Out of cigars?"

"I'll light one up, when I get to the house."

In the front of the limo, the driver reached into a storage compartment, pulling out a fresh cigar.

"Here you go, Sir."

Powell, Sr. was relieved. "The day I've been having, I needed this bad."

"I try to keep two extra cigars in the limo for you."

Powell, Sr. sniffed the cigar for freshness. His throbbing headache began to fade when he concluded that the cigar was okay to smoke. He fired it. After a deep puff, he blew smoke and was relieved. He felt ready to do whatever he had to do to protect his fortune. "I say you deserve a raise. What do you say?"

"Thanks, Mr. Powell." The driver smiled. He had been promised raises by his boss in the past, but never saw it manifested in his paycheck.

The driver did not take long to get to the Powell Estate. He parked in front of the house that showcased two huge terracotta pots with an assortment of pansies, which sat on each side of the mahogany double doors.

Powell, Sr. stepped out of the limo and strolled to the entrance. The doorman tilted his hat to greet him.

"Take the rest of the day off," Powell, Sr. said, dismissing him and other workers, wanting privacy when his son arrived home.

He took his time climbing the stairs to his suite. Once inside, he removed his dark brown suit jacket.

At the foot of a king-sized bed, he untied his shoelaces, removing his brown leather shoes. He looked up to see Jarvis standing in the doorway.

"I heard you might be sick. I rushed home," Jarvis said worriedly.

"Who's passing false rumors around the bank?"

"I called your office. I was told you left for the day. That you didn't feel good."

Powell, Sr. headed inside his closet. He fussed, "I told her to take messages, not gossip about me."

"She was worried about you, Dad."

"I'm strong as a horse," his father said, returning in the bedroom. "We need to talk."

If this was going to be another one of his father's discussions about his life, Jarvis did not want to hear it. He wished he had gone to the penthouse to be with Aniyah. "Is there an issue at the bank?"

"You got the big head a few years ago. Took my money and bought you a penthouse."

Jarvis' mouth could not open any wider when he heard his father mention his purchase. He wondered how he had discovered his secret. "I wanted somewhere I could go and relax." *Does Dad know about Aniyah and me?*

"I don't like sneaky people. And, I don't like it when my own flesh and blood tries to put one over on me."

"I didn't do it to piss you off."

"Then turn it over to me," Powell, Sr. said subtly. He puffed on his cigar.

"I bought it with the money I've earned."

"You own nothing until I'm gone. How many times do I have to tell you this? You're my heir. So first thing tomorrow, you contact Attorney Chavis."

"Dad, it's my property."

"Boy, you'll learn one day who's in control. But tonight go sweep that tramp onto the streets, where she belongs."

Jarvis loosened his tie. He wiped sweat from around his neck. "So that's what this is all about. You're been spying on me."

Powell, Sr. stepped in front of him. He blew another puff of smoke in his son's face. "You can bed the tramp. Just not at any property that's owned by a Powell. Take her to a motel."

All types of emotions flowed through Jarvis. A teardrop trickled down his cheekbone. It puzzled him what it would take to have an identity of his own. "Dad, you know you're not right. It's like you don't want me to be happy. What is it?"

Powell, Sr. rested his hand on his son's shoulder. "It's not you. It's the demon in women."

"Take the time to get to know her. I believe she has feelings for me."

"She doesn't care about you. Her love is money."

"That's not true." Jarvis stepped away from his father.

Powell snatched the flap of his son's jacket. "I tell you what. You're my heir. But you don't have an heir to carry on for you."

"What does that mean?"

"Change of plans. I have a better idea." He took another puff. "The deal is, you can keep the penthouse with her in it, in exchange for you making a baby with her."

"Dad, you want a grandchild?"

"Name it what you want. The Powell fortune must continue. And you better deliver a home run."

Jarvis could not believe his father was asking him to produce a baby with Aniyah simply for him to have someone to carry on the family's legacy. "What if it's a girl?"

"It won't work. You take charge in the bedroom and a boy will manifest."

"You really want me to do this."

He chuckled. "Hell, yeah. Go! Spend the night with her. I give you permission to stay with her until you've fattened her belly."

"Dad, can we at least get to know each other more. Get married before we have a baby?"

Powell, Sr. tossed his son up against the wall, thumping him on his forehead. "Think, Jarvis. She's not marriage material. Baby Mama, that's all she'll ever be to you. Now, you do as I say."

Jarvis held his fist tight and grit his teeth not to step out of line. He left with the sound of his father laughing hysterically. He was glad to leave rather than stay in a house where he felt like he was property, not family.

CHAPTER 14

A subtle breeze came through the opened French doors from the terrace. The penthouse glowed with flickers of light from candles. With her head resting on a cushioned pillow, Aniyah relaxed on the sofa.

She held cubes of ice wrapped in a towel against her face, soothing her pain and bruises. Her neck was too tender to touch from the soreness of the bruise that had replaced her diamond necklace.

If only the bruises would disappear before Jarvis appeared. She would not have to lie about what had happened to her. Not that it wouldn't be easy for her; she could carry it out without a sweat.

Her face became numb from the length of time that she held the ice pack against it. Aniyah decided to dispose of the ice in the kitchen sink. She ran the cold water long enough for it to get its coldest. She took the towel and soaked it. She wrung it out, tossing the cool towel around her neck.

She headed into the hallway bathroom and studied her face in the mirror. Homebound was what she would be for days. She peeped under the towel and viewed her neck. "Yuck," she mumbled as she thought of Powell, Sr. "To make you miserable, I'll never leave your son."

She again turned on the water until it got its coldest. Soaking the towel in the water again, she tossed it back around her neck.

In the living room, she turned on the radio. She danced around the floor to an upbeat song. She held her neck like a robot, moving only her hips to the music.

The fullness of the lingerie she wore swayed. With one swing of the towel, she flung it across the room. The music made her forget her injuries. She danced under the glow of the candles. The loudness of the music caused her not to hear Jarvis when he entered.

Tiptoeing, he crept up to her, grabbing her from behind. Aniyah jumped, causing a sharp pain in her neck.

"Didn't mean to scare you." He let go of her, turning her around to face him. Even though the lights were off, he saw that she was disfigured. "What happened to you?"

Jarvis hurried, turning on a lamp shaped like a football.

She put her acting into motion. With teary eyes, she made her way to the sofa.

Jarvis followed her. "Baby, what happened?"

"I got mugged."

"There's never been a crime in this building."

"No, no. Outside…I took a walk. This nut came after me. He pulled my necklace off."

Aniyah turned her face to show her injuries.

"Do you know what he looks like? And, which necklace?"

"The druggie tried to steal the presents you gave me. He was on a high."

"The diamonds?"

"Yes."

"Did you notify the police? I paid good money for that jewelry."

"I handled him on my own."

Jarvis reached into his pocket for his cell phone prepared to report the stolen jewelry.

Aniyah snatched the phone out of his hand. "No police. I have the diamonds back. A few broken pieces, but I got it back." She handed him back his phone.

"I'm confused. How?"

"He must be a rookie. The fool tripped on his own shoelaces. I beat him down with my pocketbook. He dropped my stuff and I let him go."

Laughing, Jarvis pictured her whacking at a man with her bag. "Assertive, Lady."

"I wasn't about to let no thug take from me what my man gave me."

Aniyah kissed him.

As Jarvis tasted the sweetness of her lips, he pulled her close to him. Not thinking, he placed his hand on her neck. Aniyah twitched. He came up for air. "Sorry, Baby," he said. Then he touched her on the tip of her nose. "No more walking by yourself. You'll use the limo driver. Or when walking the driver will trail next to you."

"You're being too protective." Aniyah was happy of his concern, and in return, she touched the tip of his nose.

"Call it what you want to, but I want my lady safe."

Again, they kissed and he enjoyed the sweet candy taste of her lips. He was eager to enjoy the process of giving his father what he wanted. He opened his eyes, capturing her beautiful brown eyes, staring back at him. Getting Aniyah pregnant could work in his favor. He wouldn't have to worry about her leaving him. A baby would bond them.

On the other hand, Aniyah wasn't about to let go of him without a fight. He was the only man that ever had put her needs before his own. She was gradually changing from landing him for his money into wanting him as a potential husband. His father was the only obstacle in her way. That meant, if her relationship became more threatened by Powell, Sr., she would have no choice but to use the $3,000 she had swindled from him, back against him, thanks to his own hired weapon—the private investigator.

Jarvis stood up, and her eyes darted to his scarred face. But once he undressed in front of her, the scar was meaningless. The sexy protruded muscles that had built up on his chest from weight lifting made up for it. He dropped his bottom garments. Aniyah was in heaven, feasting her eyes on his erect manhood.

She stood, ready to give him a show. Her flowing lingerie dropped to the floor. She watched how he was mesmerized by the fullness of her breasts and her full-blown garden.

They kept their eyes on each other.

Aniyah led him through the opened French doors to the closed-in terrace. She pulled down the bamboo shades to give them privacy. The cool breeze chilled their bodies, but once they connected into each other's arms, they became electric blankets for each other.

Jarvis circulated her breasts with his tongue until he captured her nipple between his lips. Aniyah moaned from stimulating pleasure. She forgot about her bruises, but he handled her gently not to discomfort her.

She stood and let him have his way with her; she was the one who always had control during sex.

Jarvis may not have been in charge of his father's business, but he took command when it came down to satisfying his woman.

Her knees buckled from the touch of his tongue gliding down her body. Jarvis came up and she held on to him for support. He eased her down on a chaise lounge. There he crawled on top of her.

Once he tried to enter her passage, Aniyah recalled they did not have a condom. "Go get a rain jacket," she teased.

"Aw. Let's do without it." He pouted.

"I will," she blurted, "when I become Mrs. Powell."

Jarvis was caught off guard with her words, and his eyes pro-truded. "Are you asking me to marry you?"

"No way. I'm waiting for the day you ask me."

"When my dad gives us his blessings."

She smirked. "Go get a rain jacket."

Jarvis hurried to the bathroom, removing a condom from the drawer. It was no time to think if he should follow his father's request and deceive Aniyah. She had revealed to him that she wanted to become his wife, so the answer was there; he would go ahead with his father's request—impregnate Aniyah. He found a safety pin and poked enough holes in the condom for his juices to flow through it and into her. He slipped it on his erect manhood and made his way back to her. "You win," he said.

Entering her, Jarvis stroked her with power. He sweated like dripping water from wet hair.

Aniyah let out a loud scream with his every move inside her; she wanted to holler to the world that Jarvis made her feel special. She wondered if this were the beginning of her turning her life around as her Aunt Tessa so wanted her to do. Or would it take one wrong move on Jarvis' part and she would gain control back in a way he would pay dearly? He stroked her one last time, and together, they reached the ultimate climax.

Worn-out from sex, Jarvis rested on top of her. Even with the cool breeze, they sweated.

With dampened hair, Aniyah said, "Let's go take a shower."

"Sounds like fun. I'll stay the night with you in my arms."

Aniyah was amazed. "You're not rushing home to Papa?"

"The hell with him. I'm willing to deal with his bitching to-morrow."

"Get off me. And let's go." Lifting up fast, she was reminded of the pain in her neck.

"To the water." He raced.

Aniyah followed, not letting her injury stop her from getting into the shower with her man.

Playfully, they poured liquid bath soap on each other, lathering up lots of suds. Every moment, they locked lips and touched each other in the right places. They rinsed the suds off their bodies. Aniyah kissed him on top of his wet forehead.

Jarvis pushed her up against the wall. He'd come prepared with another condom—full of pokes. While he worked his way inside her, he moved her hands above her head, laying kisses on her neck.

Aniyah moved her body as one with his. They stirred up their own splashes of body fluids. It did not take long before they climaxed. They repeated with the suds, helping to cleanse each other's bodies. They took turns towel drying each other off.

The night was long. Aniyah lay on the thousand-thread count, wrinkle-free sheets, while Jarvis blew out the candles in the living room.

Upon his return, they lay naked in each other's arms.

"I'd say I'm in love," he whispered in her ear.

She'd never thought of the word "love," only that she felt she was falling for him. Now he was showing her his true feelings. She had no choice but to whisper back, "Me too." But in reality, she had to keep her distance from getting her heart broken. Only marriage might secure her heart to open for love.

The morning came soon enough. Aniyah awakened to see she was in bed alone.

The penthouse smelled of a morning breakfast. She peeped into the kitchen, eyeing Jarvis, who was wrapped in a burgundy apron with his nude behind exposed. She went into the bathroom, cleansed her body, and then she found her way back into the kitchen.

His voice echoed in her ears. He whistled, while he mixed pancake batter. She came up from behind him, tapping him on his rear. "I never would've thought you cooked."

"I spent many days in the kitchen with the help." Jarvis turned around to give her a peck on the good side of her injured face. "Hope you like pancakes as much as I do."

"I do, Chef Jarvis. Scrambled eggs on the side with cheese."

"I got it covered. Sausages or bacon?"

"Bacon. I can take care of it, if you have to get dressed for work."

Checking the clock on the wall, Aniyah noticed it was almost time for him to head to the bank.

"I'm taking a day off. It's no clothes day."

Aniyah was tickled. "I never heard of that holiday."

"It's our own personal day."

"Well, if you say so." Letting her bathrobe drop to the floor, she put her arms around his waist. She sucked on his neck.

"That feels good, but baby, we don't need to do this near no hot grease," he warned. Aniyah let go of him. "Watch the bacon." He handed her a fork. "I need to call into the office."

Jarvis left to make a quick call, notifying his receptionist that he would be gone for the day. When he returned, Aniyah allowed him to finish breakfast while she set the table with napkins, silverware and glasses filled with orange juice.

Once breakfast was ready, Jarvis pulled out a chair for her and she took her seat. In front of her, he set a plate with a stack of four pancakes, bacon and scrambled eggs.

She smiled. "I feel like royalty."

"That you are." He tossed the apron, exposing his masculine goods. He took a seat across from her.

Aniyah savored the flavors of the breakfast he'd prepared. She especially enjoyed how he stroked her with his feet from under the table. In return, she tickled him with her polished toes.

"You're going to tell your papa about our day," she teased.

"That's our secret." Jarvis felt it was no need in reporting to his father. With his cell phone turned off, he figured his voicemail would be loaded with incoming calls from him.

Aniyah did not want to respond with an answer, so she got out of her seat and sashayed over to him. She loved how he feasted his eyes on her curvy body in the spotlight of the daylight.

Taking a slice of bacon off of his plate, she put one end of it in her mouth and the other end in his. She chewed it all the way up to where he chewed on the bacon to meet and lock lips. They forgot about the rest of their breakfast.

Somewhere between smooching and touching, Jarvis laid Aniyah down on the ceramic tile floor. He rested on top of her. Prepared with another poked condom, he entered her.

From the coldest of the floor, Aniyah felt a chill in her back. She kept right with him, moving their bodies as one. Her back ached to the point that it was too painful.

"Getting sore from the tile," she admitted.

Jarvis scooped her off of the floor, laying her on the carpet in the living room, where, after so much lovemaking, he prayed one of his sperms had connected with her egg—turned into a baby that would tie them together forever.

They spent the rest of the day in the nude playing cards, eating, and in between, working their bodies as one. The calls from his father went straight to voicemail.

CHAPTER 15

The wipers brushed away the pouring rain that splashed on the windshield. To avoid an accident, the limo driver reduced his speed and turned on his warning signals.

In the backseat, Jarvis looked on, but every so often, he covered his eyes to hide from the lightning that gave him the impression of daylight.

"I'm in no rush," he called. "Take your time. Pull over if you have to."

The driver never turned his head to the sound of Jarvis' voice, but heard his request. He kept his eyes on the road, driving close to the white line on the right shoulder.

It took double the normal thirty-minute time to get from the penthouse to the Powell Estate.

Once parked in front of his home, Jarvis insisted the driver stay in the limo, letting himself out. Jarvis opened a black umbrella, holding it above his head, but with a gush of wind, the umbrella crushed into pieces, letting the rain soak his tailored suit.

Hailstones began to fall, hitting him like someone was shooting him with a BB gun. He hurried under the awning, fumbling with his key to unlock the entrance door.

Finally inside, Jarvis stood in darkness. He hit the switch on the wall and the chandelier did not sparkle. He presumed the power was out.

He removed his suit jacket, pants, and black leather shoes.

In his boxers, he ran up the stairs, leaving his clothes at the front door for the maid to send to the dry cleaners. Happily for him, there were no signs of his father. He hoped Powell, Sr. was in his own bedroom, snoring under bedcovers.

Inside his master suite, Jarvis lit candles, which was a necessity in stormy weather that sometimes led to a power outage. He took a seat in a corner and watched his bedroom, brightened from the lightning. Next, he rested his eyes. He opened them once he heard footsteps.

Powell, Sr., wrapped in a dark blue robe, entered. In his left hand, he held a small dish with a lighted candle on it.

Jarvis saw that his father did not have a cigar dangling from his lips as he usual did. Instead, Powell, Sr. reminded him of an old man in a fairy tale holding a lantern.

"So you found your way home. And you disrespect me by not answering my calls." Powell, Sr. took a seat in a matching chair.

"I was doing what you ask me to do."

"You're supposed to check in with me," his father ordered. He was curious about what had happened between him and Aniyah. "Well, do you think you succeeded?"

"I did my part. The rest is up to nature."

"If she's not pregnant by next month, I say you need to go and get yourself checked."

Jarvis shook his head in disbelief. "Oh, so if Aniyah doesn't become pregnant, I must have a problem."

"If the tramp is not knocked up in a month, yes, Sir, I say you do have a problem. It must be from your mother's side of the family." Powell, Sr. held his fingers in the position of shooting a gun. "Pow! I made you in one shot."

Jarvis watched his father stick out his chest, showing how proud he was of his statement.

"Speaking of my mom, tell me more about her." The lightning ceased and the tapping from the hailstorm had disappeared.

"How many times do you want to hear the same damn thing? She ruined your face. Left me for another man. End of story."

"You get so angry when I speak of her."

"She's another tramp, like the one you're banging."

"Please, Dad, drop the word, 'tramp.' She's my mom, no matter what."

The harsh tone in his father's voice made Jarvis speculate that his father was one of the reasons his mother had left. He felt Powell, Sr. must have been as dominating with his mother as he was with him. Maybe his mother wanted to take him with her, but knowing his father, he would have put up a battle that she could not win.

Powell, Sr. was up on his feet. Jarvis watched him come toward him.

His father poked him in the chest. "Listen here. Since you were little, I'm the one who took care of you. Your mom didn't do a damn thing but run off on us. Whoring herself around. You owe me your loyalty. If I say she's a tramp, then that's what she is."

Jarvis could not dispute his father on what he had done for him. It was clear that as long as he had remembered, his father had devoted his life to him. He humbly gave in. "I'm sorry, Dad."

Jarvis left the story of his mother to rest.

Satisfied, Powell, Sr. parked himself back in the seat.

Jarvis changed the subject. "I'll be late for work in the morning."

"And, why so?"

Jarvis hesitated. "I want to check on Aniyah."

Powell, Sr. laughed. "Son, she won't have pregnancy symptoms that fast."

"She was mugged." Jarvis repeated the story Aniyah had told him.

Powell, Sr. did not show any reaction. He chuckled. "That's a joke.

She doesn't have a damn thing anybody wants; unless it was her body the thieves were after." He waited to hear whether Jarvis would tell him about the jewelry he had purchased for her.

"I can't believe you think it's funny."

"She's lying. Seeking pity to get to be a Powell."

"The baby she conceives will be a Powell."

"I'll be damned, if she will."

It had hurt Jarvis to hear his father say Aniyah could not share their name. This made him want more than ever to make her part of his life. "Dad, can we talk about anything else than Aniyah?"

"I call the shots when we stop talking about her. Your job is to keep me informed when she gets knocked up."

"You'll be the first to know." Jarvis got up out of the seat. As he passed by his father, he said, "I'm going to take a shower before the storm starts up again." He went and tried the light switch in the bathroom. The room brightened. The power was back on. Jarvis blew out the candles.

Reared back in the seat, Powell, Sr. got relaxed, pulling a cigar out of his robe pocket. He sniffed it, lit it and puffed away.

"Damn," Jarvis said, rubbing his nose. The stale smell had seeped into the bathroom.

Inside the shower, he forgot about his father and his thoughts went straight to Aniyah. He recalled the wonderful time they had spent together, wishing he were back at the penthouse with her.

He prayed his sperm had connected with her egg, as fast as his parents had conceived him. The baby would bring a bigger bond between them. His father would somehow have to accept it.

Thinking of Aniyah, Jarvis became aroused and she was not there for him to relieve himself. He turned the faucet water from hot to cold. He needed to cool off. Tonight the only thing that he would hold tight was a Lauren designer pillow.

Once he felt a sense of relief, Jarvis turned the water off. He cleared his throat from the fumes of his father's cigar.

Out of the shower, Jarvis reached for a towel, but became alarmed when he saw his father standing in the doorway. He wrapped the towel around his waist. "Dad, can I have some privacy?"

Powell, Sr. did not make a move.

Jarvis stepped back into the shower. He closed the door and dried off slightly.

"You're on my time," his father declared. "So do you think you might have enough balls to land me a grand-heir?"

"Dad, relax. You'll get a grandchild soon enough." Jarvis came out of the shower. "Pass me my robe." Powell, Sr. tossed it to him. "Dad, can you give me some privacy?"

"Put the damn robe on. You don't have anything I've not seen before on my own self."

Jarvis went into the walk-in closet where he finished drying off, covering up with the robe. When he came out, Powell, Sr. had gone back into the bedroom. He got comfortable in a chair.

"Dad, the smell is killing me."

Powell, Sr. blew rings of smoke, not caring what his son had to say.

Jarvis, annoyed, got into his bed. "I'm tired. Goodnight, Dad," he said, hoping his father would leave.

Once under the covers, Jarvis removed his robe. He turned on his side, placing the pillow on top of his head.

Up out of the seat, Powell, Sr. jerked the covers off him, slapping his rear. "You're never too old for me to give you an ass spanking."

The burning sensation of the hit stung Jarvis. His instinct was to strike back. He jumped up, but before he could attempt to do anything, his father caught him by his wrists.

"So, you're big and bad now," his father roared like an untamed beast.

"Dad, let go of me." Jarvis was amazed of the strength his father had for an old fellow.

Powell, Sr. held strong to his wrists, pushing them against Jarvis' chest. "I'll write you off, like you never existed. I better hear that tramp is knocked up by next month. No later. Get out of here and go be with her." Powell, Sr. let go of Jarvis' wrist and vanished.

Angrily, Jarvis snatched his pants and shirt off a hanger, slipping them on. It did not take long for him to pack a garment bag of suits. He got hold of a driver and made his way back to his woman.

In bed, Aniyah awakened when she felt her body being held by strong hands. She turned over, and to her surprise, Jarvis had returned to her. "What are you doing back here, tonight?"

"I couldn't go to sleep without you." He locked lips with hers. Jarvis, delighted to be where he wanted to be, held her close.

Through a long time of kissing, he made his way on top of her, exploring her body and doing what he could to impregnate her.

Aniyah, in the dark about what was going on, let him stimulate her body as if he were a masseuse. They moaned from the pleasure they gave each other.

"You'll one day be my wife," he whispered as he rolled off her.

"Mrs. Powell, that's me."

"You can have the biggest wedding ever. You'll have a whole page to yourself in the state paper in your wedding gown."

It sounded great and everything to Aniyah, but she was not about to expose herself in the media for her Aunt Tessa or anyone else to recognize who she was from the past.

She stared into his face. "I don't need that."

"You're too beautiful not to show off."

"I don't like attention. Please, let's do it my way."

"And, what do you have in mind?"

"Las Vegas." Aniyah smiled.

"All the glamour."

"Yeah, what happens in Vegas is permanent."

They grinned and somewhere through the night, again Jarvis added more reassurance to becoming a father.

CHAPTER 16

The strong scent of Pine Sol attacking her nostrils caused Aniyah to awaken. It was clear to her that the housekeeper had arrived, tidying one of the two-and-half bathrooms in the penthouse.

Coming from a home where her mother and aunt worked as maids, she had smelled disinfectants many times, and it had never affected her. But this particular morning, the aroma attacked her to the point she was nauseous with a weak stomach.

Feeling she needed to vomit, Aniyah attempted to get out of bed, but before her eyes, in a fast pace, the room moved in circles. She squeezed her eyes, then again opened them. There was no change. She lay back down.

In a panic, she cried for help. "Lady, get in here."

The housekeeper, a young woman in her late twenties, dressed in a pair of black pants and a black pullover top with her hair pulled back into a ponytail, came to her aid.

"Something wrong, Ma'am?"

"I'm feeling lightheaded. Throw away whatever you're using. It's making me feel like yuck."

"I will, right away."

"Where's Granny?" Aniyah asked before the housekeeper could leave the bedroom. She noticed the housekeeper was not the usual older lady who cleaned.

"She's sick."

"I wish someone had told me today was a sick day. I would have stayed asleep."

The housekeeper took a peppermint from her pocket and handed it to Aniyah. "Suck on this. It might help."

Aniyah unwrapped the peppermint. She put it in her mouth, sucking on it while the housekeeper went to do as she was told. Aniyah closed her eyes and relaxed. She covered her nose with the covers to block out the odor.

It did not take long before the housekeeper returned, carrying a tray with a cup of hot tea and a slice of lemon along with two slices of toast, grape jelly and butter. A silver butter knife and spoon rested on top of a folded napkin with a matching sugar bowl, half filled.

Aniyah eased into a seating position. She felt the room seemed to have slowed down from twirling but not her nauseous feeling.

The housekeeper placed the tray on her lap.

"Thanks. Your peppermint helped some."

"I'm glad, Ma'am."

"Hold up. That's the second time you called me that. I'm not an old lady. Call me, Aniyah," she said, scooping sugar into her tea. She buttered her toast and finished spreading jelly on it. "What's your name?"

"Nellie Anna Mason."

"You talk like a true Southerner."

Nellie stood upright like she was to lead the Pledge of Allegiance. "Born and raised by my daddy in the country. Ma died when I was a baby."

Aniyah envied the housekeeper being nurtured by her father. She was too ashamed to tell her that she had no clue who her father was. She wondered if her father was from the South, but switched the conversation. "My mama and aunt worked as maids. That's not for me."

"It's an honest living."

"Girl, find yourself a rich man. Get away from cleaning."

Nellie giggled. "Too late for that. I'm engaged to one of the Powells' drivers." She folded her arms across her chest. "Roy and I are in love. We do just fine."

"I won't settle for breadcrumbs. I want a fabulous lifestyle." Aniyah chewed the toast and sipped her tea.

"You're here 'cause of money?" Nellie asked eagerly.

Aniyah paused. "I'm not going to lie. I'm a pro at getting the richies to take care of me.

But Jarvis Powell is making me rethink things."

"You've caught the love virus."

"Girl, thinking of the word 'love' makes me want to choke on this toast."

Nellie laughed. "I'll get back to cleaning."

"Girl, park your butt." Aniyah patted her hand on the bed. "I can use the company."

Nellie sat at the foot, long enough for Aniyah to finish eating. "I'll take your tray," she volunteered.

"I'm gonna spit up," Aniyah said, pushing the tray toward her, causing it to tumble onto the floor. The remaining tea that was left in the cup spilled on the tray.

Not quite lightheaded as she was, Aniyah dashed to the bathroom, making it in time to stand over the toilet. She vomited up the toast, plus any food she had eaten the previous night.

Nellie heard her and entered the bathroom. She witnessed Aniyah stooped down on the floor with her head leaned in the toilet.

Aniyah tried to speak, but she continued to spew anything that was left in her stomach.

"I say you're having a baby."

Nellie caused Aniyah to turn her head and look up at her. "Save the jokes."

"I wasn't being funny. You have the signs," Nellie informed her.

"I use rubbers."

"They burst like bubbles."

"Girl, don't play with me. This is a stomach virus."

"What about your period? Have you seen it?"

"Shit." She panicked.

Too involved in lots of bed partying, Aniyah had forgotten her due date had swept right by her. She and Jarvis had been nonstop compulsive addicts to each other. Is it possible that one of the rubbers he used was defective?

Aniyah held on to the toilet to rise to her feet, but was forced to get right back down on her knees until she was convinced she had nothing else to deposit.

"You have the signs of a pregnant woman." Nellie, not wanting to smell the sourness, kept her hands gently pressed against her nose. She was thankful she did not have to clean behind Aniyah.

Up off her knees, Aniyah brushed her teeth. She washed her hands and splashed her face with cold water. Her stomach continued to feel weak. "I need to get back in bed."

"Take a pregnancy test."

Aniyah gave Nellie an evil eye. "Forget keeping me company. Go clean."

"No disrespect, but when your belly starts growing and growing bigger than a cantaloupe, you can say I told you first." Nellie took hold of the tray, carrying it into the kitchen.

Aniyah crawled back in the comfort of the bed. She looked down at her flat stomach, and was getting nausea again. She visualized herself with a huge stomach.

Was Nellie telling the truth? She could not go through the day wondering if she was or not. Aniyah decided to prove the housekeeper wrong.

"Nellie," she blabbed.

The housekeeper entered the room. "Yes."

"Let's make a bet. I'll take a home pregnancy test. If I'm right, that I'm not pregnant, you'll work a day free."

"What do I get for being right?" Nellie smiled, as she was sure of herself.

"You'll get paid double. That's how nice I am."

"I'm happy to go to the store for you."

Aniyah saw she was excited to have betted her. She handed her a fifty-dollar bill. In a flash, Nellie disappeared.

Aniyah lay in bed, praying that her body was merely going through a change. And, it would not be long before her period would start flowing. She tried to rest but tossed and turned every time she touched her stomach.

It did not take long for Nellie to return with a box that contained three pregnancy tests.

"Give it to me," Aniyah ordered, snatching the package from her.

"I've taken this test before. Go pee on the stick."

Aniyah read the instructions herself, and followed it step by step.

Together, when the time came, she and Nellie went into the bathroom and checked the strip. Aniyah's eyes popped wide open—the test showed a positive result.

"See, I told you. You're having Mr. Jarvis Powell's baby." Nellie was overjoyed for Aniyah.

"There are two more sticks. I'll try it again. This one must be no good."

Nellie laughed. "It's right."

"Get out of here."

Aniyah proceeded to read line by line. She did exactly what the instructions said on the second, and on the last test.

Nellie knocked on the door. "What's taking so long?" She was eager to see the results.

Opening the door, Aniyah showed the last two sticks in her hand.

Nellie moved her hands and feet like a tap dancer. "I told you. You're having Mr. Jarvis Powell's baby. Maybe two babies."

"Shut up. I can't take this news."

Out of the bathroom, into the bed, Aniyah placed a pillow over her mouth, screaming to the top of her lungs. Pregnancy was not in her plans.

"It's not that bad. Having a baby is supposed to be wonderful news. You have everything to give your baby a good life," Nellie said, noticing her reaction.

"I'll look like a potbelly pig. Like Jarvis' papa."

"No you won't. A woman always looks pretty carrying a baby."

"Do you have kids?" Aniyah wondered, tossing the pillow on the other side of the bed.

Nellie spoke in a low tone. "Always a negative result."

"Lucky you."

"My man and I want kids."

Aniyah watched as Nellie patted her stomach. Being a magician would be great at that moment. Aniyah would graciously pass everything pertaining to having a baby over to the housekeeper in a snap. "This yuck feeling has to go."

"I hear it lasts three months."

"No way in hell I can take this that long."

"My friends say eat crackers. It's supposed to help."

"Go get me some, please."

Nellie went to do what she was told while Aniyah concentrated on her pregnancy.

Looking down at her stomach, Aniyah thought of her mother, who, if she were alive, would have been thrilled to have a grand-child. If she wanted to give the baby away, her mother would have been willing to take the baby and care for it as if it were her own.

Then, her Aunt Tessa was alive; she, too, would take the baby if she decided not to care for it. But Aniyah would not dare give her baby to her aunt.

Abortion was not an option. In reality, she had been down that road two times in her younger years. She did not want to spend the rest of her life contemplating what another one of her babies would have looked like. She had lived her life brainstorming what her father looked like.

Aniyah stared at her stomach. With watery eyes, she thought, I'll go through with this pregnancy.

If the baby were born a girl, she would name her after her mother—Julia.

"Aniyah." Jarvis' voice echoed in her ears.

She heard him loud and clear and mumbled, "Not now, Jarvis, not now."

She jumped out of the bed, dashed into the bathroom and closed the door behind her.

Aniyah gathered up any signs of the packages from the preg-nancy tests, throwing all in a plastic trash bag. She tied a knot in it and hid it under the cabinet. "I'm using the potty," she said, once she heard Jarvis's footsteps in the bedroom.

She settled down and walked out to confront him with her bright smile. "Hi, honey. I'm surprised to see you."

"I had to pass by here to go to a meeting. Thought I'd stop. Get me some sugar." He pulled her into his arms.

They kissed until Nellie barged into the room, carrying a box in her hand. "Here's the crackers that you wanted," she said, focusing her attention on Aniyah. She set the box down on the nightstand, giving them a big smile.

Aniyah, still in his arms, cut her eyes at the housekeeper. "Thank you."

Once Nellie exited the room and closed the door, Jarvis spoke, "She's in a good mood."

"That's because she knows a hot-looking man when she sees one." Aniyah smothered his lips, giving him a sultry kiss.

Jarvis tossed her on the bed, but Aniyah sat up.

"No nasty here today. Go on to your meeting," she said.

"I won't be able to concentrate. It'll be your fault."

Pushing back down on the pillow-top mattress, Jarvis leaped on top of her. There was no life in her to give him pleasure. She thought fast.

"This is not the right week. It's that time to love red for a week."

"You're flowing red wine," Jarvis teased but wanted to faint from the thought of having to go and inform his father he'd failed in the baby-making department. He would be forced to have a complete checkup.

"Sorry. It began today."

"Damn it. Back at work," he said, frustrated. He got up off the bed, then smoothed out his suit jacket. He took two crackers from the box and exited.

Quickly, Aniyah stuffed her mouth with crackers.

Nellie entered. "I bet you didn't tell him."

"Heck no." Aniyah crunched on the crackers. "I got to see a doctor to be sure."

"I won the bet. Three tests said positive. I say it's a baby."

"I want to hear a doctor tell me I'm pregnant."

Nellie did not understand how being pregnant by a man who was loaded in the pockets did not excite Aniyah. "Since you're with Jarvis Powell, you can go see Dr. Guess." She was informative on where to seek prenatal treatments. She had worked around many women who became pregnant by men with money.

"For a person who never had a baby, you're dead on things."

"When you work in people's homes, you take on more than cleaning."

Aniyah snapped, "What you trying to say?"

"Nothing." Nellie realized she had said one word too many. To smooth things she responded, "I'll go with you. Be your support. Get dressed."

"Make me an appointment."

Nellie smirked. "I already did. He'll see you right away."

"You're really staying on top of this bet."

"I love to win."

Aniyah headed toward the bathroom. "I'll go and freshen up. A little extra soap and water."

"Yeah, good idea."

"Yes, Nurse Nellie."

Once Aniyah was dressed, Nellie called for a limo driver.

They were off to finalize the bet.

CHAPTER 17

At the ob/gyn center, through the double wooden doors, women sat in the waiting room to be called by one of several doctors. Aniyah took a seat in the first cushioned chair she had observed.

Reaching for one of the magazines stacked on a table, she opened it and hid her face. She pretended to read. To not draw attention that she was the patient, Aniyah insisted Nellie go to the sign-in desk on her behalf.

Once the receptionist noticed Nellie, she slid opened the glass window that separated the office from the reception area. "I made an appointment for Aniyah…" Not knowing Aniyah's full name, she turned around and looked at her. "What's your last name?"

If this baby was going have the last name Powell, so was she. Aniyah peeped over the magazine and proudly said, "Powell."

Puzzled, Nellie said, "Powell." She whispered, "She's having her rich boyfriend's baby. Three home tests showed positive. But she still wants Dr. Guess to confirm it."

"Please ask her to come to the desk," the receptionist said.

"Aniyah," Nellie again called. "She wants to speak to you."

Aniyah eased the magazine down from her face. She looked to see everyone in the room had attention on her, thanks to the help. She made her way to the desk, pushing Nellie to the side.

The receptionist saw her and asked, "Please give me your full name?"

"Didn't she just tell you my name," Aniyah said, wanting to hurry and be seen by a doctor.

"Sorry, my computer screen went blank for a second," the receptionist said, waiting to key in Aniyah's information.

"I'm Aniyah Powell."

"I assume it's your first time here."

Aniyah twirled her eyes. "Hello. This is not on my favorite places list."

"Take these forms and fill them out. Do you have medical insurance?" The receptionist handed Aniyah the forms attached to a clipboard.

"No. I'll give you the address where to bill my man. He's loaded."

Aniyah gave Jarvis' penthouse information. She went to return to her seat, but it was taken. She saw two seats available at the far end of the room.

She scribbled her answers to the questions, with Nellie hovering over her, catching any mistakes she made on the forms.

Back up at the window, Aniyah turned in the completed documents.

"You'll be called back as soon as possible," the receptionist said.

"I hope it don't take all day," Aniyah complained. She took her seat back next to Nellie.

"It's nice in here. When I get pregnant, I'll come here." Nellie admired the mahogany furniture and the Tiffany lamps on the end tables in the office.

"They don't take Medicaid folks." Aniyah presumed Nellie was assisted by government health insurance.

Nellie, somewhat offended, said, "Everyone should have equal healthcare."

"You know that. I know that. Girl, that's not how it is. The money people get the better care."

"I'll save the cash from our bet."

"I'm not paying you that much money."

"I'm joking." Nellie giggled.

Watching the room empty out from women going through the doors that led to the examination rooms, Aniyah wondered when it was going to be her turn, but finally a nurse uttered her name.

Tired of sitting, she got up and followed the nurse through another set of doors. She became confused, when she was led to a lab tech instead of a doctor.

Nellie stayed with her, as Aniyah took a seat.

"You have to give blood and pee." Nellie smiled.

"Oh hell, no. I don't do needles."

Aniyah saw a woman in another seat getting her blood drawn.

Nellie eased out of the lab room to wait outside the door. Aniyah was handed a tiny plastic cup.

"Do you think you can use the restroom? I need urine from you," a technician said, dressed in a white jacket.

"I might have some pee left in me," Aniyah said with a smirk on her face.

With the cup in her hand, she went straight into a nearby bathroom.

On return, she handed the technician a barely half-filled cup.

"I do need to take some blood," the technician advised.

"I'm here for a pregnancy test."

"Giving blood is part of the process. It won't hurt. I'll use what we call a butterfly needle. You'll feel a pinch."

Aniyah eased into the seat. Before closing her eyes, she rested her arm on a small table attached on the side of the chair. The technician tied her right arm with a tourniquet.

"Squeeze your hand tight," the technician instructed.

Aniyah felt the tourniquet around her arm. The technician

tapped her arm to locate her vein. "Is it over with?" Aniyah squinted and followed instructions until the technician finished up with her, covering the spot on her arm with a bandage.

"You can have a seat around the corner. The doctor will be with you soon," the technician informed.

With pleasure, Aniyah followed her instructions.

"That didn't hurt," Nellie said, walking with Aniyah to the next waiting area.

"Yes it did," Aniyah complained. She looked down at her arm making certain no blood seeped from under the bandage. "I don't know if I can deal with this."

"My ma went through nine pregnancies, you'll live through one."

"I'm not your mama."

Aniyah focused her attention on a man that passed them dressed in a short-sleeved shirt. She admired the small amount of gray strands blended in his jet-black hair. She eyed him until he went into a room that held her chart in a slot on the outside of the door.

Aniyah presumed he was her doctor. She waited for him to call her name. She was eager to know whether her troubles were going to be cured by him.

The door opened, and this time the man appeared in a Clorox-clean jacket. "Aniyah Powell," he called. The doctor waited to see which one of the women he would treat.

"The laugh will be on you," Aniyah said, grinning at Nellie.

"I'm Dr. Guess." He extended his hand out to Aniyah. In return, she held out her hand and shook his. "Follow me this way."

Instead of going into an examination room, Aniyah went into his office filled with awards and his credentials, framed like art on the wall. She sat across from his desk.

Dr. Guess opened her chart, browsing the four pages in the folder. "You did more than one home pregnancy test."

"Forget those tests. I want to know from you. Am I pregnant?"

"Yes, you are," Dr. Guess responded.

Aniyah dropped her head. "Darn it!" she mumbled.

"Now we need to get you examined to see how far along you are. When is the last time you saw your period?"

"The beginning of last month."

"Is this your first pregnancy?" The doctor noticed she had skipped the question on her medical history.

Aniyah sighed. "No. I had two abortions in my teens. I'm keeping this one. I just hate the nausea feelings. I threw up my guts this morning."

Dr. Guess informed, "That's normal for pregnancies the first three months."

On the heels of the doctor, she followed him into an examining room.

Aniyah was instructed by the doctor to get undressed and cover herself with the white sheet that was already placed on the table.

When the doctor left to give her privacy, she undressed. She sat on the examination table, not bothering to hide her jewels.

It didn't take long before Dr. Guess came back with a nurse to assist him. They were astonished to see Aniyah fully exposed. Without saying a word, the nurse went straight to her and covered her up with the sheet.

Not knowing what to expect, Aniyah sat nervously on the table. Dr. Guess took his stethoscope and listened to her heart. Next, he instructed her to lie down.

When he went to examine her breasts, Aniyah panicked, and raised her right hand. "Hold up. My man only touches my boobs."

"This is part of your examination," Dr. Guess explained. "I'll only feel your breasts to make sure you have no lumps. No diseases."

"Just relax," the nurse said, giving Aniyah a pat on the shoulder.

"Is it okay I continue to examine you?" Dr. Guess asked.

"Go ahead. I don't like this baby thing." Aniyah was disgusted.

Dr. Guess resumed examining her. "No problems here." He pulled the sheet back over her breasts. He moved down to the foot of the bed. "I want you to scoot your bottom all the way down to the end of the table. Place your feet here." He pointed to a place where Aniyah could rest her feet.

She slid down, not being able to see what the doctor was about to do to her.

He flipped the sheet above her knees.

Turning on a bright light, Dr. Guess aimed it between her legs. Her private parts were in the spotlight. He placed a latex glove on his hands. The nurse squeezed lubricant on his fingers. "I want you to relax your bottom," Dr. Guess ordered and examined her. "You're around four weeks," he informed her.

"One month," she said, glad he was done examining her. She hated the extreme pressure he applied to her insides.

Dr. Guess removed the latex glove off his hand, disposing it in the trash. "The checkout desk will make you an appointment to see me in a few weeks. Get dressed. Meet me back in my office."

Once he disappeared with the nurse following him, Aniyah scurried off the table. She went inside the bathroom, wiping off the lubricant around her private parts. She felt sicker than before she came in to see the doctor.

When Aniyah stepped into the hallway, Nellie spotted her, making her way to her. "What did he say?"

"You win. Four weeks."

"Yippee." Nellie celebrated. "Pay me."

"Girl, you'll get your money."

"I'm happy you're having a Powell baby."

Aniyah informed, "I have to go back and see the doctor."

Inside Dr. Guess' office, Aniyah was instructed on prenatal care. He gave her a prescription for prenatal vitamins.

"Take care of yourself, Ms. Powell. Make sure you stop at the checkout desk to get your next appointment."

"I'll be sick for a long time." Aniyah pouted.

The doctor patted her on the back. "Normally it lasts no more than three months."

When Aniyah finished checking out, she dashed for the exit door.

Happy to be in the limo to be taken home, Aniyah stared out the window. The driver slowly drove through the parking garage.

The driver came to a halt, letting three well-dressed women carrying designer handbags cross in front of the vehicle.

Focusing on the women, Aniyah recalled the last time she had laid eyes on them. It was the day she was hauled off to jail.

Nellie spotted them as well. "Those are the Houston sisters. They come from money. It must be the time for their yearly physical."

Balling her fist tight, Aniyah refrained from opening the door, to go after them. She just turned her head. "They're uppity snobs," she said, but was relieved she had finished her appointment before they appeared.

The first thing Aniyah did when she entered the penthouse was honored the bet. She handed Nellie two crisp hundred-dollar bills.

"This is more than our bet."

"You helped me today. And you won. Now be gone. I want to be by myself."

"Thanks. Call Jarvis Powell. He'll be happy to hear your good news."

"I do have to tell him. He'll see this out-of-shape body soon enough."

"Once the baby comes, you'll get your figure back."

"This can't be happening to me." Aniyah was annoyed.

"It'll be fine. You'll see."

Nellie gave Aniyah a hug. She left her to deal with her own issues.

After undressing, Aniyah crawled into bed. She was eager to contact the condom manufacturer and sue them for defected products.

With tears running down her face, she dampened the pillow. Before long, she dozed off.

The daylight had disappeared into darkness. Aniyah awakened, wondering was she really pregnant or was it a dream. Her swollen eyes from crying and the spot on her arm where blood was drawn showed her it was a reality.

She thought of Jarvis. Aniyah suspected he must have gone home after she'd told him it was that time of the month. Immediately, she got him on the phone.

"Jarvis."

"Aniyah." Jarvis heard the frog in her voice. "You sound like you just woke up."

"I did. Where are you?"

"Still here at the office."

"I have to talk to you. Come by here on your way home."

"I'm leaving here now. Be there before you think about falling back to sleep."

"Then you better hurry up."

It did not take long before Jarvis came into the darkness of the penthouse. He entered the bedroom, turning on the light switch to the ceiling fan.

Aniyah squinted her eyes. "You took too long. I dozed back off."

She headed to the bathroom, where she brushed her teeth. She figured he would be all over her lips once she gave him the news.

Back into the bedroom, she made her way to him, looking him straight into his eyes. "I'm pregnant."

Jarvis pretended to act surprised. "We used protection. Is it mine?"

Aniyah slapped him on the arm. "Of course it's yours."

"Wait a second. I thought you said this was your time of month."

"I lied. I went to the doctor today. Four weeks."

"I can't figure out how it happened."

"A defective rubber."

Jarvis chuckled. "Baby, it's our blessing. We're about to be, Dad and Mom."

He touched her stomach, followed by taking her into his arms. They locked lips with him circulating his tongue in her mouth. Aniyah enjoyed his luscious lips until they separated.

"You have to take it real easy from now on."

"I'm not going to break apart."

"Just tell me what I need to do for you. Name it."

"Pay the doctor bill I made today."

"Consider it paid."

"I'll let you know when it comes in the mail." Aniyah crept back into the bed. "I've been sick all day. Nellie, the new help, has been helping me. Please keep her," she begged.

"It's good to know you like her. I'll give her a bonus pay."

Aniyah did not bother to let him know about their bet. She figured the way Nellie acted about the bet that she could use more money.

"I feel like yucky yuck." Aniyah hid her face with the bedcovers.

Jarvis removed his suit jacket, easing under the covers next to her. He rubbed her stomach. "Hey, baby girl. You're going to be pretty like your mom."

Aniyah could not help but giggle. "And what if it's a boy?"

"He'll be as handsome as his dad."

Honey, I'd rather our child have your personality, not your looks.

"We have to select names. If it's a boy, it's Jarvis Powell the Third."

"Three generations of Powells. And if it's a girl, I'll name her after my mama—Julia."

"Well, that didn't take long." He snuggled her in his arms until she fell asleep. Jarvis eased his arms from around her and got up. He put back on his suit jacket. He was anxious to share the good news with his father.

CHAPTER 18

Entering the front door, Jarvis sped to the second floor of the house to locate his father's whereabouts.

"Dad, Dad. I got good news for you. Where are you?" he yelled but did not get any response. The only thing he heard was the echo from his voice.

He searched his father's master suite. There were no signs of Powell, Sr. so Jarvis returned downstairs.

Jarvis checked the study and peeped inside the kitchen. He felt he was playing hide-and-seek. His father was hiding and he was seeking him out.

The lower level of the home deemed the recreation area was built soundproof. When Jarvis opened the door, the tune of "Mr. Magic" blasted his ears. "Dad," he called, trying to speak louder than the music.

He ran down the flight of hardwood stairs, spotting his father.

Powell, Sr. sat at the bar, sipping on a glass of white wine, in between taking puffs from his cigar. He tapped the cigar occasionally against a ceramic ashtray that sat on top of the black granite counter top. He listened to the music from a CD player that was stationed behind the bar. Tuned out from everything, he spotted Jarvis, who went straight behind the bar and shut off the music.

"Turn it back on," his father roared.

Jarvis disregarded Powell, Sr.'s orders. He broke the news to him.

"You're going to be a granddad," he said.

His father showed his dentures, which looked like they had been dropped in a cup of coffee. Jarvis was satisfied he had given him good news.

"Superb," Jarvis Powell, Sr. said.

"Aniyah and I are excited, too."

"Who cares about her? The Powells need heirs."

"The baby is not a possession."

"Being a Powell is money in the bank."

Jarvis grabbed a glass. He joined his father for a drink, taking a seat next to him.

"Aniyah and I have decided on a name for the baby."

"A girl is not an option. A boy's name is a no-brainer—Jarvis Powell, the Third."

"Dad, it's no guarantee that it's going to be a boy."

"Well, the tramp better have a boy in her belly."

"Please, Dad. She's going to be the mother of your grandchild. Can you have some respect for her? At least for me?"

"If she makes a boy, I might give her some slack."

The men drank more of the wine while they talked.

"Dad, I did what you wished. Now can I get my wish?"

"And what the hell is that?"

"Aniyah and I should marry."

Powell, Sr. began to cough, choking on his cigar. "That tramp will never carry my sweat and blood fortune's name."

Jarvis was astonished. "You thought she was good enough to produce a Powell baby. That doesn't make sense. Think about it, Dad."

"Never!" Powell, Sr. slammed his hand on the counter. "You can have your way with her. But give her our name? Forget it."

The wine mellowed Jarvis. It gave him more courage to speak his opinion. "It's my choice, Dad."

Powell, Sr. swung his left hand backward, knocking both of their glasses on the floor. Jarvis' suit was splashed with wine.

Powell, Sr. raised his voice to the top of his lungs. "Do you want to be voided out of my will?" He got up off the stool and headed for the stairs. "Next time, don't touch my damn music, when I'm listening to it."

It was no sense in Jarvis trying to continue to convince his father about Aniyah. Powell, Sr. was the typical example of old folks settled in their ways. He was not about to change his view that women who did not come from money were gold-diggers.

Awakened by the phone, Aniyah saw that Jarvis had vanished— a grown man running home to his father. She presumed he was calling to check on her.

"Hey, Papa," she teased.

Powell, Sr. shouted, "I'm not your father."

"Oh it's you."

"My son told me you're knocked up."

Aniyah was no longer sleepy, so her ear was glued to the phone. Never had she thought Jarvis would get the guts to share with his father their relationship, now the pregnancy. But she would bet he had no notion his father was contacting her.

"You're stuck with me. I'm pregnant with your grandchild," she bragged.

"No need in celebrating," Powell, Sr. said, hearing joy in her voice.

"Jarvis and I are happy. So choke on your stinky cigar."

"Don't play games; you can't win."

"I think I've won already. Get over it." Aniyah smirked.

She heard a beep, letting her know another call was coming in. Without any warning to Powell, Sr., she switched over to her next caller.

"Feeling better?" Jarvis asked.

"I think I am," she said after speaking with Powell, Sr. but waited for Jarvis to share his news.

"I…got up enough nerve to tell Dad about us and the baby."

Aniyah acted surprised. "How did he take it?"

"He doesn't like any of it."

"He'll change once the baby is born."

"I feel like celebrating. Let me take you on a date to a nice restaurant."

"As long as it's not in the morning," Aniyah said, knowing that was the time of day she felt nausea.

"In the evening, Baby."

"Two babies now."

They laughed.

Aniyah held back from mentioning her conversation with his father. She did not want to burden Jarvis with his father's unruly ways.

The next morning for Aniyah was no different than the morning before. She stayed in bed until the evening when the nausea eased.

In the closet, she searched for something to look good in for her man. The red spandex dress caught her eye. The dress was a constant reminder to her of the day she had entered prison as well as the day she was released. Snatching it off the hanger, she tossed it in the trash. She was quite aware that her Aunt Tessa would be thrilled to hear that she had gotten rid of it.

From the closet, she removed another red dress. It was a more subtle one that Jarvis had purchased for her.

Into the bathroom, she jumped into the shower to cleanse her body. Once dried off, she checked the time to be on schedule for her date.

She slipped on the dress and it fit her curves. The front bodice was cut low enough to sneak a peek at her cleavage. She wrapped the red belt that came with the dress around her waistline. As she stood looking at herself in the mirror, Aniyah figured, after her date night, she would not have any use for the dress until she lost her soon-to-be baby fat.

She let her hair flow on her back. To sweeten her neck, she sprayed on Mary J. perfume. She smoothed a thick layer of red lipstick on her lips. Lastly, she stepped into a pair of red leather pumps.

With a phone call from the limo driver announcing Jarvis' arrival, she tossed a small red purse under her arm and went to meet her man.

When Aniyah came out of the building, the outdoor breeze brushed her face.

Jarvis eyed her strut in her fitted dress. Instead of the driver opening the limo door for her, he insisted on greeting her himself. Like the gentleman he was, he gave her a peck on the lips. "You look gorgeous."

"I'll be a whale soon."

"Sexy. That's what you'll always be to me." Jarvis licked his lips. Aniyah got in the limo. He closed the door behind her, and then he ran to the other side to get in.

Aniyah rubbed her exposed arms. "It's a little cool tonight."

"I'll go and get you a wrap."

Jarvis jumped out of the limo, hurrying to the penthouse. It did not take long before he returned. He draped a cream-colored shawl around her shoulders.

"Is that better?" he asked.

Aniyah, loving the attention he gave her, embraced him in a hug.

During the drive to the restaurant, they held hands, sneaking juicy kisses. She had to apply more lipstick on her lips before they reached their destination.

Jarvis was right there for her, opening doors from the limo to the restaurant. She admired the lobby. The sound of water splashed from a mosaic-tiled fountain. Vines of artificial grapes hung from a trellis nailed to the ceiling. A small-framed, elegant woman dressed in black, with her hair pulled back in a ponytail, escorted them to their seats. They sat down on soft, dark-brown leather seats.

The table with specks of brown in black granite was set with silverware wrapped in royal-blue cloth napkins.

A candle flickered at the center of the table to give off a romantic feel, among the low-voltage lights coming from a fixture that hung above each table.

They had a full view of the chefs working behind a low brick wall. It was like being in Italy, smelling the aroma of fresh baked bread and pizza cooking from a wood-burning brick oven.

Across the room, a pianist played classical melodies.

"I've got an idea." Jarvis got up from the table and spoke with the woman, who had escorted them in.

When he finally returned back to the table, Jarvis took Aniyah by the hand. "We need privacy."

"Where are we going?" she asked curiously.

Jarvis led her to a private room, not far from the bar, that was decorated with greenery and glowing lights. A long table was set up the same as the rest of the restaurant. But on the table was a bottle of chilled sparkling apple cider. Chocolate-covered strawberries filled a small basket. Red roses, not yet fully bloomed, sat in a vase.

Aniyah became overwhelmed with tears. She had never had a man to treat her like she was an ounce important. "This is so special."

"Anything for my babies," Jarvis said, wiping her tears with his cloth napkin.

A tall, young man dressed in a white shirt and black pants waited on them. For appetizers, they ate groovy mushrooms, brick-oven-baked stuffed mushrooms, topped with sushi graded salmon with Greek vinaigrette sauce. Afterward, they were served a bowl of she-crab soup, then a fresh Caesar salad.

For the main course, they tasted the tenderness of New Zealand rack of lamb with red-skinned garlic potatoes and buttered vegetable medley.

The dishes were new to Aniyah, but she loved every bit of her meal. Instead of eating dessert, they fed each other the plump ripe strawberries.

"I'm the luckiest diva in the world," she marveled.

"I'm glad to hear that. I want to be the luckiest man in your life."

Jarvis pulled a tiny red velvet box from his pocket. He kneeled down in front of her, staring into her eyes. "Become one with me. Make me yours forever."

He opened the box. Her eyes protruded when she saw the four-carat diamond ring with a platinum band.

Holding her hand out, Aniyah watched him slide the ring on her finger. She gasped for breath. "I'm yours."

Jarvis got up off his knees, pulling Aniyah out of her seat. He locked lips with hers. In the background, music serenaded them as they celebrated.

She rested in his arms to dance to a slow melody. It was not her usual kind of dancing, so she followed his moves to dance in the style of a waltz.

"This is a night to have fun. Let's leave here. Have a wild time," she whispered.

"Your wish is granted." Jarvis took care of the expenses of the meal. He figured Aniyah wanted to go back to the penthouse, where they would have complete privacy to snuggle with each other.

"Take us to a club. It's party time." She clapped her hands.

"The Yacht Club isn't open at this hour."

Aniyah laughed. "Not that type of club. I'm talking about a place where we can let loose."

Not wanting to disappoint her, Jarvis instructed the driver to take her wherever she wanted to go.

The driver drove them to a club that, during the early evenings, was a mellow, after-work spot, but at night it was pumped with party music played by a deejay.

"Wait here for us," Jarvis instructed the driver. He watched the people going inside. They were not dress in a suit and tie like he was. The fellows wore slacks and shirts. The women's clothing was short, fitted and they had a lot of junk in their trunk.

With his arms around her waist, Aniyah strutted inside the club with her man. The upbeat sound of the music made her begin to move her body. Ready to dance, she pulled Jarvis straight to the dance floor.

Jarvis felt awkward. He had no clue about the way the people were dancing. "Baby," he tried to yell over the music. "I'm not a dancer. At least not this kind."

Aniyah did not hear a thing he said. She moved her hips like a belly dancer. She fitted right in with the other people dancing.

"Isn't this fun," she chatted in his ear. "I love to dance."

"I'm far behind on dance moves." Jarvis had never seen her work her body in the way she moved on the floor. He did not want to look like a fool, being with a sexy woman and had no rhythm. He took her into his arms.

Aniyah placed her hands on his hips. "Move from side to side to the beat of the music. You're a brother. You can do it. This is soul music."

She turned around and leaned back on him, steady grinding her rear against his crotch.

"I'm goofy," he whispered. He put his arms around her waist, doing his best to learn how to move right with her, while his manhood grew, bulging from his pants.

Men's eyes were drawn to Aniyah the way she rubbed up against him. He noticed their stares and to show she belonged to him, he saturated her neck with his lips.

The music turned into a slow song. Aniyah lay in his arms. She saw how couples danced in the form of making out. She yearned for the same thing.

"Hold me tight," she whispered in his ear. She got what she wanted—Jarvis squeezed her.

After a few songs, Aniyah could tell he was not in his comfort zone. She grabbed him by the hand, and led the way to the exit door.

The heavy smoke from smokers in the club made Jarvis sick. He cleared his throat. He was glad to be on the outside to once again breathe. He smelled his good suit jacket to see if it had the aroma of fumes. "Baby, my suit is full of smoke."

"You didn't have a good time."

"Only watching you dance. That kind of club is not for me."

"I needed to let loose. I won't get to do it again no time soon."

"You're happy. I'm happy."

They got into the limo.

Spontaneously, Aniyah smothered Jarvis' lips, pushing him down on the leather seats. Her dress rose to expose her bare bottom.

She slid down the zipper of his pants, releasing his hardened manhood. She removed a condom from her bra, covering his erection.

Aniyah entered his manhood into her, riding him like a bumpy car on an uneven road.

They moaned from the pleasure, each of them exploding like an exhaust pipe.

The driver, who had witnessed their sexual act, interrupted them when they arrived at the penthouse. "Mr. Powell, we've arrived."

Jarvis juggled with his clothing to tidy himself, while Aniyah simply pulled down her dress. "You don't have to get out. I'll open the door for my lady," Jarvis said to the driver, smacking his lips to clear any smudged lipstick. He hopped out of the vehicle on the roadside to open the passenger-side door.

Aniyah winked at the driver. She spoke fast. "You're a peeping-tom. The next time I'll have to charge you."

The driver wiped sweat from around his hat. Saved by Jarvis opening the door, he responded, "Goodnight, Ma'am."

"Goodnight," Aniyah answered.

"Be right back," Jarvis said to the driver.

The couple made their way to their love nest. Again, she gave her man a juicy kiss. "I had a blast. Especially in the limo."

"Next time not around the driver. But I did have a good time."

"No you didn't." Aniyah poked her finger at him. "Not at the club."

"It was...definitely different," he said hesitantly.

She held her hand out to show off her ring. "Thank you, for the bling."

He blurted, "Baby, we should keep our engagement between us for now."

Aniyah presumed immediately what that meant. Jarvis did not want his father to know.

"I'll keep quiet only until the baby is born."

"Thanks for understanding. Dad is already upset. But hearing we're engaged, he'll emphatically disown me. I pray by the time our baby is born, he'll come around and see we should all be a family."

"Goodnight, Jarvis."

They kissed.

Aniyah watched him get on the elevator. As much as she felt Jarvis loved her, he was not about to lose his inheritance because of her. But she was willing to take a chance on waiting on the right time for them to marry.

One foot was in the door, and with the other foot, she would work on kicking the door down. The hell with his old fart, papa. Aniyah marveled the rock on her finger.

CHAPTER 19

After one week of being engaged, Aniyah was aggravated that she couldn't share her good news.

She held the ring in the palm of her right hand. Not wanting to put it back into the drawer, she slipped the sparkling diamond on her left ring finger. At the first sign of Nellie coming to tidy the house, she waved her hand in front of her face.

Nellie gave her a big grin. "You got married?"

Aniyah pointed to herself, rolling her neck. "This diva is engaged. The diamonds are the real deal," she bragged, feeling good to reveal her secret to someone.

"Jarvis Powell?"

Aniyah snatched her hand back. "Who else, Nellie? It sure isn't his papa."

"It's the biggest diamond I've ever seen. Is it too heavy for your finger?"

"It's not a brick."

Nellie giggled. "You and your man set a date?"

Aniyah took a seat on the sofa. If it were up to her, she would already be a married woman, but she had to wait until Jarvis smoothed things out with his father.

"It's a secret for now. Jarvis doesn't want to share the news with anyone, yet. "

Nellie's eyes lit up. "You told me."

"Ladies can't keep secrets like men. I had to tell someone."

"I'm glad you told me."

"I didn't have anyone else to tell. Then again, maybe…I like you." Aniyah showed a softer side of herself.

"That's nice of you to say to a worker."

"Girl, I'm telling you my business. You've become a friend to me."

"Thanks and congratulations. I'll get busy doing my work." Nellie dismissed herself. She made her way into the kitchen, running dishwater to clean a soiled cup and spoon.

Once Aniyah stood on her feet, she began to feel nausea. She dragged herself into the kitchen, taking a seat on a barstool.

"The pregnant sickness is coming on again." She rested her head on the granite counter.

Nellie took it upon herself to make her two slices of dried toast for her to nibble on.

Aniyah took all she could to keep down the bread before she had to run into the bathroom to throw up.

Lucky for her, by the middle of the day, she felt a lot better. Hungry, she made herself a salad with grilled chicken.

Nellie ended her cleaning day by sanitizing the bathrooms. She came back into the living room where she saw Aniyah relaxed on the sofa and eating. "You must be feeling better."

"Trying to see if this will stay on my tummy."

"I'll be leaving."

"Stick around. Sit down. Let's have girl talk," Aniyah insisted, wanting to share her thoughts with someone besides a shrink as she had done in the past.

"What kind of girl talk?" Nellie asked, aware that Aniyah must be lonely. She had never seen anyone come visit Aniyah except Jarvis. She took a seat and waited to see whatever more Aniyah had to say.

"I don't believe I'm saying this…I'm scared."

"Of what, having a baby?"

Aniyah paused for a moment, and then said, "I don't want my past to come between me and Jarvis."

"You're keeping secrets from him."

Aniyah chewed her food before she spoke. "I've been behind bars before."

"Jail?"

"Hell yeah."

Nellie waved her hand. "That's nothing. My man was in jail before. He got out. Got the job with the Powells. He's doing fine."

"A woman going to jail is not good for a businessman, like my man."

"Tell him. He loves you. I'm sure he'll forgive you."

"Not for trying to take money from a rich dead man and his family. I'll lose Jarvis. My butt will be thrown on the streets. Girl, I'll be homeless."

"If he truly loves you, you have a chance of him forgiving you," Nellie said, but curious if Aniyah truly was aiming for the Powells' fortune.

"Jarvis is so different than other rich men that I've dated."

"He treats you like a lady."

Aniyah smiled. "In and out of bed."

Nellie giggled. "You have nothing to worry about. Maybe he loves you enough to forgive your past."

"He knows the family I got arrested for—the Houstons."

Nellie kept a straight face. She could not believe she sat next to the woman who had portrayed herself as the daughter of one of the wealthiest men around town, but had gotten caught. Aniyah was the talk amongst housekeepers. "That day when we saw them, you didn't say a word."

"I'd just met you."

"No, he might not forgive you."

"I say this girl chat is between us only," Aniyah said harshly.

"Everything you said escaped my brain."

"I knew I could trust you. You're the only person I feel I can talk with."

"You do have an aunt." Nellie recalled reading about Tessa Sanchez.

"Please. Forget her. She's into her lawyer hubby."

"I see." Nellie stood up. "I'd better be going."

Aniyah continued talking. "Maybe after the baby is born, Jarvis will forgive me for any hateful things I've done."

"He will. Concentrate on having a healthy baby."

"I have another confession."

"You have more dirt?" Nellie scratched her neck.

"When I met Jarvis, I played the game of landing another rich man to take care of me. But I never thought I would start getting attached to him. He's a nice guy. He doesn't dog a lady. I do feel a connection to him."

"Everything will work out for the good. Have faith." Nellie watched the tears build up in Aniyah's eyes. She figured maybe Aniyah had changed—bitten by Jarvis' love.

"Girl, I only have luck with the devil," Aniyah said.

Nellie embraced her. "Think positive," she said, and headed to the elevator, hitting the button for it to arrive. "I must go to my next client."

"You may leave when you agree to be my maid of honor and take this plate to the kitchen."

With her mouth opened wide, Nellie relieved Aniyah of the empty plate. "You're kidding me…me?"

"Hell yeah."

"I'm a maid."

"So what. You're a person first."

"What will the Powells say about this?"

"I'll handle that. Yes or no?"

"Of course, yes. See you next Friday." Nellie gave Aniyah another hug, ready to get on the elevator.

"Hey, don't steal the dishes." Aniyah giggled.

Nellie looked to see she held on to the plate. She ran to the kitchen, placing it in the sink.

It had always been men that Aniyah had associated with. She was happy that she had a female, whom she could talk to as a friend.

Outside on the streets, Nellie stared at her cell phone. She was confused whether to make her call but decided to.

Powell, Sr. had approach her after Aniyah had become pregnant to spy on her. He'd fanned a few hundred-dollar bills in her face. The greed to get paid more money made her go ahead and call him, even though she felt guilty betraying Aniyah.

"You got some news for me," Powell, Sr. grumbled. He recognized her number.

"Yes, Sir. Aniyah told me she's been in jail. Also, she's engaged to your son."

"Engaged?" Powell growled.

"Your son gave her a fancy diamond ring. She showed it to me. They're keeping it a secret."

"Anything else?"

"She told me she got with your son for his money."

"I knew it," he shouted.

"But Mr. Powell, she now has fallen in love with him. She's afraid he'll find out about her past and won't want her."

"That tramp knows nothing about love. There won't be a marriage if I can help it. Keep being her friend. I need a pile of ammunition on her to get her the hell out of the Powells' life once my grand-heir is born."

"Sir, it could be a girl."

Powell, Sr. snapped at her. "Do your job. I didn't ask you for your opinion."

They hung up.

Nellie decided to keep her being in the wedding her secret.

CHAPTER 20

*I*n the fifth month of the pregnancy, the nausea feelings that Aniyah suffered had stopped. She felt flurries of movement in her stomach, which had grown into a small bump.

During her appointment with Dr. Guess, he was prepared to reveal the sex of her baby. Nellie accepted her offer to go with her. She was all ears and prepared to report back to Powell, Sr. his new heir's sex, but the gender was not revealed. Aniyah had informed the doctor she and Jarvis had decided to wait until the birth.

Months continued to fly by, and by the ninth month of pregnancy, Aniyah no longer could look down and see her toes. Her breasts overfilled her bra, which she did not mind. It was plenty of pleasure for her man. They, at times, witnessed how the baby stretched her stomach.

Aniyah, slouched on the sofa, turned the television from channel to channel. It was a routine she had become accustomed to on a daily basis. She refused to go out in public, unless it was for her scheduled doctor's appointments.

Nellie busied dusting the furniture. She had played many roles: being Aniyah's personal assistant, running errands from time to time, as well as keeping Powell, Sr. updated on Aniyah's involvement with his son.

Exhausted from watching Nellie, Aniyah sighed. "You're making me tired, just looking at your ass."

"I'm doing what I get paid for."

"Take a break. Give me a rest from looking at you."

Nellie dropped the cleaning cloth on a cherrywood end table. "Pregnancy is keeping you grouchy. No more babies for you."

"Girl, I'm not traveling this road again."

Nellie giggled. "That's what us women say."

"I mean it." Aniyah was disgusted.

"No need to get excited. You have a few weeks to go."

"Girl, that's like a year to me."

Off the table, Nellie scanned the state newspaper. "You saw the paper today?"

"Not into news."

Taking a seat in a recliner, Nellie turned the pages until she came to the metro session. Her eyes lit up. "It's time for the ball at the Powell Estate."

"That old grouch knows nothing about having a good time."

"It's right here in writing." Nellie turned the page toward her.

Aniyah read the title to the article out loud. "Annual Powell Black and White Ball." She scrambled to get up off the sofa, snatching the paper out of Nellie's hand. She read the rest of the article. "It's this Saturday. Invitation only." Aniyah crunched the paper into a ball. "Damn you, Jarvis. I wasn't invited."

"Your man didn't ask you to be his date? I know that hurts."

Aniyah flung the paper on the floor. "Shut up, Nellie."

"Don't get mad. Stay calm for your baby."

The housekeeper picked up the dismantled paper, placing it on the coffee table.

Aniyah sat back down. In the middle of a carpet cleaning commercial, she put the television on pause. She picked up her cell phone, keying in the number on the dial pad.

"Calling your man?"

"You got that right. His mean-headed papa probably told him not to tell me."

The office rang a few times before the receptionist answered. Aniyah cut to the chase demanding to speak to Jarvis.

On the other end he answered. "Hello, Baby."

There was no room for sweet talk. Aniyah went straight to what she wanted to know. "The Powells are having a party...and I'm the last to hear about it."

"Please don't be upset. I can explain." It was clear to him that Aniyah had found out about his father's event.

"It's either your papa or my swollen belly is not sexy enough to be seen with you in public."

"It's not like that, Baby."

She argued. "Save the 'baby' for the one in my belly. Were you planning on going to the party without me?"

Jarvis was stunned by the feisty tone of voice that Aniyah spoke to him. He did not answer her question; instead he tried to make her see his point. "You know how my dad is. He won't accept you being there. On the other hand, I do have to attend."

"And your baby's mama has to stay in hiding."

Aniyah did not wait for a response. She hit the end button to cease their conversation.

"Men," she fussed. "They want what they want and the way they want it. But it doesn't go like that for me."

Nellie watched how Aniyah went from nice to nasty.

"I'll show him and his damn papa that I do what I want to do, not what they say."

"What are you going to do?"

"Show up in my black and white."

"Pregnancy is making you crazy. Mr. Powell will be furious."

"Girl, Papa Powell can sit on one of his cigars...let it burn his ass."

Nellie laughed. "You're a brave person."

"Come right along. See me in action," Aniyah invited.

The phone rang. Aniyah saw it was Jarvis ringing her back and answered him. "Are you calling to tell me to go buy me a dress?"

"Baby, you know my dad won't allow you to come. Please don't take it out on me," he begged.

Aniyah decided to change her tune. In a soft tone, she responded, "I'm sorry for getting emotional. You have to promise to come here after the party."

"I'll be in your arms, right afterward," he said, relieved that the tension had turned smooth between them.

Nellie was confused. Once Aniyah ended the call, she said, "I thought you were going."

"Ain't that what I said?" Aniyah wobbled out of her seat. "Join me. It'll give you a front-row ticket to drama."

"I can't lose this job."

Aniyah patted her stomach. "You forgot I have a Powell in my belly."

"Money in the safe." Nellie patted her stomach.

They laughed.

"Let's go shopping. I got you covered for a dress to wear."

"I can't take that risk."

"Girl, don't be scared. I'll handle the Powells."

This was not information Nellie would share with Powell, Sr. It was her chance to get a fashionable outfit whether she attended the glamorous event or not. "I can use a new dress," Nellie said.

"Call the limo to be here in twenty minutes. I have to throw something on this pot belly."

The driver drove approximately one hour to Charlotte, North Carolina for Aniyah to find something special to wear to the ball.

All fears of being caught seen with an oversized stomach left her. Her cell phone was shut off from receiving any calls from Jarvis. His calls or text messages would have to wait until she returned back to Columbia.

Dressed in a pair of elastic stretch jeans and an off-the-shoulder maternity top, with Nellie by her side, Aniyah wobbled inside a boutique store full of dresses from upscale designers in black and white. She headed straight to the counter for assistance.

"I need the hottest black-and-white dress you sell that a pregnant diva can wear."

The slender tall woman smiled. "I'll have a fashion consultant come and work with you."

"That's what I need. And hook my girl up, too, with a sexy dress." Aniyah pointed to Nellie, dressed in her work clothes like she was there to dust the store.

"Follow me." The saleswoman led them over to the area where they could relax and look at dresses that would be shown to them by the consultant. "What price range are you looking to spend?" the saleswoman asked.

Nellie did not open her mouth.

Aniyah, annoyed, flopped down on one of the peach-colored lounge chairs. "I bet you don't ask every customer that question."

"I only ask so that we don't waste your time showing dresses out of your price range."

"Woman, go get the fashion consultant." Aniyah rolled her eyes.

The saleswoman turned her nose up. She walked away to get them help.

"She thinks we can't pay."

"She's right, I sure can't," Nellie whispered to Aniyah.

"You can today. Hell, I'll try on the dresses. Then, leave with zero. Go somewhere else and get us dresses. That woman better not play with me. I'm pregnant and miserable."

As Nellie burst into laughter, a short woman, with dark hair, in her mid-sixties, dressed in a navy St. John skirt-suit, approached them.

She shook Aniyah's hand, first. "Hello, I'm Mary Sweden."

"I'm Aniyah Powell." Aniyah pointed at her guest. "She's Nellie, my friend."

"Nice to meet you," the saleswoman said, shaking Nellie's hand. "I was told you ladies would like to see a collection of our black-and-white dresses."

"Yes. We're invited to a black and white party. I need help looking sexy with a big belly."

"I have lots of dresses you ladies will fall in love with." The consultant turned to Nellie. "Any particular styles?"

"I..." Nellie was lost for words.

Aniyah jumped in and spoke for her. "She needs something to show off her body. Real sexy. But, not sexier than mine."

"Give me a moment. I'll select a few dresses, I think you'd be interested in," the consultant said, leaving them for no longer than five minutes. She came from the back with two racks of dresses covered in garment bags.

Aniyah eased out of her seat. She browsed through the rack, finding three dresses that she wanted to try on. She handed the dresses to the consultant.

Nellie had only pulled one dress off the rack. Aniyah went to her aid. "Let me help you," she said and pulled two more dresses off the rack. "I like these for you."

The consultant took charge of the dresses, hanging them inside the dressing room.

"You try yours on first," Aniyah said to Nellie.

"There is more than one changing room," the consultant informed.

"I'll wait. I want my friend to pick out her dress, first." Aniyah took a seat, while Nellie changed into a dress.

It didn't take long before Nellie appeared in her garment. She stepped up on a platform in front of a three-way mirror. She showed off the white dress with a black band around the waist. "I'm a ballerina." She twirled around.

"You won't catch a man in that poufy dress." Aniyah disapproved.

"You know I have a man."

"It makes you look like a teenager. Try another one on."

Off to the dressing room, Nellie changed into the next dress. She walked out in a low-cut black dress with a V-neck in the front and back. It showed off her curves. The low cut front exposed her tropical-looking skin tone.

"Girl, you don't need to try on anything else. That one says… I'm available."

"Too much of my body is showing. Don't you think?"

"Trust me. That's it. That's the one that'll make them high-class hussies scared you're going to take their man."

"I'll be pretty as them."

"They don't have anything on us."

"I'll wear it." Nellie went and changed back into her clothing.

Aniyah headed into her dressing room. She grabbed the dress off the rack that she thought would look good on her, to try on first.

When she slipped it on, the dress glided down her body. Aniyah looked into the mirror. Right away, she smiled. Her pregnancy was not going to be an obstacle in the dress.

Out in the boutique, Aniyah stepped up onto the platform in front of the three-way mirror. The dress hugged her body, laying off her shoulders and showing off her neckline. The wide, three-quarter-length sleeves had slits. She thought the peek-a-boo, open lower back was totally sexy.

Nellie returned to see her in her dress. "You look beautiful."

"Thanks." Aniyah turned to the consultant. "I'll take this one." She figured she would get the attention of as much men as Nellie at the ball.

Aniyah danced in the mirror.

"Do you need accessories?" the consultant wondered.

"Diva pumps for the both of us." Aniyah stepped down off the platform.

"We're going be the prettiest ladies at the ball," Nellie said.

"Men stoppers."

Aniyah went to change back into her jeans, then returned, handing her findings to the consultant, who turned the dresses over to the clerk.

Aniyah and Nellie did not take long before they found shoes and accessories. It was one-stop shopping for them.

The salesclerk added the bill. "That'll be twenty-five hundred dollars."

Nellie nearly choked when she heard the total. "That's a lot of work hours of money."

"We deserve to look good." Aniyah handed the clerk a Platinum Visa, compliments of Jarvis for her shopping needs.

"ID, please?" the clerk asked.

Aniyah pulled out her old temporary job ID from Powell Bank. The clerk studied the ID carefully. "No other credit card?"

"That's it. I'm not a thief," Aniyah said. She recalled that was her past life. She was not about to be a jailbird again.

"It's nothing personal. It's the store's procedure," the clerk explained.

"Whatever? Hurry up before I leave and go somewhere else."

The clerk saw Aniyah meant business. The transaction went through. She handed Aniyah and Nellie their dresses stored in garment bags. Their accessories were given to them in another bag.

Strutting to the exit door, like she was on a catwalk, Aniyah hollered back at the consultant, "At least you got sale skills."

Once on the road, and closer to home, Aniyah checked her cell phone. She had at least fifteen calls and texts from Jarvis. She presumed he was at the penthouse, waiting on her—nervous about where she was.

"No more sleep. Wake up." Aniyah shook Nellie, who had dozed off.

Nellie stretched her arms. "We're back?"

"We're almost there," Aniyah said, and then she spoke to the driver. "Get this straight. You're not to say where you drove us to, if any Powell asks you. Your answer should only be, you drove us to Greenville to visit Nellie's sick aunt. That goes for the both of you," Aniyah said, turning to Nellie.

"I hear you," the driver said.

Aniyah took a hundred dollars in twenties from her purse. "Give this to him," she said, not wanting to get out of her seat to go hand the driver the money. Nellie passed the cash to him.

"My memory just went dead." He smiled, welcoming the bribery.

"Nellie, your dress and invitation to the party are your keep-your-damn-mouth-shut present."

The driver dropped them off. Nellie went to her old Ford Escort to go home.

Still cautious that Jarvis might be inside the penthouse, Aniyah had insisted the clothes stay in the trunk of the limo until the next day.

Feeling exhausted, Aniyah dragged into the penthouse. She was not surprised when she saw Jarvis sitting on the sofa; with his mouth pouting like a mad little boy.

Without hesitation, he made his way to her. He pulled her into his arms, but fussed, "Baby, you're trying to stress me out? I've been calling you. Why didn't you answer your phone?"

Aniyah kissed him on the lips. "Relax. I know you've been blowing up my phone."

"I thought something had happened to you and the baby."

"I was with Nellie. She needed my help. Her aunt is sick in Greenville. I took her there to let her spend some time with her. Without thinking, I left the phone in the limo. I'm sorry if I scared you. See, I'm fine and the baby is, too." Aniyah patted her stomach. "So damn tired."

She walked away with him following her into the bedroom. She dropped her purse on a chair and removed her clothes.

Jarvis came up behind her. He rubbed her shoulders.

"A personal massage is what you need," he said.

The touch of his strong hands felt good, penetrating her shoulders. He went on to unhook her bra to give her breasts freedom. She took deep breaths, feeling relaxed from her bra being removed. She turned around to face him.

"You have a big bustline," he said, placing his lips on one of her breasts. He tickled it with the tip of his tongue.

Aniyah moaned. She yearned for more, but the unborn baby with lots of movement interrupted her sensual feeling. She placed her hand on her stomach. "It's play time for the baby."

Jarvis came up for air, placing his hand on top of hers. They laughed at the baby's movement.

"I think it's a boy," she said.

"A feisty girl, like her mom."

"Oh, no you didn't say that." Aniyah pushed him away. "No goodies tonight. I need to calm the baby so I can get rest. You're staying the night?"

"I wish I could. But I'm overseeing the arrangements for the Powell Black and White Ball."

Aniyah turned her lips down. "I don't want to hear anything about the party. I'm not invited."

On her heels, Jarvis followed her into the bathroom, where she ran water to take a bath. He took her by the hand. "Baby, you know it's not me. It's my dad that's calling the shots," he explained.

"He won't rule our baby. He'll catch hell from me."

That was another obstacle Jarvis speculated was going to be a tough challenge for them. He realized his father was going to want to groom his grandchild for the banking business. "Things will get better," he said hopefully.

"See you when you have time for me."

Aniyah walked away from him, turning off her bath water. She went to the oval mirror that hung above the sink. She tossed her hair up in a knotted bun.

Jarvis came closer to her, placing his arms around her. He caressed her breasts while he placed mushy kisses on her neck. He moved his hands down to her stomach and whispered in her ears. "Always know I love my babies. After the ball, my attention is focused on you and the baby."

"We're not taking second place to your papa."

"Never. Now see me out."

Aniyah walked with him into the living room. They waited for the elevator to arrive.

"Keep your eyes off those hussies at the party," she said with authority.

Jarvis pointed to his face. "My eyes are stuck on you."

"You better. I'll turn psycho on them."

"You have no worry."

The elevator arrived. Aniyah placed her hands around his neck and pressed her lips on his, taking full control of the kiss. It was a moment she wished she was not tired and pregnant. She wanted to have passionate sex right at the elevator door.

CHAPTER 21

Dreaming of the loss of her baby awakened Aniyah. She placed her hands on her stomach to reassure the bump was still there. Was the dream a sign that there was going to be trouble if she attended the ball? Would her past be there to haunt her? Then, there was her Aunt Tessa and hubby, Baron; would they be there to rat her out? And, if she did not run into her former life, Aniyah would have no choice but to face old man Powell.

Mixed emotions continued to storm her brain. She contemplated whether to attend the ball or not. But one phone call from the penthouse security, notifying her that the glam squad she had hired was in the lobby, determined her answer. There would be no turning back. She would attend the ball.

It was noontime, and every minute counted for her to be ready on time.

Aniyah dragged out of bed, covering herself with a bathrobe. The first voices she heard stepping off the elevator were the masseuses.

"Hey! I'm here to loosen any tight bones. Hurry, Hurry," Rarlon, a muscular man, called.

"Cut the noise. You're on my time," Aniyah scolded him.

Preparation for the ball was going to be a daylong event in itself. Aniyah wanted the pampering to make her into the hottest-looking woman, even being pregnant. She would be there in grand style.

Once she made eye contact with the second masseuse that she had hired to pamper Nellie, she realized she had forgotten to inform her to come by early.

On her cell phone, Aniyah scrolled through her contacts. She hit her dial pad to make her call. "Get over here," Aniyah ordered her.

Nellie recognized Aniyah's voice. "You're in labor?"

"Not yet. I forgot to tell you to be here at twelve o'clock."

"This is my day off. Why so early? The ball starts at seven."

"We have a lot to do. I'll send a car for you."

"I was leaving my apartment to spend some time with my boyfriend."

"This is more important. Tell him we have to get glam for the party."

"I can't do that," Nellie whispered into the phone. "I didn't tell him about it."

"Tell him whatever. Be ready when the driver comes to pick you up. Girl, I spent money on you."

Nellie gave in when she heard the authority in Aniyah's voice. "I'll come."

"Ungrateful," Aniyah muttered, ending their conversation.

In the living room, Rarlon and the other masseuse had set up portable massage tables. Aniyah entertained them until Nellie arrived, with the driver carrying the bags from their shopping spree.

Under her instructions, the driver carried her bags into the master suite. Nellie handled her own bags, and dropped them off in the guest bedroom, decorated in soft shades of blue.

Back in the living room, Nellie stared at the masseuses. They stood next to tables that were covered with white sheets. She went over to Aniyah and whispered in her ear, "I told you I have a man. And so do you."

Aniyah was tickled. "Girl, they're here to give us a massage."

Rarlon handed Nellie a white robe to change in, the identical style Aniyah had already wrapped herself in. "Keep your panties on," he instructed Nellie.

Aniyah's attention went to the driver. He tilted his hat as to say he was leaving.

Once the driver was gone, there was no shame in Aniyah showing off her body in front of the masseuses. She removed her robe, tossing it to Rarlon.

Up on the table, Aniyah lay on her side, facing the other table. Rarlon fanned her with a white sheet, covering her bottom. She watched the other masseuse snap his finger twice.

"You can lie over here. My name is Anten," he said, noticing Nellie had returned.

Aniyah looked up at her and saw that the belt from the robe was snug around her waist. Nellie, fully wrapped in the robe, eased on top of the table.

Aniyah laughed. "Nellie, take that thing off."

"In front of them?" Nellie asked excitedly.

"Girl, we want no parts of you. Now, your man, that might be different," Anten teased.

They all laughed, except Nellie. As fast as she dropped her robe to the floor, she flopped down on the table, covering her body with the sheet. Anten, however, snatched the top back down to her waist.

"Relax," Aniyah instructed her. "You'll love a massage."

The masseuses began to do their jobs, penetrating their fingertips into every bone in their clients' necks down to the middle of their backs.

"Babe, your body is on lockdown," Anten said to Nellie. "Take a nap or something. I don't bite."

"Please be gentle," Nellie requested but wanted to tell him to stop.

"This feels so good." Aniyah absorbed the motion of every stroke from her masseuse's hands on her back.

"Girl, I can tell you're a diva," Rarlon said. "You're going to be hot at the party tonight."

"Rich men going to need bibs when they see me," Aniyah bragged.

"They'll be slobbering," Rarlon teased.

It didn't take any longer than an hour before the masseuses finished. They shut down their temporarily massage stations, got paid and headed out.

"Our lunch will be here soon," Aniyah said. She had ordered food.

"That sounds better than that massage." Nellie was thankful the men were gone.

"Look, you know how many workers around here would die for a chance to have a day like this one. And on top of that, get to go to a party the Powells are giving. So stop complaining."

"I'm sorry. I ain't used to this."

"Girl, I lived your world. Once I got a taste of this one, I don't ever want to go back to that time in my life."

"Even if you were happier?"

"The thing is...I wasn't." Aniyah's sadness turned into smiles. "This is supposed to be a fun day. We're doing things best friends do together. We'll get our hair done, feet and nails polished. Our faces will be made up like celebrities."

"Cute like them gals on TV." Nellie touched her hair.

They went their separate ways into the bedrooms to get dressed.

Aniyah was startled when her cell phone rang. She saw it was Jarvis on the line and closed the bedroom door for privacy.

"Hello, Baby," he said before she could speak, "I called to make sure you and the little one are okay."

"Baby and I are quiet."

"Not here. It's chaos around the ballroom. Decorators, caterers and some of every kind of business are at work to get this place ready by seven."

"Handle your stuff."

"Wish you could attend."

"Maybe the next one," Aniyah said, but under her breath she mumbled, "I'll be there."

"I'd have a better time if you could be here with me."

"Jarvis, do what you gotta do." She didn't want him pacifying her to try to make her feel good. The house phone rang as she spoke. "Got to go." She abruptly cut their conversation short.

Nellie beat her to the phone, yelling outside her door, "The guard said the food you ordered is here. The deliverymen are on their way up."

Aniyah opened the room door. "Have them put the food in the kitchen on the bar counter."

She closed the door again. She hated that Jarvis had called. It was like he was rubbing it in her face that she wasn't invited.

Would he cheat on me with another woman at the ball for the heck of it?

The thought gave her a feeling of jealousy that she had never experienced. She patted her chest to settle her heart. His kindness was getting to her. She channeled her attention to a white lounge robe and slipped it on.

The counter looked as if the ball was going to be at the penthouse instead of the Powell Estate. Aniyah and Nellie feasted on chicken fingers and shrimp, dipping them into cocktail sauce. Trays of fruits and veggies were there for their delight. They sipped on a bottle of sparkling apple cider. Aniyah stayed away from the alcohol for the baby's sake.

"Our feet and nails will be done next," Aniyah announced. She chewed her last bite of a kiwi.

"I never had anyone to do my feet before."

"Girl, your feet are going to feel and look so pretty. Your man will want to lick your toes."

"Mr. Jarvis Powell licks your toes?"

"Jarvis licks...No, I better not say it. I might be giving away too much information."

"Aniyah, no way. That's nasty."

Aniyah stuck out her tongue. "I love every bit of it."

They laughed.

The phone rang again from security, letting them know the manicurist had arrived.

"Clean hands," Aniyah said.

They hurried to wash their hands.

Two young women, no more than twenty, entered.

The manicurists worked magic on their feet. Aniyah chose a deep-red polish for their toes and nails.

Nellie looked down, admiring her painted toes. "My feet do look pretty."

"See, I told you. Tonight, put your feet up on your man's lap. I guarantee he'll kiss them first, and then..." Aniyah stuck out her tongue, wiggling it.

"No, no." Nellie covered her eyes after she saw Aniyah's tongue.

The manicurists laughed, along with Aniyah.

"I see I got to teach you a thing or two." Aniyah giggled.

Once finished, the manicurists packed their tools, got paid and left, passing Jarvis, who had stepped off the elevator into the penthouse.

Relaxing back on the sofa, letting her toes dry, Aniyah panicked when she saw him. She wanted to leap to her feet but feared she would smear her polish.

Nellie, with her toes pointed upward, tiptoed into the kitchen. She busily picked things off the counter to tidy the mess they had made from their meal.

"Jarvis, what are you doing here?" Aniyah asked frantically.

"I had to come by and see for myself if you were okay with everything." He walked over to Aniyah, kissing her on the lips. "You're doing fine. You and the help are having a personal spa day."

"A girly day. Go back and do whatever you have to do. This is a girl's thing going on here."

Jarvis laughed, relieved Aniyah was not upset with him. "See you later on tonight." He gave her another peck on the lips.

Jarvis was back on the elevator, waving goodbye until the doors closed shut.

Aniyah's eyes watered, knowing that he had stopped what he was doing to come and check on her.

"I'm getting nervous." Nellie tiptoed back to her seat.

"Please. I'm ready to surprise him. I'll be diva'd up for my man."

"You're brave."

"I see I'll have to be for the both of us."

"My worry is losing my job."

Aniyah quickly turned into a psychotic mood. "You're still complaining? I can fire your ass right now myself," she fussed.

"You're not serious, are you?" Nellie panicked.

"You keep being an ungrateful bitch."

Aniyah fanned from the fumes of the nail polish.

Nervously, Nellie said, "What next for us to do, friend?"

"That's better talk. We have another break before the hairstylist and makeup artist come. We'll let our nails dry, then go take a shower before they come. You can use the guest shower," Aniyah said, returning back into a mellow mood.

"You go through all this for a party. It only takes me no more than an hour and a half to get ready at home."

"Nellie, when you want to be grand, it takes a day. I may have a big belly in front of me, but I want to have the men staring at me. They'll be jealous that Jarvis has me."

"I don't care if they don't look at me."

"You say that now. Wait until tonight when the money men around town are right there for you to pick from. Girl, you'll turn into another person. Trust me on that one." Aniyah winked her eye.

It did not take long before they finished grooming. The next crew of glam squads arrived.

Nellie, with grown-out roots from an old hair-perm, had to be given a touchup.

Once their heads were shampooed and blow-dried, the hair-stylist used a flat iron to straighten their hair.

The makeup artists made their faces up, brushing eye shadow on their eyelids. Black eyeliner extended their eyelashes. Lastly, their lips were painted with deep-red lipstick.

Most of the glam squad left except one, to stand by for last-minute touchups, if needed.

Teenagers going to the prom were the way Aniyah and Nellie acted. They paraded in front of the mirror. They were flattered about their looks, snapping photos with Aniyah's cell phone.

CHAPTER 22

It was a night out on the town for the elite in South Carolina. Their stretch limos pulled up in front of the entrance of the ballroom of the Powell Estate.

While the drivers held the doors opened, women stepped out, dressed in flowing gowns, mostly in black. A touch of white gowns flowed among them. They lifted their gowns up, in fear of tripping on the wide staircase that led up to the ballroom.

Men suited down in black tuxedos and bow ties escorted many of the women.

Everything was simply grand from the white lights that brightened the walkway up the stairs into the ballroom to tall white pillars with large crystal vases of freshly cut white roses. A huge crystal chandelier brightened the foyer and glittered like stars.

Finally, Aniyah and Nellie arrived. They, too, stepped out of a limo, but were not escorted by gentlemen. They were two ladies on their own, crashing the biggest ball of the year.

Aniyah wobbled up the stairs, with Nellie at her side.

"I'm getting nervous." Nellie's hands trembled.

"Don't start that again. You're with me. I got this under control."

"I really hope so," Nellie said worriedly. She knew tonight could be the night she could become jobless. But she banked on Aniyah to keep her employed. After all, she hoped Powell, Sr. would not get mad at her. She was doing what he had asked of her—to keep her eyes and ears open to what Aniyah had planned for his son.

As they entered, Aniyah looked out among the crowded ballroom, scoping for anyone who might be a threat to her future. There were a few women not on the arms of men. Most were in the age bracket of old man Powell. She could tell by the way they were dressed in sequined gowns that fully covered their bodies and their frosty-colored hair.

There were a few women who were younger, wearing low-cut dresses. They were the ones she worried would easily want to take her place in Jarvis' bed. Aniyah realized she had made the right move in showing up.

Nellie became excited. "Wow! Everything is so pretty. Look at the roses around here. The Powells must have bought out every flower shop in town."

"Yeah, they're nice," Aniyah had to admit.

A waiter dressed in a white shirt, black bow tie, vest and pants approached them. He held a tray of drinks in crystal wineglasses. "Champagne?" he offered.

"Sure will," Nellie said. The waiter handed her a drink.

"None for me, as you can see." Aniyah patted her stomach.

The waiter stopped another waiter who held a tray in his hands. "Give the lovely lady a glass of sparkling white grape juice."

Aniyah smiled. "Thanks, Cutie." She held the glass up to her mouth and sipped on the drink, pretending to sip on the real stuff.

Across the room, like a magnet, she was drawn to Powell, Sr. They locked eyes. She watched him conversing with a gentleman and whisper something in his ear.

It did not take long before Nellie also spotted him. "Oh no, Mr. Powell is coming toward us. He doesn't look glad to see us."

"Who cares? Let me handle the jerk."

Aniyah decided not to make another move. She steadily sipped on her drink.

Powell, Sr. confronted them. He argued, "You have no right to be on my property. Leave or I'll have you thrown out of here. And you," he said, cutting his eyes over at Nellie, whom he had to admit looked very nice in her attire and makeup.

With her right hand on her hips, Aniyah raised her glass with the other hand. "We are not going any damn where. This baby in my belly is a Powell. That's our invitation."

"I'm warning you," he said. He stood close to her, speaking in a low tone. "Leave."

"Make me!" Aniyah snapped back, cutting her eyes at him.

Not far away, Jarvis turned around to discover his father at the door, exchanging words with Aniyah. He swallowed the last bit of champagne that he was drinking and rushed to her rescue; he was surprised to see her. "Baby, what are you doing here?" he asked, approaching Aniyah.

"I couldn't take being at home, while you're here around these hussies. They want to get their paws on you."

Powell, Sr. chuckled. "You're no way equal to the young socialite ladies in this room."

"Dad, please. She's carrying your grandchild. Have respect."

"Handle this situation or else. Get her out of here," Powell, Sr. ordered. He grabbed Nellie's right arm. "And you?" he said, staring at her. "I recognized you. You belong to one of my drivers, Roy." Powell, Sr. pulled her to follow him. "Come with me. I need to have a private word with you."

Nellie nervously went along with Powell, Sr.

Aniyah yelled, "Don't be scared of him, Nellie. He's all bark."

Jarvis took Aniyah by the hand.

"Baby, you know how my dad feels? You're only making things worse for us. You shouldn't have come," he said.

She whined. "I wanted to be with you tonight." Aniyah smothered his lips with kisses. "Don't I look hot to you?" she flirted, turning to show him the peek-a-boo, open lower back of her dress.

Jarvis drooled over how sexy she looked from behind. He admired how the dress hugged her around the hips. He could not help but smile. "You look gorgeous."

"Your white suit turns me on." Again, she kissed him.

Jarvis enjoyed her lips against his; quite aware the women around the ballroom were watching them. A tap on his shoulder interrupted their kiss. It was one of the waiters who needed assistance in the kitchen. He turned to Aniyah. "I have to go take care of business. You can stay. But, please keep far away from my dad. Get lost on the other side of the room."

"I'll wait right here for you to escort me."

Jarvis left while Aniyah made her way in the direction she saw his father had taken Nellie. She made it to the room that they had disappeared into and stopped at the door, listening in on their conversation.

"I repeat. I'm not paying you extra to come to my affairs. I'm paying you to get whatever information you can get out of that tramp," Powell, Sr. scolded Nellie.

"But, Sir, that's why I'm here, to keep close by Aniyah," Nellie explained.

"My estate is where I draw the line. Got it. Tell her you want to leave. I don't give a damn what you tell her. Get lost!" Powell demanded.

"Yes, Sir. I'll try. But Aniyah is bullheaded like you."

"That tramp isn't nothing like me. Go on. Do as I say. Get her out of here."

Aniyah could not believe what she had heard. Nellie, who she thought was her friend, was backstabbing her. She hurried away from the door, when she heard Nellie's footsteps, coming toward it. Aniyah moved fast, looking around as if nothing was going on.

She smiled with her eyes once Nellie came back to join her. "Is everything okay?"

"Mr. Powell gave me a warning."

"Let's go to the ladies room. I want to put some more lipstick on. Jarvis licked it off."

"Maybe we should leave."

With a false grin on her face, Aniyah pulled her by the arm. "I say we go to the ladies room." She saw a waiter and tapped him on the shoulder. "Where's the ladies room?"

"Down the hall, Madam." The waiter pointed in the direction.

"Lead the way." Aniyah pushed Nellie in front of her. She followed her into a bathroom with three stalls.

Aniyah listened for any sound of someone else stirring around. They were alone. Immediately, she grabbed a chunk of Nellie's hair in her hands, shoving her up against the wall, covered in cream wallpaper.

"You're hurting me," Nellie cried. "What did I do?"

"You're been playing me for a fool."

"It's not what you think."

Nellie was quite aware Aniyah had somehow discovered about her dealings with Powell, Sr. Her eyes watered. She was more scared of Aniyah than him.

"All I have done for you and you're out to get me with that fat head," Aniyah said, while she kept her slammed up against the wall.

"I didn't give him any dirt on you. I just took his money."

Aniyah yanked her hair. "You ratted me out."

"I told Mr. Powell you do care for his son. Honest, I did."

Aniyah let go of her, pointing to the door. "Get the hell away from me. Find yourself another job."

Nellie cried, "Please don't fire me. I am your friend."

"I like enemies better. And you're one of them. Go before I…"

Aniyah did not have to say another word; Nellie left like she had roller skates on her feet.

Aniyah walked to the vanity, took a tube of lipstick and refreshed her lips with a new coat. She picked up her purse, ready to go back into the ballroom, but a sharp pain struck her under the stomach, causing her to drop the purse back down on the counter.

She grabbed onto the vanity, taking deep breaths. The pain lingered. "Please. My sweet baby, don't do this to mama. Okay for tomorrow but not tonight."

To Aniyah it was like the baby in the womb had heard her plea. The pain ceased. She grabbed her purse.

The noise of footsteps caused her to look in the mirror. There she saw the image of a woman, dressed in a flowing white gown, hair combed back off her face, twisted up into a bun. Diamond stud earrings sparkled in her ears.

"Oh no, not you, Aunt Tessa," she blurted.

"Rosie Aniyah Sanchez. I've been so worried about where you disappeared. You abandoned the apartment. What are you doing here at this ball?"

"That rat hole?"

"It wasn't that bad. You had a place to rest your head until you could do better."

"Look at me." Aniyah turned around, showing off her belly. "I'm doing great."

"You're with baby?" Tessa's eyes popped open. "With what man?"

Aniyah proudly said, "That's why I have a VIP invite to this party. Jarvis Powell is the papa."

Tessa became weak at the knees, convinced Aniyah was back to her old ways. "I bet he has no idea about your past. You seduced him."

"He loves me. And don't you go running your chops. I paid my dues."

"I won't have to say a word. Someone will eventually recognize you and tell him the truth."

"I'll be Mrs. Powell soon enough. I already have a part of him inside me."

"You owe him the truth."

"Stop telling me what I should do," Aniyah stated firmly. "Get it through your head. You have no say-so in what goes on with me."

"I'm nervous for you."

"Shut up," Aniyah demanded. "Get out of my way." She shoved her aunt to go past her.

"We're family," Tessa reminded her. She wanted to run after her niece, but after drinking two glasses of champagne, she headed straight into the stall.

The signs of trouble were stirring up. Things were not going as she had expected. Aniyah wanted to at least get to shake her hips on the dance floor with her man. Then again, she wondered, was the dream she'd had becoming a reality?

Back into the ballroom, people stood around chattering while soft music played. There was no real partying going on, or so she thought. It was a showcase for the community to show off their fashion and rides. It was time for her to leave, hoping Jarvis would join her.

Aniyah spotted him near the door, engaged in conversation with a gentleman, whose back was turned to her. As she approached them, Jarvis extended his hand out for her to come and be by his side.

"Mr. Chavis, let me introduce you to my lady." Jarvis put his arms around her waist.

The stare Baron gave her was the sign that she was in jeopardy of being busted. But she said nothing.

Jarvis spoke, "Baby, this is Mr. Baron Chavis. Big-time attorney."

"You might want to hire me. Jarvis, you've got your arms around the devil," Baron blurted.

Jarvis was confused. "Mr. Chavis, that's no way to talk to my lady and soon-to-be mother of my child."

"He's mistaken me for someone else. Honey, it's okay." Aniyah patted Jarvis on the arm, hoping Baron would keep his mouth shut.

Baron chuckled. "I know exactly who I'm talking to." He looked at Jarvis. "Do you remember that woman who preyed on the Houstons' fortune?"

"I don't remember her name. She's your wife's niece. Isn't she still serving time?"

"Hell no. She's on your arm."

Jarvis dropped his arm from around Aniyah's waist. "Nah." He stared into her innocent face. "He's mistaken. Isn't he, Baby?"

Aniyah stood frozen. She did not know whether to run for the door or faint on the floor. She knew one day, she would have to face the flames of her past. But she hoped it would have been later, after the baby was born or maybe after she and Jarvis were a happily married couple.

Tessa came out of the bathroom and joined her husband. She saw that Baron clashed with her niece—the lies would not be protected by her husband.

Baron turned to his wife. "Tell Jarvis, this is your crazy niece," he said, pointing the glass he held at Aniyah.

Tears flowed from Tessa's eyes. She had to reveal the truth. "Rosie Aniyah Sanchez, be honest. No lies."

Aniyah became hysterical. Her voice escalated throughout the ballroom. Tearfully, she said, "Yes, it's me."

Jarvis became outraged. "My dad was right. You're a tramp."

Aniyah cried, "I'm not that person anymore. I love you, Jarvis."

"My God, you're carrying my baby," Jarvis said, staring at Aniyah's protruding stomach. "I can't believe I've been made a complete fool." Overwhelmed, he shoved Aniyah aside, leaving frantically.

She tried to run behind him, but Tessa caught her by the arm. "Let him go. He must cool down."

"Get your hands off me." Aniyah jerked away from her aunt. She turned and faced Baron. She scolded him, "You hurt my man for nothing."

Baron chuckled. "I'm letting him know who he's dealing with."

"Because of Jarvis, I've changed."

"You expect me to believe that," Baron argued.

"I don't care what you believe," Aniyah said, turning her head toward the dance floor to lock eyes with her past—the Houstons.

Aniyah watched the three elegantly sisters dressed in flowing gowns, with suited gentlemen as their escorts, parade off the crowded dance floor in her direction. It was obvious that they had overheard her dispute with Baron.

The youngest sister, Kenley, confronted Aniyah first. "Why aren't you still rotting in jail? And, what madman would want you for a mother of his baby?" she asked, noticing Aniyah's stomach.

"I've served my time. Now I go as I please. Get used to it. I'm having Jarvis Powell's baby," Aniyah bragged, rubbing her stomach.

Kenley laughed. "Poor Jarvis is trapped by a whore," she said, rolling her eyes. She stormed away with her date.

Any other time Aniyah would have leaped at her, but she stayed put not to jeopardize the safety of her unborn baby. "That's right, get lost," she told her.

The oldest sister, Milandra, turned to Baron. "Attorney Chavis, why didn't you alert us that she was released?"

"It's my fault," Tessa admitted. "Baron didn't tell because I asked him not to."

"We agreed. We didn't want to bother you and your sisters. We thought Aniyah was rehabilitated and wouldn't be a threat to anyone," Baron explained. "I guess we were wrong."

Aniyah shouted, "Stop talking about me like I'm the worst person on earth. I love Jarvis."

"You love no one but your greedy and crazy self," the middle sister, Noelle, said.

"Call the police. Have her thrown back in jail," Milandra suggested.

"She hasn't done anything legally wrong. At least that we know of," Attorney Chavis said, cutting his eyes at Aniyah.

"I'm sick of you," Aniyah said, turning to face the guests in the ballroom. "May I have everyone's attention?"

Powell, Sr. overheard her voice. He had rushed from the main house, after hearing there was a disturbance at his ball. "You don't get to make announcements here," he shouted.

"This party has turned into my fiesta," Aniyah argued back. "Tell them, Grandpa Powell, you already knew who I was. And…"

Before Aniyah could say another word, Powell, Sr. abruptly stated, "You've said enough. Leave here or I'll have you thrown out," he threatened, gripping her by the arm.

"Get your rusty paws off me." Aniyah pushed his hand away. She decided to save the rest of her revelations about Powell, Sr. for Jarvis' ears.

"I'll be glad to represent you," Baron offered his colleague.

Aniyah cut her eyes at the attorney. She turned her attention to the males in the room. "Rich men, they want me to let ya'll know that I'm the diva who tried to con money from these uppity Houston sisters."

Milandra lashed at Aniyah. "Watch your lowlife mouth."

"And you, high and mighty attorney Chavis, tell everyone you and I have had a few rounds in the bed. And now you're mad, because I didn't want you. Sorry you got stuck with second best." Aniyah darted her eyes at her Aunt Tessa, then at Baron.

"You're crazy," Baron barked.

"Rosie Aniyah, please, you're embarrassing yourself and me," Tessa pleaded.

"I hate you, Aunt Tessa. I'm your only blood, and you treat me like dirt. Go on and be a puppet for your hubby. My baby is my family," Aniyah bellowed, pointing to her stomach.

Aniyah eyed the guests to see all eyes were on her. The music had stopped. She switched her mood on the guests. "None of you have anything to do beside be nosey."

Tessa begged. "Rosie Aniyah. Please hush. That's no way to speak."

"No one is rude to my guests, Missy. I said get the hell out of here," Powell, Sr. threatened Aniyah one last time.

"I don't have to listen to any of you. I'm my own woman," Aniyah announced. "Jarvis will forgive me," she said as she turned to leave, but buckled to her knees, when another sharp pain struck her in the bottom of her stomach. She let out a fierce scream. Water began to trickle down her legs like she was a toddler, wetting her pants.

Aniyah tried to stand back up, but the pain kept her down on her knees in a crunched-up position. Tears flooded her face, causing the black mascara to smear under her eyes.

Tessa came to her aid. She pleaded, "Someone, please help me get my niece to a car. She's gone into labor."

"A Houston doesn't put their manicured nails on trash," Milandra Houston said, brushing her hands against each other. She walked away on the arm of her husband, as did her sister, Noelle.

Powell, Sr. rushed over, only to help secure his investment in his grandchild. He tried to lift Aniyah but she pulled away from him.

"Let go of me, you old fart," she yelled, squeezing her eyes closed to bear another pain that had followed behind the first. There was nothing she could do. She was at the mercy of her enemies for the sake of her baby.

Tessa wiped the sweat off Aniyah's forehead with the sheer scarf that went with her gown. "I may have to deliver the baby," she said.

"The hell you will. Get me to the hospital," Aniyah demanded.

"Hey, you two," Powell, Sr. flagged his waiters. "Give her a hand." He ordered the waiters to help Aniyah outside and into the closest parked limo.

"I'll ride with her," Tessa volunteered. She held on to Aniyah's arm.

Baron reached for his wife's other hand. "We're going home. There's nothing you can do."

Tessa was annoyed at her husband. "I will not leave my niece to be alone. She's still my family. Sorry, but honey, this is where I draw the line."

"She doesn't deserve your kindness." Baron watched his wife leave, aiding her problematic niece.

Tessa was accompanied by Nellie, who had never left the ball. Nellie introduced herself as Aniyah's friend. "You may need help," she informed Tessa.

"My niece is a handful," Tessa said. She got into the limo following Aniyah, who was in agony.

"Get away from me," Aniyah screamed at her aunt. Then her attention went to Nellie, who had opened the door, pushing her to the middle of the backseat. "Where the hell did you come from?"

"I never left. My boyfriend is working tonight. He caught me here. He's your driver," Nellie explained. "Hurry, Roy, and move this limo."

"You and my aunt, get lost. I don't need ya'll."

Aniyah felt like she was held hostage between two women who obviously, at this moment, she despised. She wanted so much for them to disappear and leave her to have her baby in peace. But that was not going to happen. Her Aunt Tessa was not about to let her give birth to her first great-niece or nephew without her. And Aniyah figured Nellie was there to keep Powell, Sr. abreast of his first grandchild.

Aniyah no longer put up a fuss. She concentrated on getting to the hospital so that her baby could arrive and she would be relieved of the labor pains.

Relaxed, resting her head on the back of the seat with her eyes closed, Aniyah held her stomach tight, taking deep breaths, per her Aunt Tessa's request. She thought she may not have been in control at the moment, but once at the hospital, she would demand from the nurses and doctors to keep her aunt and Nellie away.

"How did you and Aniyah become friends?" Tessa curiously asked Nellie.

"I work for the Powells," Nellie said.

"She's a spy." Aniyah jumped into their conversation, even though her aunt ignored her comment. She listened as Tessa updated Nellie on the moments, leading up to her going into labor.

CHAPTER 23

Being pregnant had its benefits. When Aniyah arrived at the hospital, she felt like a superstar—she was in the spotlight.

A male volunteer greeted her. He assisted her into a wheelchair. He pushed her down a long corridor that led to the elevators. Tessa and Nellie, moving fast in high-heels, rushed right alongside.

"Go away," Aniyah hollered, "I have no need for you, haters."

"I'm not going anywhere," Tessa said, overlooking her niece's nasty comment. "Concentrate on your baby."

Aniyah looked over her shoulder at the volunteer. "Can't you tell them to disappear?"

"I'm not getting in the middle of a family feud. My job is to get you to the maternity ward. I'll let the nurses handle ya'll's feud," the volunteer said, pushing Aniyah right along.

The pain became so intense that Aniyah could no longer bear it. Her tears turned into a downpour. Never in her life did she think bringing a baby in the world would cause such severe pain.

As she rode the elevator, she was curious whether Jarvis was somewhere grieving because of her. She thought of all times, her past would ruin a time when they should be sharing this joyous moment—the birth of their baby.

When the elevator doors opened, a nurse was there.

"Hello, I'm McGillan. I'll be one of the nurses on duty to take care of you."

Aniyah continued to cry in agony, but got in a few words. "Please tell these two," she pointed her thumbs at her aunt and Nellie, "to get to stepping."

The nurse was familiar with what Aniyah meant. Labor pains were a time when she witnessed patients wanting to have a private delivery. She turned to Tessa and Nellie. "There's a family room down the hall on the left. You can wait there."

"I wish to stay with my niece," Tessa said.

"Get it in your head, I don't want you here," Aniyah cried.

"I'm sorry, but the patient doesn't want you to go with her. Ma'am, don't take it personally," the nurse said.

Tessa begged, "Please let me know as soon as my niece has the baby?"

"Someone will inform you," the nurse responded, pushing Aniyah down the hallway.

Everything went fast for Aniyah. The nurse got her settled in her room. Her new evening wear was stripped off of her, replaced with a hospital gown, and her stomach was strapped with a monitor that gave her music of thumping sounds of her baby's heartbeat.

In so much discomfort, she became hysterical. "Get this baby out!" She repeated the words over and over, but the nurses that monitored her did not pay her any attention. They continued to prepare her for the delivery.

"Hello, Ms. Powell. Your baby is eager to come into this world," Dr. Guess said, entering the room.

Relieved to see him, Aniyah was hopeful to be long gone of her pain. In a matter of minutes, she would not only be responsible for herself but for a child, too.

Without any substantial income, the remaining money she had

in the bank would not be enough to take care of herself, much less a baby. *I must win Jarvis back. First thing is to deliver him and I a healthy baby.*

Dr. Guess covered his hands with sterile gloves. He instructed Aniyah to move her bottom to the foot of the bed, which converted into a delivery table. Aniyah eased her feet into stirrups.

"Baby is ready." Dr. Guess informed her, once he finished his examination.

Nurse McGillan stood by her side. Across the room was a group of other nurses from the nursery, on duty to make sure the new arrival was physically okay. They stood by a portable crib on wheels, ready to roll the baby into the nursery for care.

"Open your legs wide," Dr. Guess instructed, "then on the count of three, I want you to sit up and push as hard as you can."

"Shit. Knock me out and take it," Aniyah demanded.

"I think you're capable of handling a vaginal delivery."

Nurse McGillan easily lifted Aniyah in an almost sitting position, as if Aniyah were three pounds.

Dr. Guess counted to three. Then he ordered, "Push."

With her eyes closed tight, Aniyah's ears captured Dr. Guess's voice, again saying, "push." Nurse McGillan joined in with the doctor, giving her orders to push as well.

Aniyah gritted her teeth. She did what she was told to do, but became exhausted.

The doctor saw the agony in her face that displayed she needed a time-out.

"Take a quick break," he said.

It felt good to Aniyah to hear him give her permission to rest her head back on the pillow. But before she could get too comfortable, it was time for her to get pushing.

Again, she used all her strength and did as she was told. After several pushes, a baby with a head full of ebony hair fell into Dr. Guess's hands.

He smiled. "You have yourself a fine baby boy."

"I have a son," Aniyah wept. So exhausted, she fell back on the pillow. She realized things were going to turn in her favor. She glimpsed at her baby cuddled in the doctor's arms with closed eyes. Aniyah stretched out her arms. "Give him to me."

"You'll have plenty of time to hold your son. He needs to be examined, first," Dr. Guess informed her.

Aniyah listened for the first cry from her baby, knowing babies let out a cry when they arrived into the world. Her smile disappeared once she did not hear any sound coming from her baby.

Nervously, she kept her eyes on her son. She watched the nurse rest his tiny body in the portable crib, under a warming light—still, she heard no crying.

When the nurse started caring for him, Baby Jarvis let out a loud cry, echoing throughout the room.

Hearing his voice, Aniyah was relieved, opening up her mouth to form a big smile.

It didn't take long before the staff finished treating mother and newborn. Aniyah got her chance to hold her baby for the first time. "Jarvis Powell, III," she whispered in his ear.

Aniyah placed a kiss on his forehead. Holding the baby made her understand that her life could no longer be about her needs. Baby Jarvis' needs were her priority. And that meant she had to find a way to get his father back into her life. The baby, she hoped, would bond her and Jarvis back together.

Tessa and Nellie entered the room. They had been informed of the baby's sex by one of the nurses. Aniyah witnessed tears flowing down her aunt's face.

"Oh, he's so handsome. My new great-nephew." Tessa came closer to the bed.

Aniyah proudly pulled Baby Jarvis closer to her bosom. "I'm his mama," she bragged.

"Yes you are," Tessa agreed.

"Congratulations," Nellie said, fascinated by the news. She could not wait to report to Powell, Sr.. She had no doubt that he would be willing to pay extra money, when she delivered him the good news of the second heir to his assets. She listened for any other news that would bring her extra pay.

"He looks like you, Rosie Aniyah," Tessa suggested, "and his dark hair comes from our side of the family."

Dr. Guess, who washing his hands in a sink, heard a familiar voice. He turned around. "Tessa Chavis."

"Yes," Tessa said. She took her focus off the baby on to Dr. Guess.

"How is Attorney Chavis?" he asked.

Aniyah jumped into their conversation. "He's a creep."

"Rosie Aniyah, please hush," Tessa said, turning back toward Dr. Guess. "Baron is always busy." Tessa grinned, speaking of her husband.

"Isn't there any other lawyer besides your man?" Aniyah asked. *Of all the doctors in the world, my aunt has to know the one that is treating me.*

Small towns always equal people in the same circle know of each other, she thought.

"There are others around. Baron happens to be one many trust." Tessa defended her husband.

"I wouldn't use him if he represented me for free." Aniyah rolled her eyes.

Dr. Guess watched as they disputed. "Are you relatives?" The doctor directed his question at Tessa. He saw how his patient resembled her.

"This is my niece," Tessa said.

"I delivered your great-nephew. That's even more special to

me," Dr. Guess said, staring at Aniyah. He did not want to ask more questions, but the only niece he recalled that Tessa had was the one in jail for embezzlement. Never did he put two and two together. This patient had no characteristics of the ugly things that he'd heard in the news. "I'm confused. You have two nieces? This can't be the niece that…" Dr. Guess stopped what he was about to say.

"You can say it, went to jail," Aniyah admitted, throwing up her hands in frustration. "Everyone in this damn town won't let me forget it."

"Watch your mouth, Rosie Aniyah Sanchez," Tessa scolded.

"Geez. Can you just call me, Aniyah?"

With nurses still in the room, Dr. Guess did not want gossip spread on the ward about one of his patients. "Nurses, please give me and my patient some privacy."

The nurses dismissed themselves. Aniyah noticed Nellie. She was skeptical of her. "You can get lost, too." Aniyah fanned her away.

"That's no way to speak to your friend," Tessa said, lightly tapping Aniyah on the hand.

"She's not my friend. A traitor is what she is. Nellie, go wherever. Leave!" Aniyah demanded.

"I want no problems," Nellie said. She stormed out. When she stepped outside the door, she stayed put, hoping Aniyah would say something she could make money off of.

Dr. Guess turned to Aniyah. "I'm not here to judge your life. My job as your doctor is to look after you and your baby's health," he explained.

Tears flowed down Aniyah's cheeks, feeling good to hear that the doctor did not judge her like others did. She wiped her eyes. "Thanks for taking care of me and my baby."

"You're welcome. I'll leave and give you your space. Good seeing you again, Tessa."

"I'll tell Baron I saw you," Tessa said.

Outside the door, once Nellie heard Dr. Guess saying his good-byes, she hurried away.

Aniyah held her baby and played with his tiny fingers.

"I'm a mama now," she said.

"That you are," Tessa said joyfully. "But you do need rest. I'll take the baby," Tessa volunteered, wanting to get a chance to hold her great-nephew.

Aniyah pulled her baby close to her bosom. "You can't touch him," she said spitefully.

"I'm not against you." Tessa wiped a tear that eased down her nose. "We must solve our differences at another time."

"Leave, Aunt Tessa." Aniyah was annoyed.

Tessa did not want to argue on such a joyous occasion. She grabbed her purse and let Aniyah be. For the first time, mother and son were left alone. Baby Jarvis slept peacefully in her arms. Aniyah gave him a lovable peck on his forehead.

It was times like this that made her think of her own father. She didn't want her baby to suffer some of the pain of not having a father around like she had lived her life. It made her yearn for reconciliation between she and Jarvis.

She rubbed her baby's arm and continued to ponder what was going to happen once she was released. The penthouse was now off limits to her. The credit card was probably voided like a bad check. And she was on borrowed time with the use of his cell phone. *Damn*. Her life was again on a downfall.

A nurse entered the room. "Delivery can make you tired. You need to get some rest."

"I have to watch my baby. I can't sleep while he sleeps."

"I can take him to the nursery. The nurses will look after him."

"Keep him safe," Aniyah said, giving the nurse a quick stare in the eyes.

Baby Jarvis went from his mother's arms into the nurse's arms. The nurse rested his small body inside the portable crib. With his fist balled up to his face, Baby Jarvis, tired from his own delivery, stayed asleep.

"I'll bring him back when it's time for his next feeding."

"How soon is that?"

"You'll have plenty of time to rest. Feeding time again is in three hours."

"'Night-'night, 'lil fellow," Aniyah waved goodbye and turned on her side.

CHAPTER 24

Outside the hospital, Nellie paced the walkway until the shiny Mercedes-Benz parked in front of her.

She noticed the man's white tuxedo as he stepped out of the vehicle. Not knowing who he was, her conclusion was that he was one of the guests that attended the Powells' ball.

"Hi." She waved. "Coming from the Powell estate?"

"Yes, I was there. And, who are you?"

"I'm Nellie. I work for the Powells."

"I'm Baron Chavis. That's my wife's niece who went into labor."

Nellie smiled. "You're the proud great-uncle of a great-nephew. Your wife and I waited for Aniyah to have the baby."

"Poor kid." After giving his opinion of Aniyah, he noticed Tessa, coming through the revolving hospital doors. He pointed. "There she is."

Nellie turned around to see Tessa, who directed her attention at her, not her husband.

"After Aniyah's nasty ways, I thought you were long gone," Tessa said.

"Waiting on my ride. My boyfriend is a little late," Nellie said, steady watching what vehicles drove up.

"We'll be glad to take you home," Baron offered, willing to give a beautiful woman a ride.

"That's nice of you, but my boyfriend will be here soon." Nellie told half the truth; her boyfriend would most likely be the driver for Powell, Sr.

Still being his spy, she had informed old man Powell of the delivery of his grandson. It was he that she waited for. She wanted the Chavises to be gone. She did not want them to have any clue that she was in cahoots with Powell, Sr.

Finally, the Chavises said their goodbyes, got into their vehicle and sped off.

The next vehicle that pulled in front of the hospital was the limo with old man Powell in it. As Nellie figured, her boyfriend, Roy, was the driver.

In the backseat, with the window rolled down, Powell, Sr. called to her. "Get in." He opened the door.

Nellie hopped in. She waved to say hello to her boyfriend.

"Is that heir of mine as handsome as I am?" Powell Sr. simpered, exposing his dentures.

Nellie concluded that the old man might have been good-looking in his younger years, but in his old age, full of wrinkles, his looks had deteriorated. "Yes he is," she said, wanting to make him feel good.

"Who delivered the baby?"

"Dr. Guess."

"Is the doc still in the room with her?" Powell, Sr. continued to question her.

"No one is with Aniyah. Her auntie just left."

"Then she should be alone. I need to pay her a visit."

"What about your son? Does he know she's had the baby?"

"That's no concern of yours. What's the room number?"

"Three twenty-six."

"Find a park. This may take a little while," he said to the driver and grabbed the doorknob once parked. He opened the door and stepped out, still dressed in his tuxedo.

Powell, Sr. placed dark shades over his eyes. He did not want to be recognized in the hospital he had donated funds to in the past.

The maternity ward was quiet. He moved fast through the hallway and followed the signage on the walls that led him to the nursery.

Once he arrived in front of a huge windowpane, he was thankful the blinds were drawn. He heard a few cries from some of the babies, while others slept.

Reading each label on the cribs, Powell, Sr. searched for the name Sanchez. To his surprise, he saw his last name on one of the portable cribs toward the back. He mumbled. "The tramp used my last name." *I hope that son of mine didn't get married without my knowledge. Jarvis can't be that dumb.* He prayed not.

A nurse noticed him. She was headed to greet him, but he scattered. He found his way to room three twenty-six.

The door was closed. He listened for any sound coming from inside. Once he was assured the coast was clear, he entered and noticed Aniyah was in a private room. He saw that she lay on her side with her back to the door.

Easing up to the bed, he slapped his right hand over her mouth.

Aniyah felt his touch and woke up, smelling the strong odor of tobacco. She tried to scream, while turning over on her back to see who held her hostage. Once she recognized Powell, Sr., she forcefully shoved his hands away.

"Get your freaking paws off me," she snapped at him.

"Shut your mouth," he whispered, placing his hand back over her mouth.

Aniyah tried to speak, but this time he held a tight grip on her.

"You listen carefully. That boy you pushed out of you is a Powell. Name the price and turn him over to me."

He lifted his hands off of her mouth so that she could respond to him.

"Never."

He placed his hands back over her mouth. "You have no choice. I'll turn you into the police. Using my name as your own. Big-time gold-digger. Name your price and be gone."

Again, he lifted his hands off of her mouth for her answer.

She cried, "I've changed. Jarvis and I will get back together. And, I'll tell him you know where his mother is."

"You empty-head tramp, don't try to blackmail me. You'll be back in jail before you get anywhere near my son. Believe me, you can't take a baby with you." He chuckled, removing his cell phone from his pocket. He was eager to call law enforcement.

Aniyah tried to grab the phone, but had no success. "You win this round," she surrendered. "Now get the hell out."

"You'd better not play games with me. You'll get paid enough to take a flight to wherever you want to go. Go far away from here. Are we in agreement?"

Aniyah submitted one last time. "Yes."

Powell Sr. disappeared, like he had never come to visit her.

Once Powell Sr. returned back into the limo, Nellie wanted the scoop on what had occurred between him and Aniyah. But she dared not ask the old man any questions. She dismissed the thoughts only to bring up her payment for her good deeds.

"Roy and I are saving for a house. I would like my money," she said.

Lighting up a cigar, Powell, Sr. cut his eyes at her. He took a couple of puffs, blew smoke, then decided to respond. "In due time," he grumbled.

The driver gazed into the rearview mirror. "Where to?" he asked, interrupting them.

"Home," Powell, Sr. ordered. He rested in the seat.

The foul smell of the cigar made Nellie want to gag. She came to the conclusion that no woman would ever deal with Powell's habit of smoking one cigar after another. She had never seen him without one. The habit was like a person who never left their glasses behind.

Her nose stayed turned up until they reached the Powell estate. Some relief came of the odor when her boyfriend got out of the limo, opening the door for his boss.

"Wait here," Powell Sr. ordered, "I'm going to check to see if my son is home."

Nellie was convinced that Powell Sr. was going to break the news to Jarvis about the birth of his son.

There would always be a doorman who opened the front door of the house when Powell Sr. arrived home. Once inside, he screamed Jarvis' name, but got no response.

An elderly caretaker came immediately; she had been with the Powell family for many years. "Mr. Powell Jr. isn't home, Sir."

"Has he been back here since the ball?"

"No, Sir."

He trotted back to the limo. "The Penthouse," he ordered his driver, "and make it snappy."

"Yes, Mr. Powell," the driver said.

"It's late," Nellie said, yearning to go home.

"Pumpkin," the driver called her. "Hush."

"Thank you. At least she's not only getting on my nerves," Powell Sr. said, irritated.

Nellie pouted but said nothing else.

When they arrived at the penthouse, Powell Sr. did not wait for the driver to open the door for him. Instead, he jumped out with his cigar hanging from his mouth. He went straight into the lobby and spoke to the security guard.

"I'm here to see my son. Let me up," he ordered.

"Sorry, Mr. Powell, but I've been instructed by your son that he wants no visitors."

Powell, Sr. reached in his pocket. He took out a hundred-dollar bill, slamming the money down on top of the guard's desk.

The guard scooped up the bill, giving Powell, Sr. access to visit the penthouse.

Powell, Sr. entered and saw that the only light that glowed in the room was coming from the outside lamps on the terrace. He flicked on the light switch and spotted Jarvis, slouched on the sofa.

"I know darn well, you're not sobbing over that tramp," he fussed. He noticed his son's tearful face.

"Dad, please leave."

"I told you she wasn't any good. So get your ass up. Stop weeping."

Powell, Sr. snatched him by the arms, but Jarvis jerked away.

"Would it make you feel better if I told you, you're a dad yourself."

Jarvis jumped to his feet. "Aniyah had the baby."

"She went straight to the hospital from the ball." He slapped his son across the back. "It's a boy."

"I need to go and see my son." Jarvis forgot about wailing in his sorrows. He slipped on a pair of black leather shoes.

Powell, Sr. grabbed him by the shirt. "We need to talk."

"Dad, what now?"

"That baby doesn't belong with her. He belongs with you."

"She's his mom."

"Get ahold of yourself. You have rights, too. Soon or later, she'll be back behind bars. Your son will be tossed into foster care or Tessa Chavis will try to get her claws on him," Powell, Sr. argued.

Jarvis thought about Aniyah's history. As much as he wanted to disagree with his father, he understood what he was saying was true. He submitted. "I'll take claim of him."

"That's my boy." Powell, Sr. patted him on the back. He got on the elevator with a big smirk on his face. Things were working in his favor. He had his son and Aniyah right where he wanted them to be, giving him full access to groom his grandson to carry on the family tradition of becoming a banker.

Back in the limo, Powell, Sr. ordered the driver to take him home.

"You found your son?" Nellie asked curiously.

"You need to keep her in her place," Powell, Sr. said to the driver. "She's got too much mouth."

"Pumpkin, stop it," the driver said, calling Nellie his pet name for her.

"I'm ready to go home," she whined, resting back in the seat. The ride from the penthouse to the estate was quiet, but the smell again from Powell, Sr.'s cigars left her nauseous.

Once arrived, Powell, Sr. did not jump out of the limo; instead he waited on the driver to open his door. Reaching into his pocket, he pulled out two tens and a five-dollar bill. He tossed it onto the backseat. "Keep the change."

Nellie counted the money. "This is it," she yelled, widening her eyes.

Powell, Sr. turned around, focusing his attention to the driver. I warned her about her mouth. You can't keep her in her place. You're both fired."

"Yo, Mr. Powell, I need this job. I got bills," the driver pleaded, cutting his eyes at his woman. "Damn, Pumpkin, keep your trap shut."

Nellie yelled, "All the work I've done. I get twenty-five dollars. Roy, we're not stupid enough to fall for this."

"I'll get another driver to drop you and the chatterbox off at the nearest bus stop," Powell, Sr. hollered back at them. He had made his way into the house, ordering another driver to drive them off his property.

CHAPTER 25

The hospital room, frigid like the inside of a refrigerator, caused Aniyah to cover her shoulders with a lightweight blanket. She smothered her face into the softness of the pillow, dampening it with her tears.

"Damn that old fart to hell." She pressed her fingers into the blanket, holding a tight grip on it. She hated that old man Powell had turned her into a crybaby.

No way is he going to get my baby boy.

Aniyah brushed away the tears. It was no time to feel pity. She needed to put things in perspective. First and foremost, Baby Jarvis was her priority. Then again, why not go for it all. She had to admit in the past she was a devil in heels, but since she had met Jarvis, he'd made her want to become a better person. Her heart fluttered; he no longer wanted any dealings with her. It felt unreal not having the urge to get revenge on him.

On the other hand, his father was another story. If he wished to play dirty, so did she.

From time to time, powerful men like Powell, Sr. had to have a history of diving into ruthless things. She needed something more to get him to back off from claiming her baby to use as a pawn; the way she thought he had used Jarvis.

"The private investigator," Aniyah mumbled. "He's the answer to my problem."

Next to the bed, she reached for the phone that set on a small stand. She was about to call the number but realized she did not know it off-hand.

Easing out of the bed, she made her way to the closet, where her belongings were stored. She searched in her purse for her cell phone. Browsing through her contacts, Aniyah came across the number, pushing the SEND button.

"Hello," the investigator grumbled.

She could tell by his harsh tone, she had awakened him.

"Hi, this is Aniyah. Do you remember me?"

The investigator yawned. "Call me in the morning. I'm closed."

"Man, I need help."

"After hours will cost you big bucks."

"I need toilet crap on Mr. Powell."

"Stinky dirt. Like, where's the woman he's sending checks to?"

"You're turning me on," Aniyah said vindictively.

"One thousand dollars. I'll map the path to her."

"Five hundred dollars," she responded, doing her best to get his fee down.

"No negotiation. One thousand. Take it or leave it."

Aniyah gave in. "Deal," she mumbled. "I'm in the hospital."

"Give me a call when you go home."

All of a sudden, Aniyah assumed he was ending the call. "Don't hang up." She spoke quickly. "You get the info. Be ready to take me to her. Deal?"

"Cash equals a deal."

"Go back to sleep." She ended their conversation.

Slipping back into bed, Aniyah prayed that the investigator would locate Jarvis' mother. Anything to keep old man Powell, Sr. from taking claim of her baby. She also wanted to win back her man.

She tossed the blanket back over her shoulders. Aniyah felt

relaxed enough to try to fall asleep. The door opened and she turned to see who had entered the room. To her surprise, Jarvis stood in the doorway. She eased into an upright seating position. Tears watered her eyes. "I'm so happy you came. We have a baby boy."

"I saw my son," he said with authority.

Jarvis had visited the nursery. He'd identified to the nurses that he was the father of Baby Jarvis. He wore a band on his arm to give him free access to the nursery to see and feed his son.

"I'm so sorry. I should've told you about my past."

"You deceived me. A fool. That's what I was." He spoke to her from the foot of the bed.

"No you weren't. It's all me. At first, I met you for the wrong reasons. Your kindness and love made me see things differently."

Looking at Jarvis, Aniyah was quite aware that he was a man every woman dreamt of having in their life: well groomed, compassionate and a great lover.

"I defended you to my dad. And he had you figured out."

"That's the person I used to be. I've changed. Jarvis, I truly have."

"Forget the tears. I'm not buying it. It's time you taste hurt."

"What are you saying?" Aniyah asked frantically.

"I won't let my son be raised by an unfit mom."

"You don't mean that."

She hopped out of bed and went to him, placing her arms around his neck. Never had she thrown herself at a man. If anything, she made men drool for her. But for Jarvis, she would do anything to get him back. She began to kiss him.

The softness of her lips against his, made Jarvis kiss her in return. With her breasts pressed against his chest, he grabbed her by the back of her hair, circulating his tongue in her mouth. His manhood began to harden. Not to be back under her spell, he let go of her hair and removed her hands from around his neck. As he wiped his lips with the back of his hand, he stepped back from her.

"Goodbye. See you in court," he said.

Aniyah watched him exit the door. With her hand on her wet lips, she felt worse than ever.

Back into bed, she cried until she fell asleep. Even then, she was not at peace, dreaming about her life growing up in Mexico as a little girl with no father, only her mother and Aunt Tessa. She played on the grounds of hotels and rich folks' homes, while they cleaned, washed and ironed. She vowed not to be caught as an adult doing such work; people would work for her.

She continued to dream about the day she thought her wish had come true, running away from home as a teen with a tourist, who she thought would give her a good life. Instead he introduced her to the streets; making her not only special to him, but men who were willing to pay the right price. It took a new incoming girl to get the attention off of her, giving her the opportunity to escape. Not having anywhere to go and limited funds, she used her body to lure men into her web. And that's the life she'd lived until she landed in prison.

"It's feeding time," the nurse said, awakening her.

Aniyah jumped. She imagined that she was in prison with the correctional officer waking her up for the morning breakfast. Instead, the nurse held her baby and a tiny bottle in her hands.

"Jarvis the Third," she said, reaching for him to give him his after midnight feeding.

"Nice name for a boy."

"It's his father's name."

The nurse gave Aniyah instructions on how to feed the baby. Jarvis was to drink at least two ounces of milk, followed by a rub on his back to let him have a nice burp, instead of spitting up the milk. "I'll be back to see if you want me to take him back to the nursery. That's your option."

"Thanks."

Aniyah took the plastic lid from off the bottle, gently placing it in her baby's mouth. His little jaws began to move, drinking his milk.

"And thank you, Baby Jarvis, for waking me up from my crazy old life."

The nurse returned the baby to the nursery. After a nap, Aniyah peeked from under the covers and saw Dr. Guess standing at the foot of her bed.

"Hello there." The doctor locked eyes with hers. "How are you feeling this afternoon?"

"Happy my baby is here."

Dr. Guess examined her stomach and vaginal area. "Any pains or discomfort?"

"No. My sleep was awful."

"Most ladies claim after they deliver, sleep is the best."

"Dreams and more dreams."

"Want to share?"

"It's personal."

"Things look good. You'll be discharged tomorrow." Dr. Guess removed the plastic gloves that covered his hands. He tossed them in the trashcan. "Any questions before I go?"

"Going home is what I needed to hear." Aniyah wondered where home would be.

After the doctor left, Baby Jarvis was brought to her again for feeding. He sucked most of the milk out of the four-ounce bottle before she insisted that he be taken back to the nursery.

Aniyah wanted to get things moving. She called the investigator. He answered, "Hello."

"I get out of the hospital tomorrow."

"Doll face, give me a time? And have my cash."

"I'm in a hospital, not at a bank. I don't know what time yet."

"Don't get smart. We'll talk after I get the cash."

They ended the call.

Aniyah rested on the pillow. She turned on the television for the first time, flipping the channels until she turned to the inspiration channel. The minister gave his sermon. She heard him as he spoke of how God truly loves and wants everyone to have a full abundance of joy in his or her lives. Listening to his words made her feel good until Nellie walked in.

Aniyah flicked off the television. "Oh hell no. You know how to ruin a person's day. Get lost," she fussed.

"I know you don't trust me. But I'm your friend." Nellie carried a blue-and-white gift bag. She handed it over to Aniyah.

"Giving me a present won't make us friends."

"It's something for the baby."

Aniyah took out a blue two-pieced short set, small enough to fit a doll. She smiled for a second. "He'll be handsome in this." Aniyah cut her eyes at her. "That's if I let him wear it."

"Please forgive me. I was wrong. But I needed all the money that I could get. Roy and I want to buy a house." Nellie got comfortable in a chair, determined not to leave until Aniyah heard her out. "Mr. Powell is nothing but a user. He paid me twenty-five bucks."

Aniyah had to laugh. "That's what you get. Even though, he's a jerk."

"He made me think he'd pay me well, if I spied on you."

"He was here last night. Was it because you went back and told him I had the baby?"

"Yes," Nellie admitted. She looked down at the floor. "I'm so sorry."

"He ditched your ass last night. That's why you're here, begging for me to forgive you."

"Okay, yes, it wasn't right. I did it for the money."

Aniyah could relate to what she had done. It was like listening to how she had acted in the past. She decided to forgive her, but never forget. She waved her hand at her. "Girl, it's squashed."

"I'll make it up to you somehow. I'll tell Jarvis Powell you have changed for the better. And, his father is manipulative."

"Jarvis knows how his old fart papa is. He's weak when it comes to him. Hey, I'll pay you thirty bucks, if you go and convince him that I love him. That's more than his cheap papa paid you."

They both had no choice but to laugh. Nellie gave Aniyah a hug.

"Get lost." Aniyah pulled away from her, pointing to the door for her to leave. "I'm sleepy."

Nellie exited the door with Tessa coming in not too long behind her.

Tessa carried a box in her hand wrapped in blue metallic paper. A blue rattle was tied to a blue bow on the box. "I saw your friend leaving."

"I'll never get any sleep." Aniyah had closed her eyes for a second, but opened them to stare at the rainbow of colors in her aunt's skirt. "Auntie, when are you going to get rid of them wide skirts with hundreds of colors?"

Tessa spun around. "This is the way I like to dress."

"You're married to a freakin' lawyer. Get sophisticated. A nice suit or something."

"Never mind my clothing. Here's a gift for my nephew."

Aniyah opened the box. Inside were a variety of blue-colored outfits.

Tessa sat in the same chair where Nellie had. "You have any idea when they'll let you go home?"

"What home?"

"I wish I could bring you and the baby to my house. Baron won't hear of it."

"Put your foot down. Take charge. It's partly your house, too."

"He's loyal to his clients and friends. Letting you live in our home would betray them."

"Forget it. I'm out of here tomorrow," she snapped. "I'll walk the streets with my baby in my arms until I find a place for us. I'll do whatever I have to do."

"Don't speak like that. It only gets you into trouble. I'll get you another apartment where you used to stay."

"My baby is a Powell. He can't live in a rat hole."

"It's a place to rest your head."

One month in the apartment won't hurt. It'd give me enough time to win Jarvis back. "I'll go back there. But you get me a bigger place. One bedroom is not enough. Two bedrooms." Aniyah closed her eyes. "I'm tired. Aunt Tessa, go get the apartment."

"Not leaving, yet."

"No peace, even in a hospital." Aniyah eased back down in the bed, covering up her face with the blanket.

A catnap was the only sleep that Aniyah got during the day. The nurses were in and out of the room. Blood was drawn from her arm from a lab technician. Her Aunt Tessa did not help with her getting rest either, awakening her, when she applauded for a contestant that had won a vehicle on a TV game show. Then feeding times for the baby came around pretty fast, between her hot breakfast, lunch and dinner. Rest was not an option.

Before Aniyah swallowed the last bite of apple pie on her dinner plate, Tessa decided to leave. She tossed her bag on her right arm.

"I've made the call for your apartment. You and the baby have a place to live."

"That creep, old fart Powell, wants to take my son away from me," Aniyah admitted.

"Over my dead body," Tessa said with beaming eyes.

"He's going to use my mistakes against me." Aniyah softened up.

"Let me handle Mr. Powell," Tessa suggested. "He can be bull-headed."

"You mean that?" Aniyah was overwhelmed. She thought her aunt never would want to help her again.

"One day you'll believe I do love you." Tessa went to her niece, giving her a hug. "Maybe that old mean niece you used to be may finally be somewhat gone. Being a mama can make you change. Believe that, Rosie Aniyah, good things will happen for you. Trust in God."

"I want my baby's papa. You think God will see to it that Jarvis forgives me?"

"Pray. If your heart is sincere, He'll make it happen."

"I hope so," Aniyah said, wiping her watery eyes.

"I'll bring the key for the apartment. See you tomorrow around twelve."

It wasn't long before Tessa left the hospital. Aniyah hoped once she was discharged, she would be able to handle her business without her aunt trying to huddle around her.

Following her aunt's advice, Aniyah closed her eyes and prayed.

Dear God. Sometimes I can be a little messy…all right, a lot messy, but I'm tryin' to be a good girl. I need to keep my baby and win back my man. They're my only hope of getting right. Can you please help me? Amen.

CHAPTER 26

No matter how busy the workday was, Powell, Sr. saw to it that he puffed a cigar. To alleviate the stale smell, he constantly sprayed vanilla air freshener. He coughed from the fumes, counting the butts in the ceramic ashtray that sat on his desk—four butts left. It was time for him to go home. He hurried, scribbling his signature on the last document that came across his desk for approval.

Powell, Sr. signaled for his secretary to not put through any late callers whom wished to speak with him.

For his travel home, he lit up a fifth cigar. He stood up, slipping on his dark-brown suit jacket, which he never buttoned. One attempt and he would need a seamstress to sew the buttons back on. His secretary paged him before he could come from behind the desk. He pushed down the flashing amber button to receive her message.

"You have a visitor, Mr. Powell," she announced.

"Shit," he muffled, then responded to her out loud, "Who is it?" He was not expecting any walk-in clients.

"It's Tessa Sanchez-Chavis. Attorney Chavis' wife."

Good Lord. He figured right away, Tessa wanted to speak of their shared interest in the new arrival to their families. "Send her in." He flopped back down in his chair.

Tessa entered the office. Her eyes landed on Powell, Sr., who reminded her of her businessman husband—sitting behind a huge office desk tended to give businessmen so much authority and power.

"What do I owe the pleasure of your visit?"

"It's the baby," she said, getting right to the point. She had made her way up in front of his desk, but didn't bother to take a seat in a nearby chair. "My niece tells me you want to take him from her."

"I say you and I should be on the same page about that. She's unfit," he said, but in his head, he called her a tramp.

"My Rosie Aniyah has been troubled before, but the baby will help her to change for the better."

All that rambled though his brain was that Tessa was a pushover. She had nothing of her niece's dominant ways.

"Your own husband doesn't want her near your home. Doesn't that count for something? I need to take control of this situation. I'll handle her and my grand-heir."

Tessa was annoyed. She could not believe Powell, Sr. did not have the sense to identify the baby as his grandson.

"We should give my niece a chance to show us she can be a good mama," she said.

"Not taking any chances on my grand-heir. The kid belongs in my home with Jarvis and me."

While he reared back in his chair, holding his head up high, Tessa witnessed Powell, Sr.'s determination to take custody, which could trigger Aniyah to strike back at him. It could ultimately cause her to return to prison. "Please. Let's keep peace," Tessa begged.

Powell, Sr. pointed his cigar at her. "Tell your niece to hand my grand-heir over to me. And there won't be any problems."

"I may be out of place. I believe you're speaking out of greed."

"Your own niece has been an embarrassment to you, and you still want to help her."

"Aniyah has not been the greatest person. The baby will change her," Tessa said, praying what she said was the truth.

Powell, Sr. got back out of his seat. "I'm sure Baron would agree with me. Run along and go ask him," he said, flagging his hand for her leave.

"I'm aware of how my husband feels. Rosie Aniyah is my blood," Tessa tearfully said. "I see there's no need in speaking to you." She stormed out of his office.

Powell, Sr. chuckled. "The kid is mine. Heir to the Powells."

Tessa had heard rumors how protective and possessive Powell, Sr. was of his son. And he would no doubt be the same with his grandson. She was also convinced that he would follow through with every word he said. Her hands sweated for she feared Aniyah might disappear in order to keep her baby. But Tessa did not want that to happen. If things got too ugly, she would hire another attorney besides her husband to represent Aniyah's case. She prayed Baron would not betray her and instead be on the side of the defense, representing the Powells.

That evening at home, Powell, Sr. contacted Dr. Guess, inviting him for breakfast, and he accepted.

The following morning, he stood up from the table when he saw his guest had arrived. He extended his hand to give a handshake.

"Hello, Dr. Guess."

"Nice meeting you, Mr. Powell. Thanks for the invitation to your home. It's awesome out here." Instead of dressing in his white jacket for work, the doctor wore a short-sleeved shirt and a pair of gray slacks. Upon his arrival at the Powell estate, one of the servants greeted him, escorting him to one of the few outdoor patios in the home, which reminded him of an outdoor café.

Powell, Sr. patted him on the shoulder. "Join me on my yacht sometimes. Have you ever experienced cruising on Lake Murray?"

"Not at all. I'm a golfer."

"I play a little. Doc, pull up a chair."

Dr. Guess sat at the table, set in white and gold china. The silverware was wrapped in white cloth napkins. Two crystal pitchers, one with orange juice and the other with apple juice, were there to quench their morning thirst.

Powell, Sr. sipped on a cup of hot coffee from a sterling silver coffee pot.

The servants came out, serving them each a plate of grits, eggs, sizzling bacon and sausages.

"I had a grand-heir, born last night, at the hospital. I hear you delivered him."

"Aniyah Powell is the mother."

"That tramp using the Powell name. She's not married to my son."

"She seems like a nice young lady. Great patient." Dr. Guess chewed on a piece of sausage.

"Don't let that pretty face fool you." Powell, Sr. took a bite of his bacon and chewed while he spoke. "She has spent time in jail for embezzlement. Now she's up to her old tricks again. That tramp thinks she's going to dip into my family fortune. I told that metalhead son of mine she wasn't any good. That chest hanging out of her clothes and those curves of hers took him for a loop."

"I can see why your son fell for her. She's very attractive," Dr. Guess said. If he were a single man, Aniyah would have captured him as well, he thought.

"Jarvis sees her now for what she is—a slut."

Dr. Guess swallowed the orange juice that was poured for him by one of the servants, but at the same time, he kept his eyes on Powell, Sr. as they chatted. He did not have a slight idea why he was invited to the businessman's home. In a steady pace, he began to shake his right leg, not bothering to make a comment about Aniyah's past.

"Your grandchild is being discharged this very second."

Powell, Sr. placed his unlit cigar in an ashtray. He stood to his feet, pointing at the doctor. "You have to stop that discharge."

"Why should I stop mother and baby from going home?"

"That baby boy belongs to me and my son. He's a Powell. I need to help my son take him away from her."

"You need to take that up with a lawyer. I'm a doctor."

Powell, Sr.'s eyes popped wide open. "Doc, don't smart-mouth me at my own table."

Dr. Guess dropped his napkin on his plate. "I see clearly why you invited me to your home. You want me on your side in case there's a court battle."

"You're certainly correct. I want my grand-heir away from that jailbird."

Dr. Guess could not believe what he was hearing. "My patient hasn't given me any reason to say she's a bad mother. She's made some mistakes. And so have we all. Personally, you shouldn't be trying to take her baby."

"I see she's already punked you. Leave my home!" Powell, Sr. ordered.

Dr. Guess jumped up and leaned over the table. He pointed his finger. "No kid should be in your hands."

"I ought to see you're stripped of your medical license."

"You bastard." Losing his cool, Dr. Guess charged toward him, gripping Powell, Sr.'s tie. "You make any problems for me, mister, and you'll be in the hospital grasping for your life," he threatened. He let go of the tie and saw his way out.

Powell, Sr. did not take his threat seriously. "I'll get my grand-heir." He burst into laughter while he fixed his crooked tie.

CHAPTER 27

It didn't surprise Aniyah when her aunt arrived early for her discharge day. She eased by her aunt, who carried a Macy's bag in her hands. "I have to go to the potty," she said, but in reality, she wanted to make a private phone call.

Inside the bathroom, Aniyah took her cell phone out of her underwear. She called the private investigator. Then she turned on the faucet to drown her conversation, not wanting her aunt to hear her.

"Hey, I'm leaving here today," she whispered into the phone.

"I can use some cash."

"I can't meet you right now. I have to first get rid of my aunt."

"Hey, don't call me anymore, unless you're ready."

"Will do." She hung up.

Aniyah was eager to put her plans into motion. She would use her last resource, to make sure the Powells did not take custody of her baby.

Out of the bathroom, she saw her aunt holding up an infant suit.

"This is a cutie." Tessa showed off her purchase.

Aniyah admired the blue outfit, but then she focused on the bulge in her stomach. "I'm fat. No more babies for me."

"In due time, you'll be back to your normal size." Tessa handed Aniyah another bag. "Here's something for you to wear home."

A present was what Aniyah needed to forget her bulge. She pulled out a dress that easily could be pulled over her head. "It's not me." Aniyah threw the dress back in the bag.

"Can't you be grateful for once?"

Aniyah turned, noticing an orderly bringing a breakfast tray into the room. "No food for me. I'm leaving here."

The orderly exited the door.

Not having a dress to wear to replace the ball gown, Aniyah decided to wear the garment her aunt had bought for her. "I'm stuck with this sack."

She snatched the dress back out of the bag.

"It'll look fine," Tessa said. She went to the portable crib, where Baby Jarvis rested on his back. She began dressing him in his new outfit for his trip home.

Back into the bathroom, Aniyah slipped on the dress. She glanced at the mirror. She mumbled, "If I was a man, I'd divorce my wife for wearing a disgusting dress like this one."

Aniyah came back in the room. "Aunt Tessa, I look like an eggplant."

Tessa giggled. "It'll get you home."

As Tessa drove into the neighborhood where Aniyah used to live, Aniyah eyed the freshly painted gray on the row of apartments. Going to the left of the complex would have taken her to her old place of residence. But her aunt drove to the right, near the playground, where children played.

Does Lenvy still live here? Aniyah wondered. If he still did, she would stay clear of him. *Maybe he moved and is freeloading off his girlfriend.*

Aniyah's eyes focused on the gardeners that busily trimmed the hedges below the windowsills of the first-floor apartments. Tessa parked nearby, where they worked.

"This is home for you and your baby."

"Back to the rat trap," Aniyah said.

"They're remodeled. It's a place for you to rest your head."

Aniyah stepped out of the car and slammed the door behind her. She lifted Baby Jarvis into her arms, while her aunt grabbed the car seat.

The noise of the machinery awakened Baby Jarvis.

"You're making my baby cry. Shut that stuff off," Aniyah demanded.

Tessa waved her hand. "Go quick. Let's get him inside." She handed the baby to Tessa.

Instead of making her way to the front door of the first-floor apartment, Aniyah hurried over to one of the gardeners using an electric hedge cutter. "Hey you," she tapped him on his shoulder, "Cut it off or you're fired."

The young gardener turned off the motor, once he noticed her. He pointed to another gentleman for her to speak to, and then he turned back on the motor.

Aniyah followed the cord until she saw the outlet it was plugged into. Without hesitation, she yanked it. Baby Jarvis continued to cry.

"Rosie Aniyah." Tessa, who had witnessed her niece's wrong behavior, had unlocked the door to the apartment and carried the baby inside.

"No one upsets me or my baby." Aniyah stormed inside the apartment with the men calling her nasty names.

After calming Baby Jarvis, Aniyah made her rounds throughout every room. The apartment suited her better than the previous one. The kitchen was upgraded to black appliances. The furnished living room was decorated with a sofa, coffee table and end tables with lamps. The bedroom had a queen-sized, iron-rail bed. Tessa had set up the second bedroom with a full-sized mahogany crib and chest to store his clothes.

"I hope this is to your liking." Tessa stood in the doorway. "You won't run away."

"A lot better." Aniyah rested the baby in the crib on his back. "He's going back to sleep."

"You need rest, too," Tessa whispered.

"I'll take a nap while he's asleep," Aniyah said, leaving the room for Baby Jarvis to rest while her aunt followed her into the living area.

"I can stay and help you."

"Aunt Tessa, I can handle this."

"I'll leave then." Tessa was willing to give Aniyah her space. "I do have errands to run before I can get rest for my tired bones." Tessa decided to let Aniyah in on what she had done on her behalf. "I paid a visit to Jarvis, Sr. He's determined to take the baby away from you. I'm going to speak to a lawyer to see what rights you have."

"Aunt Tessa, you're married to one."

"You mean you trust Baron?"

"Hell no, but he knows the law."

"He's my husband and I adore him. But, he'll help, Jarvis, Sr. before he ever helps you."

"Divorce the jerk."

"Nonsense." Tessa grabbed her handbag. "Call me if the baby gets to be a handful. Bye."

Aniyah opened the door and her aunt exited. She closed the door behind her, racing for her cell phone. She turned it on. *Thank God, I still have service.* She slouched down on the sofa with the phone ringing several times before she got an answer.

"Hey, lady," the private investigator said.

"Let's do this. I have no time to waste."

"Bank first. Info after."

"I got you covered."

"Where do you want me to pick you up?"

Aniyah gave him the information of her location—ready to leave once he arrived.

The roaring motor made Aniyah hurry out of the house to the investigator's compact vehicle. She placed the car seat in the backseat, strapping in Baby Jarvis. "Good baby," she said. He continued to sleep.

The children in the playground covered their ears from the unusual noise that came from his car. Aniyah eased down in the seat. "Drive this thing."

"To the bank we go." The investigator put his foot to the pedal, while smoke blew out of the exhaust pipe.

Aniyah looked behind to see nothing but fog. "Give up the info."

"Cash and carry."

Double-parked at the bank, Aniyah looked into the backseat. Baby Jarvis' eyes opened, but he didn't fret.

"Mama will be right back," she said.

"Take him with you."

"He'll hold me up from getting your money. You just don't drive off with my baby."

The investigator chuckled. "That ain't happening. I'm not the father." He waved his hand, giving her the okay to leave. He looked back at Baby Jarvis to see a slight grin on his face.

It did not take long for Aniyah to handle the bank transaction.

She handed the investigator an envelope. "Now, what you got? Where is Jarvis' mama?"

The investigator pulled a sheet of paper from his coat jacket. He handed it to her.

Aniyah read the information and looked up at the investigator. "Sina Cole lives in Columbia."

"All these years," the investigator said, recalling how he'd discovered her residence. All it took was flashing a few twenties in front of the night-duty security guard working for the Powell Bank, and he received access to Powell, Sr.'s office.

"Take me to her," Aniyah pleaded.

"My job ends as soon as I drop you off back at your house."

"But I need to go this address. It's important. I'll give you gas money."

Roaring the engine, the investigator chuckled. "Get out here or at home?"

"I can give you a bonus," she said, licking her lips. She glided her right hand against the flesh between her breasts.

"I don't mess with a woman that just delivered a kid. Get out here or at home?" he repeated.

Aniyah folded her arms and did not bulge.

The investigator put his foot on the pedal and zoomed off.

Back at the apartment, Aniyah was discouraged. She had no way of getting to Sina's home.

While she fed Baby Jarvis his bottle, her mind raced about why Jarvis' mother would leave her son. Her cell phone startled her. Once she looked down at the number displayed, she recognized the caller. "What's up, Spy?"

"Will you ever forgive me?"

"You owe me, Nellie. Get your butt over to my new crappy place. I need a ride."

"You're home from the hospital?"

"Yes. Girl, I need your help." Aniyah explained to Nellie where she resided. "Hold on a minute." Aniyah put the phone down long enough to lay Baby Jarvis across her lap, on his stomach. "I'm back. Are you coming or not?"

"You need a ride to the store?"

Aniyah did not want to explain so she brushed her off. "Of course."

"I'm not too far from you. Be there soon."

Before Nellie could hang up, Aniyah looked down at her dress code. "Bring me something to wear. Not one of your cleaning outfits."

Nellie laughed. "I have a sassy dress that you can fit into."

Five minutes and Nellie arrived with a dress on a hanger. Snatching it from her, Aniyah slipped it on. She stood on the bed, looking into the dresser mirror. She turned to see her rear. The dress hugged her enough to her satisfaction.

"I want to see the baby." Nellie sat comfortably on the sofa. She admired a vase of fake tulips on the coffee table.

"Girl, in a minute. You, me and baby are hitting the road."

"You want to shop at Publix?"

"Not today. I got dirty dirt on Papa Powell."

Nellie cried, "I don't want to get in any trouble. No jail."

"Been there and done that. Not going back there." Aniyah held out her hand. "Give me your cell phone."

Nellie was curious what Aniyah was getting herself into. But still she handed her phone to her.

Aniyah took it with her to the baby's room. Then she returned with Baby Jarvis in her arms.

"May I have my cell phone?" Nellie asked.

"It's safely put away. I still don't trust a backstabber."

"But my man might call me."

"That's not my problem."

Aniyah stuffed a diaper bag with bottles, pampers, and other items for Baby Jarvis' needs. She tossed the bag on her shoulder. She dashed to the door, with Nellie on her heels.

"Where are we going?"

"Wild...something." Aniyah gave her the slip of paper with the address jotted on it.

"Beautiful homes in that neighborhood."

"Let's get out of this dump." Aniyah went to the door.

"I'm not driving a baby without a car seat." Nellie noticed the only thing Aniyah carried was her handbag and diaper bag.

Aniyah had forgotten it. "It's in the room." She went and retrieved it. Aniyah strapped the baby in it, and carried him while Nellie lugged the diaper bag.

They walked out into a ray of sun beaming on their foreheads. It felt like a heating pad to Aniyah. "I hope you have A/C." Aniyah placed her left hand over the baby's head, blocking him from the sun.

After arriving to the car, Nellie turned it on to cool it off, while Aniyah secured the car seat in the backseat.

Aniyah noticed a neighbor in the street staring at her every move. She lashed at him. "You're the neighborhood eye spy. Spread the word, I won't be living here long. Now is that info worth you getting a heat stroke." Aniyah did not wait to see if the man would answer. She got into the vehicle and Nellie pulled off.

Mini mansions are what came to Aniyah's mind when she eyed

the homes in the neighborhood where Sina lived. Nellie drove up to a two-story brick home. She parked in the driveway behind a parked vehicle. "Are you going to tell me what we're doing here?"

"Your job is to stay here until I come back. Don't flip on me."

Aniyah scrambled in her purse for a pen and jotted the license plate down, then hopped out of the car.

With a sound asleep Baby Jarvis in her arms, Aniyah walked up four steps and rang the doorbell. The chimes echoed in her ears. She rocked her baby as she waited.

A woman dressed like she had been working in the garden greeted her. "Yes, may I help you?"

"I'm here to see Sina Cole."

"She's sitting out back on the porch. May I ask who's calling?" the woman asked.

"I'm an old friend," Aniyah lied.

"Come on in. That's a sweet baby in your arms." The woman admired Baby Jarvis' tiny face. "I'm Sina's neighbor, Paige. I keep an eye on her. Bring her cut flowers from my yard sometimes."

"That's nice of you." Aniyah grinned.

The woman moved for Aniyah to enter, then she pointed to the rear of the house. "You go straight to the back. I'll be back soon. I need to run home. Clean some of this dirt off me. It's nice meeting you."

"Same with you." Aniyah waited for the woman to close the door behind her. *Dummy, letting in a stranger in your so-called friend's house. Some neighbor you are.*

Down the hallway, Aniyah walked past the dining and living rooms, adjacent to each other. She passed through the kitchen, outside the French doors to find Sina, sitting in a wheelchair. Aniyah couldn't stop staring at her. Jarvis' wide nose and thick eyebrows resembled hers—two features she did admire about her man.

Sina turned to face Aniyah. Not alarmed, her attention went to Baby Jarvis. "Who are you and who's that fine baby you're holding?" she asked in a mellow voice.

"I'm Aniyah. This is your grandson."

Sina showed no signs of being moved by Aniyah's words. "I'd love to claim that baby as a grandchild. But, I have no children."

"Sina Cole, meet Jarvis Powell, the Third."

Sina spun the wheels on her wheelchair, causing Aniyah to move out of her way. She went inside the house. "Go and forget you ever came here." Sina made her way to the refrigerator.

"For God's sake, did you hear what I said? This is your grandson."

Sina's voice escalated. "I...want no trouble." She took out a glass filled with water. Holding the glass with one hand, she took a swallow. Then Sina rolled herself over to the table with the other hand. There were three chairs around it, and an empty space for her wheelchair to get closer to it. She rested the glass on it.

Aniyah got closer to her. "Your grandson needs your help."

She attempted to place Baby Jarvis in her arms, but Sina gently pushed the baby away. "I don't know how you found me. I gave up my rights a long time ago. Take that baby back to his father."

"Oh, how quick your memory comes back. What's the real deal here?" she blabbed. "You ruined your son's face with a scar. He thinks you ran off and left him and his crazy papa. But all this time you're receiving checks from his papa. I need answers."

"I'm older. Arthritis has set in these old bones. I say my life is my own business. No one else's."

"Between you and Papa Powell, I'm getting pretty sick of the bull."

"It's time you leave. No respect for your elders, young lady." Sina was frustrated. "Let yourself out." She took more swallows of the water to cool off from her unexpected guest.

Aniyah exited the kitchen, but did not make it past the living room. She laid Baby Jarvis, wrapped in his blanket, down on a chaise lounge, and then she went back into the kitchen. Aniyah grabbed the wheelchair by the handles, catching Sina off guard. She rolled her into one of the bedrooms; it appeared to Aniyah that it was a guest bedroom.

Sina panicked and screamed, "Lord, please help me."

"Shut...the...hell...up," Aniyah shouted, "before you wake up my son."

The screams ceased. Tears flowed from the helpless woman's eyes; fearful harm would be done to her.

Aniyah sat on the edge of the bed facing the front of the wheelchair. She pulled it toward her, holding tight to the rails. "Woman, I'm not going to hurt you. I need you to tell me why Papa Powell has been sending you checks for years."

"It was the arrangement...they...we made." She stumbled over her words with trembling hands.

"You said, *they* first. Who in the hell is *they*?"

Sina dropped her head. "Powell and Houston."

Aniyah felt like a tennis racket had cracked against her head. Never did she suspect, Powell and dead man Houston, two bullheads, to scheme together on a woman.

"Spill the beans. And don't leave a damn thing out."

Sina did not disappoint Aniyah on the details of her encounter with both men. Aniyah wanted to celebrate and party throughout the house. She had gotten the information she needed to keep her baby.

She lifted baby Jarvis into her arms and brought him back to his grandmother. She rested him in Sina's arms. She watched his grandmother turn her fiery tears into joyful ones.

Aniyah left promising Sina that she would keep her secret. In return, Sina vowed to Aniyah that she wouldn't tell anyone she'd come to visit her.

The sun disappeared to be replaced by rain clouds, but the warmth of the heat gave off a temperature of about eighty-five degrees.

"I was about to leave. You took too long," Nellie complained.

"No you weren't. I got your cell phone." Aniyah strapped Baby Jarvis in his seat.

"Who lives here?"

Aniyah got in the vehicle and buckled her seat belt. "Stop asking questions. I need to think." She thought fast as to how she would handle the news she had discovered. "Take me to the Powell Estate."

"That's on the other side of town."

"I'll buy you some gas. Get driving."

Aniyah turned on the radio. She danced in the seat, leaving Nellie confused.

CHAPTER 28

Nellie drove around the winding road that led to the Powell Estate, while Aniyah surveyed the beauty of the pine and hearty oak trees.

Nellie stopped the vehicle, once they had reached the security checkpoint. Nellie flashed her old employee ID badge. Familiar with her, the guard opened the black iron gates. She drove off, overlooking acres of land, where ten houses could easily fit on the lot. The sprinklers were shut off from giving the plush grass a quench of thirst. The scent of the grass had fragranced the air. Nellie sneezed.

"Bless you," Aniyah said.

"I never know when my allergies will go crazy."

Palmetto trees lined the road that led to the front of the home. It was unlike the ballroom entrance; there weren't any steps to climb. There were two terracotta pots that housed miniature cypress trees on each side of the walkway.

"How can a jerk have so much?" Nellie spoke.

"'Cause he's got dummies like you to make a fool of."

"I'm not going in," Nellie warned, and she parked behind a limo.

"Girl, I got this covered. You'd better be here if I have to make a run for it."

"No jail for me."

Aniyah looked in the backseat at Baby Jarvis. She was too afraid to take him inside with her, fearing she would be locked out with him kept inside.

"Watch my baby for me," she said.

Nellie was surprised. "You trust me with him?"

"I have no choice but to leave him with you. Don't be here when I come back, and you'll see the beast side of me," Aniyah threatened.

Out of the vehicle, Aniyah went into the backseat and un-strapped the car seat, lifting Baby Jarvis into her arms. She handed him to Nellie. Aniyah gave her a bottle of milk from his diaper bag. "Feed him."

Nellie pushed a button, and the driver's seat moved backward. She fed the baby while Aniyah set forth to do her duty.

Aniyah rang the bell more than once before a female servant greeted her.

"Welcome to the Powell Estate; who may I say is calling?"

"I'm here to see Jarvis." Aniyah pushed her way inside.

The smell of baked blueberry cobbler went up her nose. Aniyah wanted to run into the kitchen to get a taste, but duty called.

"Ma'am, I must first announce you," the servant said frantically.

"Isn't Jarvis here?"

"Yes, he's somewhere in the home."

"Which way is his bedroom?"

"Ma'am, you can't freely walk through this home."

Halfway up the stairs, Aniyah shouted back, "I'm the mama of a Powell. I can run through this place if I want to." She got to the top of the stairs and looked back down. "Which way is his room?"

The servant submitted, pointing to the right. "Third door."

Aniyah eased open the closed door, and then she peeped inside. The room was empty. She called Jarvis' name, and she then went from room to room, but got no answer.

Back downstairs, she ran into the servant, again. "He's not up there. Where else can he be?"

"Ma'am, sometimes he watches movies in the theater room or exercises in the gym."

The servant pointed Aniyah in the direction of the recreation area. The theater room was quiet However, in the home gym, Aniyah saw a beam of light. Walking in, if she did not know any better, she would have thought she had entered a commercial gym.

Lying on a weight bench, Jarvis bench-pressed. She went over to him. His exposed chest caught her eyes. The sweat on his muscles made her want to fall on top of him. But with one wrong move on her part, he would drop the weight on his chest.

Jarvis noticed her right away. "What are you doing here?" He placed the weights back on the rack and sat up.

"I'm here to win my man back."

"Make more of a fool of me?"

"I love you, Jarvis."

He stood, showing off his buffed body.

Jarvis went to grab a towel that hung on the handle of a workout bicycle, but Aniyah beat him to it. Instead of handing him the towel, she began to dry the sweat that dripped from his shoulders. He stopped her, snatching the towel away from her and dried himself.

Aniyah took her chances. She moved closer to him, staring into his eyes. Then she rested her hands on his chest. "I truly do love you," she admitted.

"You only know how to rip a man's heart to pieces."

"Not you, Honey. I realize I could never do that to you."

She placed a kiss on the scar side of his cheekbone. Jarvis wiped his chin of her wet kiss. She did not give up. Nothing was going to stop her from getting her man and to live back at the penthouse. Again, she placed her lips against his. This time she did not let up, forcing her tongue into his mouth.

Jarvis became almost weakened by her touch. He shoved her away, with Aniyah landing on the floor. "I need to get away from you."

As if he were being chased, Jarvis rushed for the door. Jumping up, she went after him.

"Leave, Aniyah," he yelled, turning to see she had followed him up to his bedroom.

"You know you love me, Jarvis. Admit it."

"It doesn't matter anymore."

He went into the bathroom of the master suite. Aniyah waited on him in the doorway.

He stood over the sink, splashing cold water on his face. He moved past her, back into the bedroom, where he sat down in a chair. Off a table, he picked up a bottle of wine from his father's wine cellar. Pouring a glass full, he took a swallow, then he placed the glass on the table.

Aniyah grabbed the bottle and took a swallow from it.

"I need my son. Where is he?"

"Our baby has made us a family," she said.

"Where is he?" he repeated.

"Safe."

Aniyah forced her way onto his lap. She kissed him passionately until Jarvis again pushed her away.

"I want to be the one to raise him," he argued.

"Together, Honey. He needs both parents."

She pressed her lips again, against his, moving her hands down to his crotch.

Jarvis rested his head back in the seat, moaning from her touch. His body hungered for her. "Why am I letting you make a jerk out of me?"

She whispered, steadily stroking him. "You love me."

Jarvis scooped her up. He laid her on top of the unmade bed that had been off limits to the servants for tidying, due to his sobbing.

Aniyah held tight, in case he decided to escape from her again. She worked her hands into the muscles of his chest.

He pushed his sweats down, exposing half of his butt, when he was forced to stop. A scream coming from outside of his bedroom echoed in their ears.

"Take this baby." They heard Nellie and were baffled.

Jarvis pulled his sweats up. He ran into the hallway with Aniyah following him, pulling her dress down to cover her exposed thighs.

Nellie was frantic. "He won't stop crying."

"You're supposed to be feeding him." Aniyah was disgusted.

"As soon as you left, he stopped taking the bottle. Started crying."

"Give me my child." Aniyah took the baby. "Get lost," she mumbled to her.

Nellie turned around and left.

"Let me hold my son." Jarvis perked up once Aniyah passed their son to him.

Aniyah saw the love in his eyes that he had for their baby and placed her arms around her man's shoulders. "Family, Honey, that's what we are."

Jarvis comforted his son in his arms and rocked him, carrying him back into the bedroom. He thought about whether he should let Aniyah's past get in the way of taking her back for the sake of their son. He sat on the bed.

Aniyah handed him the baby's bottle. Baby Jarvis' tiny jaws sucked his bottle.

Without Jarvis expecting it, Aniyah rested her hand on his lap. No conversation was held between them. They took the time to enjoy, watching the life they had created.

Outside, Powell, Sr. drove up in his limo. Nellie did not drive away. She locked her vehicle doors. Like an explosion, he stormed over to her.

Powell, Sr. banged on the tinted glass window. She submitted and rolled the driver's side window down. "I fired you. Get this piece of a junk off my property," he scolded.

Nellie squealed, "I'm waiting on Aniyah. She's inside talking to your son."

His forehead wrinkled once he heard Aniyah's name again. He had already gotten the call from one of his servants that Aniyah was at his home. It did not take long before Powell, Sr. stormed in on Aniyah and Jarvis. He watched his son feeding the baby with Aniyah sitting close to him.

"That's it! I've given you fair warning, Tramp. And you, Son, how stupid can you be to let her near you?" Powell, Sr. roared.

"Dad, stop yelling. You're going to make the baby cry."

"Give me my grand-heir," Powell, Sr. demanded. He took charge of his grandson, without Jarvis putting up a fight.

Aniyah watched as Powell, Sr. took control of baby Jarvis, causing her to go into a frenzy. Attempting to reach for her son, Powell, Sr. jabbed her with his elbow. She fell back on the bed.

"Dad, control yourself," Jarvis fussed. He went to Aniyah's aid. They watched Powell, Sr. rush out of the room.

"Dad, where're you going?" Jarvis hurried after his father.

Aniyah ran past Jarvis. She dashed at old man Powell from behind, beating him on his back. "You potbelly pig. You won't have my baby. I hate you."

"Psycho, get out of my home," Powell, Sr. yelled.

"Aniyah, let go of Dad," Jarvis pleaded, pulling her off his father. "Settle down for our baby's sake."

Powell, Sr. turned toward his son and ordered, "Call the police.

I want her arrested. Back behind bars where she belongs." His cigar dangled from his mouth.

Aniyah ran at the old man again, snatching the cigar from between his lips, throwing it on the floor. She stomped her shoe on the cigar, mashing it to pieces.

"Get this crazy tramp away from me and my grand-heir," Powell, Sr. said, scurrying down the hallway into his master suite.

Aniyah was ready to run after old man Powell, but Jarvis pulled her into his arms, consoling her. "Dad won't hurt him. Please let him spend some time with his grandson."

Tears watered her eyes. "He won't give him back."

"He will. Dad wants a private moment with him." He was weakened by how sad she looked and comforted her with a kiss.

Aniyah threw her arms around him. They passionately continued to kiss with him brushing the loose strands of her hair that had fallen on her eyebrows.

"Go back to the penthouse. You and our son can live there. Please let him stay here for one night. It would make my dad happy."

"Are you serious? I don't care about your dad's feelings."

Jarvis held her by the shoulders. "Our baby is the only chance we have of getting his blessings for our relationship."

Aniyah stood in a frozen position. She didn't want to lose out on Jarvis letting her back into his life. As much as she was scared to leave her baby, she had to give in to keep peace with him. She figured this would also give Powell, Sr. the sense that he had outsmarted her. Change of plans. She took a deep breath and said, "One night."

One last kiss and her hands on his crotch, Aniyah left empty-handed, but had her man craving her.

CHAPTER 29

Stepping out of Powell, Sr.'s home, Aniyah stepped into Nellie's car without looking back.

Nellie was astonished she had returned alone. "Where's your baby?"

"Thanks to you for bringing him in the house, I had no choice but to let him spend his first night home with his papa and crazy grandpa."

"Sorry, but I couldn't stop the baby from crying."

"You're lucky that I agreed to let him stay." Aniyah sat back in the seat and then with a big grin, she blurted, "Jarvis is letting me stay back at the penthouse."

"That's good news. I would be scared to leave my baby with Mr. Powell. He's mean," Nellie said, driving off.

Aniyah laughed. "He's all wolf. He won't hurt his grandson."

"I'll take you home."

"I don't think so. The fun has just begun."

"You're not telling me a thing."

"You're my driver, not partner, in this."

"You're right. No jail for me. Keep your secrets." Nellie was anxious to know more of what she was up to.

"I'm in a good mood. Let's get a bite to eat on me. Then I need you to take me downtown to Attorney Baron's office. Do not ask why. And here," Aniyah said, returning Nellie her cell phone.

"I bet Roy has called me. I'll give him a ring."

Before Nellie could touch the dial pad, Aniyah snatched the phone from her. "Not while you're driving," Aniyah informed.

"I'll wait to call later." Nellie took back control of her phone.

They drove to Bert's Southern Cooking, and ordered two barbecue turkey wing dinners to go. Instead of going to the apartment, they went to the penthouse.

Nellie chatted with her boyfriend while she ate, while Aniyah sorted through her wardrobe for something to wear. She took precautions, calling her Aunt Tessa to keep her from meddling in her life.

Aniyah changed clothing, trying on several items before she found the perfect dress to wear. She made her face up, pampering her eyes with black eyeliner. Her hair was brushed to one side of her face, falling over her breast.

When she returned back into the kitchen, Nellie was shocked to see she had changed clothing. "Going on a hot date?" Nellie was curious.

Aniyah handed her the dress she had loaned her. "Got to fire up a man's grill." Aniyah giggled. She twirled around.

Aniyah had made an anonymous call to Baron's office, verifying that he was at work. She had Nellie park a half-block away from his law firm.

"Wait here and stay in the car," she said.

"I don't want trouble for me," Nellie reminded her.

"Talk to your man or take a damn nap. Be back as soon as my mission is settled."

Aniyah got out and strutted down the block. She picked up her phone, contacting her Aunt Tessa. She spoke in a deep voice, to disguise her vocals. "Hello, Mrs. Chavis. I'm calling from your husband's office. He asked that you come down to his office immediately. I'm not supposed to tell, but he has a surprise for you. It's a big one."

Tessa was thrilled. "Tell my hubby, he has his wish."

Aniyah threw her head backward, full of laughter.

It had been a long time since she had visited Attorney Baron Chavis' office. She recalled the last time that she was there was for the reading of Rupert Houston's will, granting her everything but eventually landing her in jail for fraud.

The receptionist was gone for the day. Aniyah walked in on Baron, who sat behind his desk, deep into a file of one of his clients.

"Hello, Darling," Aniyah said in a low-toned voice.

Baron looked up to see her. His eyes were glued to the strut in her walk. She stood on four-inch heels with her dress falling below her hips. The dress gathered around her waist to tone down the bulge in her stomach that made her still look pregnant. Her juicy red lipstick made him lick his lips. He closed the file and rested his back in his reclined office chair.

"What are you doing here? Shouldn't you be home playing mother?" he asked.

Aniyah walked around his desk. She rested the toe of her shoe in his crotch. "We have unfinished stuff to take care of?"

"Get off me." Baron tapped her foot for her to move it.

Aniyah pressed her foot into his crotch. "I call the shots here."

"You're insane. Never should've been released from behind bars."

She eased her foot off of him. Next, she moved her hips from side to side. As much as he tried, Baron could not keep his eyes off of her.

Aniyah turned to face him. Leaning forward, she stuck her breasts in his face. "You know you want me," she teased.

"You don't have any respect for your own aunt. Remember I'm married to her."

Aniyah pulled him by the tie. "Aunt Tessa is a traitor. She gets what she deserves."

He snatched his tie from her hands. Aniyah pushed the papers off his desk. He tried to stop her, by grabbing her by the arms.

She eased closer up on him and he let up on her, giving her the advantage to throw her arms around his neck, pressing her lips against his. He tried to pull her arms from around his neck, but she held on, shoving her knees up his crotch. As much as he tried not to let her touching affect him, his manhood reacted. She felt the bulge in his pants. *Right where I want him.*

While she kissed him, she stroked his face with the tips of her fingers.

From the sweetness of her lips, he fell under her spell. "Forgive me, Tessa," he mumbled, sliding his hands up her dress, caressing her inner left thigh.

"Out of order," she whispered, moving his hand. "Milk is only being delivered today." She flipped her right breast out.

Once he eyed her hardened nipple, he covered it with his lips. Sucking on it, Baron had his first taste of baby's milk.

Aniyah continued to let him have his way with parts of her body above her waistline, while she unbuckled his pants, then ripped his shirt open. She stroked his chest down to his bulge.

Baron, caught up in the act, hungered for more of her. He pushed his pants down to his knees; he was so lost in her body, he didn't notice his wife had walked in on them.

Tessa stood in the doorway witnessing her niece and husband tangled in a sexual position.

Baron finally felt her presence. Looking over Aniyah's shoulder, he locked eyes with his wife. "Oh my God, Tessa," he yelled. "It's not what you think." He toggled to pull his pants up on his waist.

Aniyah did not bother to adjust her clothing. She burst into laughter. "Welcome, Aunt Tessa."

Her aunt focused her attention on her husband. "Baron, you betrayed me?" He ran over to her, trying to hold her in his arms. "Never touch me again." A tearful Tessa jerked away from him.

"She came on to me," he said.

"Liar," Aniyah stated.

Without warning, Tessa dashed at her niece, slapping her across the face. "I have done so much for you. You're so ungrateful. No more!" she screamed with watery eyes.

"All you've done is treat me like secondhand furniture," Aniyah said, raising her hand to her aunt, but Baron came between them.

"No fighting. Aniyah, get out of here. My wife and I need to talk," he said.

"No talk for us. My despicable niece can stay. I'm leaving. Go back to your dirty ways." Tessa cried and vanished.

Aniyah laughed. "Did you see her face?"

"You have no remorse for the rotten things you do. I warned Tessa. I knew you coming back into her life would be trouble."

"And you represent rich folks who do in the little people."

"My clients have nothing to do with what is happening here."

"I say it does. Pig head Powell and dead man Houston. Two of your clients you protected their dirt for money. You're as crooked as they are."

"I'm not going to debate with you." Baron slipped on his suit jacket. "I've got to go and find my wife. Make her see it's nothing going on between us."

"It sure isn't. Jarvis Powell is the only man I have the hots for."

"From what I hear he doesn't want you now that he's found out what type of bitch you are."

"We're back together," Aniyah bragged. "You and my aunt are broken up."

"You did this on purpose." Baron understood he was set up. He caught her by her arms and shook her. "Did you or not, do this to hurt me and your aunt?"

"Let me go." Aniyah scrambled away from him. She hauled out of the door. The night air felt good to her. She strutted back to her ride.

Nellie unlocked the door when she saw Aniyah. "You took long enough. You have to be tired."

"I feel revenged." Aniyah got in the vehicle. She looked in the overhead mirror and straightened out her disarrayed hair. "I broke up my aunt and uncle's marriage."

"You went and teased her man?"

"You know it. Had him all over me. Auntie walked in and that's the end of their marriage."

"I say you need to be on a soap opera."

"Yeah, it'll be called the Slick and Luscious."

"I'll watch it every day."

They laughed.

"Take me to that raggedy place my aunt put me in."

With Nellie's help, Aniyah gathered up Baby Jarvis' things from the apartment. She left behind the crib and chest her aunt had bought for her. Stepping out on the walkway, she ran right into Lenvy.

"Oh snap. Rich man kicked you to the curve. Baby girl back where the real folks live," Lenvy said with a sleek smile, showing off his gold grill.

"Go polish your teeth, Lenvy. I'm visiting my friend." Aniyah pointed to Nellie, who waved at him.

"You still looking tasty." Lenvy stared at Aniyah's smooth, silky legs, making him lick his tongue.

"So trifling." Aniyah, annoyed, strutted to the vehicle.

"Bye, baby girl." Lenvy chuckled.

"He has a crush on you," Nellie teased.

"I'll never come back here. Take me to the penthouse."

CHAPTER 30

In the corner of her bedroom, arranged to resemble a religious sanctuary, Tessa lit three candles—one for her, Baron and Aniyah. She dropped to her knees, staring at a statue of her God. She spoke in Spanish asking for the Holy Father to comfort her in her time of pain. She begged to rid the evil spirit within her niece.

Tessa moved her hands to form a cross and kissed her rosary beads. She got up off her knees, blowing out the candles. From the closet, she carried a suitcase, placing it on top of the bed. She tossed one garment after another into it.

Having no idea where she was headed to, Tessa wasn't going to stay another night in a home with an unfaithful husband. She carried the suitcase with both hands down the stairs, placing it near the door. She looked back at the home she kept clean, one of her duties of a good housewife. Tessa turned the doorknob, opening the door. She picked up her suitcase, ready to leave, but Baron appeared from the living room and blocked the passage of the doorway. Staring into his eyes, she replayed him and Aniyah entwined in each other's arms.

"You're not leaving me before I have my say," he said, spotting the suitcase that she held with both hands. He grabbed the handle, relieving her of the weight.

"Let go of me, Baron. I must leave," she said angrily, trying to retrieve the suitcase, but he pulled her by the arm back into their home. "Do not touch me," she screamed. "I want no part of this marriage."

He slammed the door closed behind them. "This is what your niece wants. Don't you see she set us up? She wants us apart. Make our lives hell."

"You didn't stop her," Tessa argued. "Tell the truth. If I hadn't come sooner, you would have…"

Baron waited for her to finish her words, but Tessa could not say any more. She sat down on the bottom step of the staircase. In tears, she dropped her head into her lap.

"Go on, say it…had sex with her. Damn it, yes, I would have."

It did not take long before Tessa hopped back on her feet, flying to her suitcase.

Baron stood in the doorway, blocking her from leaving. "It wouldn't have meant a damn thing to me. I love you. Only you."

"I must go," she screamed, while she fought to move him but could not compete with his strength.

Again, he pulled the suitcase from her and set it down. Tessa did not want to hear what he had to say; she picked the suitcase back up. She made her way to the kitchen door that led to the backyard.

He followed behind her. "Damn it, Tessa. I said I love you."

Once again, he snatched the suitcase from her. They tussled until it unlatched. Her clothes landed on the floor, looking like a pile of dirty clothes to be washed.

"Look what you've done now. Baron, please let me leave," she cried, and got down on the floor to gather her belongings.

"Not until you tell me you don't love me anymore."

Up off the floor, Tessa punched him in his muscular chest. "Why'd you hurt me? I've been a good wife. I cook your meals. Run your bath. Iron your clothes. I've been nothing but a fool for you."

Baron pulled her in his arms, caressing her back. His eyes watered. "You're a good wife. I'm the crazy one for allowing your niece to seduce me. I'll sleep in the guest room. Our bedroom is yours. Please don't leave," he begged.

Tessa jerked away from him, but was quite aware that if she walked out of the home that very moment, it would mean she was leaving her marriage for good. She decided not to make a hasty move. It would give her time to think. "I'll stay for the night until I make other arrangements." She kneeled down to the floor, tossing her clothes in the suitcase. Baron assisted her.

With her husband carrying her suitcase, Tessa headed to their master suite.

Inside the guest bedroom, being a guest in his own home, Baron took the pillows off the bed and stacked them on the floor. He pulled back the covers on the bed. He walked around the foot of the bed and accidentally stomped his big toe into the solid wood bedpost. He let out a loud scream. "Shit!" Baron hopped on his foot.

Tessa, settled in the master suite, heard his scream. She came running. "What's wrong?"

Although Baron hurt, he was pleased to know that she cared enough to check on him. He sat on the bed, studying his swollen injury. "I bumped my toe."

"On the poles, I bet. I told you they'd be a problem."

"I should have listened to you."

"I'll nurse it." She went down the hallway to the bathroom to come back with a first-aid kit. She sat on the bed next to him. With his foot rested on her lap, she rubbed down his toe with an alcohol swab. "You should be fine in the morning."

He reached for the bun in her hair, loosening it to let her hair fall. "I love only you." His words sounded sweet to his wife. He leaned over, placing a kiss on her neck. "Forgive me."

"Goodnight," Tessa said abruptly, while she gathered up the kit. She hurried out of the room before she submitted to him. Her heart fluttered. She wanted more than ever to turn back around to be close to her husband, but the vision of him and her niece brought tears to her eyes.

It had been a long time since she lay in bed by herself. Once in bed, she tossed and turned. Every so often, her eyes popped open, restless from not having the warmth of her husband's body next to her. Most nights they snuggled in each other's arms.

Tessa wondered if her husband was having the same problem. Curious, she went to take a peep at him. On her tippy toes, she leaned over and looked into the room. There was no light inside and no signs of his usual snoring.

Back into the master suite, she got back in bed. Again, she tossed and turned, yearning for her husband. "Go get your man," her conscience told her. She did not hesitate. Tessa made her way back to him. "Baron," she called, running into the guest room. She flicked on the light.

With one eye open, he looked up to see his wife, pulling her gown over her head to show off her jewels. Tessa snatched the covers off him, exposing her husband in his pajamas. She crawled on the bed like a sneaky cat. She ripped his top off and unsnapped his bottoms.

Baron did not know what had gotten into his wife. But he was relieved she did not let Aniyah win. He slipped out of his bottoms, pulling her into his arms. He caressed her body, while he tasted the sweetness of her lips.

Tessa was willing to do what it took not to lose her man to another woman. She pulled away from him. Standing up on the bed, she danced, moving her hips to her own beat, shaking her breasts and freely showing off her goods to her husband.

"Come to my bed," she said, dancing her way to the master suite.

Baron followed her, hopping all the way, not letting his swollen toe touch the floor.

Once in the suite, she attacked his lips with force. She made him feel like his lips were about to be chewed off. But when she squeezed his manhood, Baron spoke, "Easy."

Tessa let go of the grip she had on him, then she started to laugh. "A woman that is wild turns you on. That's what I was giving you, hubby."

Baron had thought his wife snapped in that short of time. "I love our usual lovemaking." He picked her up, gently resting her back on the bed. He crawled on top of her, pampering her body with his tongue. Tessa moaned from his touch, but cried out once he entered her. Together, they hit the highest peak of their marriage.

CHAPTER 31

The radio came on, awakening Aniyah. With her eyes closed, she pressed the off button and the noise ceased. She peeped out of one eye at the clock, noticing both hands pointed straight up. In two hours, it would be time for her six-week checkup.

Aniyah got out of bed and fumbled toward the kitchen for food. After eating, she slipped on anything that would fit her body.

Happy to regain privileges to use the Powells' limo services, she called for a ride to take her to her doctor's appointment.

Baby Jarvis' sleepover at his grandfather's home had turned into weeks. The baby was in the care of a nanny at the estate, compliments of his grandfather. As much as Aniyah missed her son, she did not make a fuss. If things went the way she anticipated, in due time, she would have what she dreamt of and more.

The ob/gyn office was filled wall to wall with patients. It took Aniyah longer than she expected to be seen, but finally, she was called and taken down a long corridor, where her doctor greeted her.

"Hello there, good to see you," Dr. Guess said. He browsed her chart. "How's that baby boy of yours?"

Aniyah smiled. "He's great."

"Any pains or any other problems since delivery?"

"All good. I would like to get back to normal. You know what I mean, Doc?"

Dr. Guess nodded. "Let's get you checked out."

After the examination, the doctor checked her, giving her the news she wanted to hear. "You can add romance back into your life."

"Thanks, Doc...There's one more thing." Aniyah hesitated, but spoke. "I do need your help."

The doctor held her chart in front of him with both hands. He nodded his head. "What type of help?"

Aniyah went on to explain in detail what she needed. Never did she expect Dr. Guess to agree to help her with her situation.

Once back in the limo, she contacted her man. In the past few weeks, Jarvis had gravitated back closer to her, even without them being sexually active with one another.

His phone rang three times before he answered. "Yes, Baby."

"I went to the doctor. He says we can, you know what," she flirted.

"I'll see you tonight."

Aniyah was excited about the date but wanted information on their son. "How is Jarvis, Jr.? I miss him so much."

"Dad went to a meeting. The help is feeding him."

Aniyah was jealous and in a squeaky voice, she said, "That's my job to do."

"Come visit your son," he suggested.

"I'm on my way." She perked up. She had wondered would Jarvis ever get enough muscles in his back to stand up to his papa.

Aniyah ordered the limo driver to take her for a quick stop at the dollar store, then on to Lake Murray.

Once Aniyah arrived at the estate, Jarvis, holding their son, greeted her. She rescued Baby Jarvis from his arms. "My little fellow."

Aniyah cuddled her baby, giving him a peck on his forehead. "And my big fellow." She kissed Jarvis on the lips.

"He just finished his bottle."

"I smell food." The aroma went up her nostrils.

"Lobster, salad and roasted garlic red potatoes."

"Sounds delicious."

Aniyah followed him out onto the covered patio. She took a seat on a black cast aluminum chair, with cushions that were covered in outdoor Sunbrella fabric.

The view of the beaming sun, highlighting the waves of the lake, mesmerized her. This was the type of world, step by step, that she was aiming to have.

Everything was peaceful, until the nanny came over to her, holding her hands out, ready to take charge of Baby Jarvis. Aniyah pulled the baby close to her bosom. "I'm his mama."

"Sorry, Ma'am, I thought you might want to be free to have your lunch," the nanny said, placing her arms down by her side.

"Aniyah, she'll bring our son back to you when we finish eating," Jarvis said.

With another kiss from his mother, Baby Jarvis was handed over to the nanny.

"Your figure looks great," Jarvis complimented Aniyah. He admired her fitted jean skirt and sleeveless blouse.

"I'm holding my tummy in. We'll work off this extra weight together." Aniyah winked.

Jarvis reached over and kissed her.

The servant brought them two plates of lobsters and set them on the cast aluminum table covered in white linen. On another two small plates were potatoes and two more bowls with a fresh salad of romaine lettuce, apples, pecans, tomatoes and cucumbers. To quench their thirst, a pitcher of cold iced tea was placed in the center of the table. The servants replenished their glasses when needed.

"This is some good food." Aniyah chewed.

"Eat as much as you want."

"The hell she will. Get out," Powell, Sr. yelled, making his presence known. "When are you going to learn, Son? I don't want this tramp in my home."

"Dad, calm down. She's here to see our son."

"It's my grand-heir."

"Glad to see you, too." Aniyah sucked her teeth at Powell, Sr.

The servant returned back to replenish her drink. Powell, Sr. stepped in front of her. "Let the tramp pour her own drink. You get paid from me. Pour me a glass," he demanded. The servant dashed and brought back him a glass. Powell, Sr. gulped downed the tea. He set the glass on the table. He pointed at Aniyah. "Be gone by the time I come back."

"I'm so sorry." Jarvis rubbed his right hand across his mouth in disbelief. "I thought Dad was gone for the whole day."

"He's a pig."

Jarvis stood. "I'll go have a word with him. Be right back."

Aniyah waited until he left and opened her oversized handbag. She pulled out aluminum foil and two large plastic freezer bags she'd purchased from the dollar store. She wrapped her food in foil, tossing it in her bag. She picked up a set of stemmed glasses, placing them in the freezer bags. Without saying goodbye to Jarvis, she took a hike.

Back on the patio, Jarvis returned to see she was gone. Her cell phone rang and she answered. She prayed he didn't realize that she had stolen the stemware. Before she could say a word, Jarvis spoke. "You disappeared on me."

"I don't want any trouble with your papa. It's time our son comes live with me at the penthouse."

"That's what I want to talk to Dad about. He's being bull-headed. Give me another day."

Aniyah did not challenge Jarvis about the baby; she did not want to make friction between him and his father. She was quite aware, in due time, her baby would be back with her.

Inside the limo, Aniyah requested that the driver take her to her next destination that would hopefully help end the feud between her and old man Powell.

CHAPTER 32

Aniyah slouched across the made-up bed. Being away from her baby at times put her in a depressed mode. To get moving, she turned on the radio. The upbeat song by Rihanna had her snapping her fingers and dancing on her feet from the bedroom into the shower.

Once finished, she sprayed her body with a fruit-scented spray, yearning for her man to treat her neck like an orange and suck on it.

She opened a medium-sized gift box. It was one of many gifts that she had received from Jarvis. She removed a sky-blue baby doll gown, wrapped in white tissue paper. She slipped on the top, throwing the bottom back into the box. The gown fell right at her hips. Her shapely body showed through the sheer fabric. She slid her feet into four-inch, open-toe pumps and strutted out of the bedroom to the tune of thc music.

Stepping off the elevator, Jarvis walked into her web. His eyes feasted on the fullness of her nipples, revealed through the gown. "I like what I see." He drooled, coming closer to her. He sniffed the aroma of her body scent. "I can use a juicy orange."

Aniyah leaped into his arms. Jarvis twirled her twice around in a circle. Once he stopped, she felt his hands caress her bottom, and his lips devoured hers. She had no worries; his strong arms held her up off the floor until he carried her to the sofa, resting her back against the cushion.

This was the perfect time for her to make a demand from him. She was satisfied that he hungered to get his groove on.

"Not so fast," she said, brushing his hands away. "Let's finish this in Vegas."

"Las Vegas?" He was startled. "What about this?" He pointed at his erection.

"It'll be worth the wait."

Jarvis smothered her neck with mushy kisses while he rubbed his manhood against her thighs. "I've been waiting over a month."

"It's been a long time since I've had a vacation. Stuck right here in this penthouse." She pouted. "I hear Vegas is wild. One night is what we need to make sparks."

"You're serious, aren't you?"

Aniyah gave him a blank look.

He hopped off her. "Pack an overnight bag. I'll make the arrangements," he said, frustrated, but he understood that Aniyah deserved a vacation after giving birth to his son. And, for once, he wanted to be spontaneous. He was willing to wait a little longer before he would make love with her on silky sheets in a hotel suite.

Overjoyed, Aniyah dashed to pack, while Jarvis got on the phone, pulling strings for a private jet to Las Vegas.

Flying high in the sky reminded Aniyah of her first flight when she had left home as a teen with tourists, full of happiness as she was with Jarvis—but this time things were different.

Her ears clogged up several times during the flight. Jarvis tried to seduce her. She held him off, though her body yearned for his muscular body.

Once they landed, limo services were there to greet them. The driver drove them to the strip, where there were more lights lit up at night than at the South Carolina Fair.

"This is party city." Aniyah could not keep her eyes off all the glamour around her. Jarvis escorted her into a five-star hotel.

They checked in. Up in the suite, Jarvis tossed his one bag on the floor. He grabbed her. "We're in Vegas."

Aniyah pulled away. "The night is young. Let's go party at the bar. Gamble or something," she suggested.

Jarvis viewed the bed from where they stood; ready to have his way with her in it. He turned back to face her. "No more excuses after this." He decided to play her game—getting him more aroused for her.

Down in the casino, Aniyah took the lead when she heard party music playing in the dimly lit lounge. They hurried through the crowd of people to get to it, but the ringing of the machines from players that were winning caught her attention. "I want to try that machine," she said, pointing to an empty chair in front of a game of Lucky Sevens. She took a seat.

Jarvis entered a hundred-dollar bill in the slot. He placed the bet, and then pulled the lever, demonstrating to her how to operate the machine. Nothing came up. "You try it," he suggested.

"Give me a kiss for luck." She perked up her lips, receiving a whopper kiss from him.

The bet was set. Aniyah pulled the lever. Three sevens came across the middle row. The machine went off like an alarm.

"I won. I won!" Excitedly, she bounced in the seat.

"Two thousand dollars." He threw his arms around her neck, placing kisses on it.

They waited for an attendant to cash her out, leaving some of the money on the machine for a few more plays. After several tries, the machine did not pay off, Aniyah pressed the button to cash out. "Let's go party." She placed the winning slip in her bra.

In the lounge area, Aniyah pushed through another group of people to get to the dance floor.

Jarvis watched her move her hips, then dance her way off the floor to pull on him to join her.

"No dancing for me," he said.

"Stand still. I'll dance for us."

Aniyah shook her hips in front of him, swinging around him. Not letting up, she put her arms around his neck, staring into his eyes, keeping him under her spell.

The music stopped. She wiped her forehead of sweat. "I need a drink." They went to the bar and she ordered. "Two Tequila Sunrise Margaritas."

"Baby, you know I only drink wine."

"Come on, Jarvis. You're in Vegas. Let loose. Drink one with me." The margaritas arrived. Aniyah handed him one. "Please." She batted her eyes and sipped on the other drink.

"I'll taste a little." One sip turned into an empty glass for him. Aniyah ordered two more. Jarvis gulped his down faster than she did. The alcohol kicked in, causing him to drag her back on the dance floor. He moved several kinds of ways with no beat.

Aniyah laughed at him but danced right along. Once the music slowed down, she was drawn like a string into his arms. She took her chance and whispered in his right ear, "You want another man to have me?" she asked, slipping out of his arms. She went to the first free man she saw, diving into the other man's arms to dance.

"Hey, sweetie," the man said happily, holding her close.

"She belongs to me," Jarvis said jealously. He pulled his woman back toward him.

"Is this your wife?" the man argued.

"Yes."

The man let go of Aniyah. "You crazy chick." He headed off the dance floor.

Jarvis grabbed Aniyah by the hand and escorted her from the floor. "I didn't bring you to Vegas to disrespect me."

Aniyah yanked loose of him. "What are you going to do about this?" She held her finger up, showing off her engagement ring. "I'm the mama of your son, but I'm not your wife. You lied to that man and said I was. I say you have to live up to your words."

"Vegas is loaded with chapels." Jarvis pulled her into his arms and kissed her before he led the way to make her his wife.

Mission accomplished, Aniyah thought.

They staggered into the suite. Aniyah was the first to discard her clothes.

Jarvis flung his shirt to land next to a trashcan. "Come here," he said with slurred speech. "I want you."

She giggled. "I bet you can't catch me."

Chasing Aniyah around the coffee table was like playing musical chairs to Jarvis until he decided to break the game rules. He leaped across the table. "Got you," he said, once he caught her and tackled her on the sofa, exploring her body with the tip of his tongue.

"Jarvis," she moaned. Her body tingled in the right places. Never had a man made her feel so good.

Making his way up to her lips, she opened her mouth to receive his wandering tongue. But once she felt his fingers stroke the most sensual parts of her body, her fingers clawed into his back. She screamed from the pleasure. For the first time, with Jarvis, she didn't make an issue about him covering up, letting him thrust inside her.

Aniyah moved right along with him. At times, she slowed down, not wanting him to explode, but with her easing up, Jarvis could not hold back any longer, and she received the injection of his fuel inside her. From the heat that had built up between them, her breasts caught his dripping sweat.

They dragged their way onto the bed. Their clothes were left scattered on the floor. It did not take long before Aniyah heard him snoring. Loud as he was, it turned her on. Things were in reverse for her. She believed she yearned for him more than he did for her. Not being able to sleep, she eased her toes up his leg, stroking his manhood.

The snoring stopped and Jarvis woke up. "Am I missing out on something?" He felt his manhood hardened.

Aniyah pulled him by the shoulder and he turned over on his back. She rested on top of him. "I feel naughty."

From under the pillow, she reached for a bottle of baby oil. Dripping it on his chest, she massaged the oil into his muscles, working her way down to his toes.

"Aniyah." He spoke her name, as he loved every bit of what she was doing to him.

She stood up over him. With her legs spread on each side of his waist, she poured the oil on her body. Then she rubbed it into her skin while she moved in a sensual manner. It drove him to pull her down on top of him. Next, he stroked her hair, while he pressed his lips against hers.

Aniyah sat down on his saddle. She galloped, stirring them to the highest leap that they had ever had. The ride left them pouring in sweat and exhausted. Aniyah spread out on top of him, and fell asleep in the midst of his snoring.

The morning after, Jarvis woke up with headaches. "No more Margaritas for me. I'll stick to wine." He held his head.

"You have to get used to the drink."

"Not my cup of tea. We'd better get back home. Dad will be looking for me."

Aniyah smiled. "Yeah, and our little man needs us."

"I hate to spoil things. Dad is drawing up papers for you to sign. He wants custody of our son."

Aniyah became excited. "The hell he does. Jarvis, the Third is our baby."

"If I defy Dad, he'll cut me off. I have to be able in the future to have a stable home for you and the baby." He took Aniyah in his arms. "We also have to keep things quiet about us for now. Things will soon go our way."

"I won't sign the papers. Never, ever."

Too disgusted, Aniyah got dressed. Quietly, they gathered their things and headed home.

Less than ten days later, Aniyah entered Dr. Guess' examination room. She went through procedures, checking her weight, which had gone down a few pounds from afterbirth.

The nurse led her into the doctor's office where Aniyah took a seat.

Right behind her, Dr. Guess entered. "I have the results for you," he informed her.

She became anxious when she noticed the sheet of paper in his hand. He handed it to her. She took a quick look and read it. Her eyes popped open when she saw the different numbers on the page. "I don't know how to read this." Aniyah tried to hand him back the paper, but the doctor pushed it back to her.

"Read the percentage."

At the bottom of the page, Aniyah read to herself. "Probably zero percent." Her eyes stayed glued to the numbers; they rattled in her brain.

"It's true. Sina Cole was telling the truth."

"You can go get your son. You can use this paper in a court of law."

Aniyah bear-hugged Dr. Guess, dampening his doctor's jacket with tears. "I thank you so much," she said.

"You did the work. You got the DNA from the glasses and took it to the lab. I'm only giving you the results. Anything to keep a mother with her child."

"I'll do whatever it takes to keep mine." Aniyah wiped her flowing tears.

"Be careful," he said warily.

"I'm street smart. That old pig can't handle me," she said with her hands propped on her hips.

"Mr. Powell is a man that will do what he has to do to protect his own," Dr. Guess said, giving his opinion.

"And wants to make me miserable." Aniyah folded the paper and put it in her handbag.

"I say this appointment has ended. Go get your kid." Dr. Guess smiled and escorted her out of the office.

Aniyah left with her only concern being the last action of her plans—the grand finale.

CHAPTER 33

The day came for fireworks to spark the city of Columbia. The biggest cookout would be at the Powell Estate on the backyard lawn. Labor Day was one of the holidays that Southerners came together to get down on Southern food.

No invitation came Aniyah's way. Jarvis did not bother to ask his father's permission for her to attend the Powells' annual BBQ. It would only cause an argument. But he informed Aniyah that his father would introduce his new heir with the setoff of fireworks. Baby Jarvis was three months old.

Inside the bathroom, Aniyah got dressed, sporting a DKNY pair of shorts that fell below her butt cheeks. The off-the-shoulder top hung below her waist.

Her phone rang. The call was from the security office, informing her that her guest had arrived.

Nellie had come to visit. They had put their differences aside, with her being rehired by Jarvis at the request of Aniyah. She entered the penthouse. "Aniyah," she called.

"Come in the bedroom."

Nellie entered. She saw Aniyah playing in her hair in the mirror. "You're in love with your own self."

Aniyah spun around, showing off that she had trimmed her baby fat and more. "Hey, when you look this good, you have no choice."

"Let's get going. My cousin's barbecue has started."

Aniyah's cell phone rang, interrupting their conversation. She ran to answer it. "Not you, Mr. Powell," she said, annoyed.

"I've waited long enough. Sign the papers today or go to jail," he shouted.

Aniyah had dodged the legal issues of the papers long enough. The time had come for her to face off with him. "I'll sign your stupid papers. But I still get to be with your son."

Powell, Sr. paused for a second. "See him whenever you want. There won't be any marriage. Stay away from me and my new grand-heir."

She was eager to reveal, "I'm his wife," but instead, she said, "I'll come by today and sign your stupid papers. You'd better pay me big money."

"We'll discuss the price when you get here. Hurry up. I don't want you here when my guests arrive. You know, like the ones you tried to rob," he said jokingly.

Aniyah hung up. Things could not be more perfect. She would also once again confront her past—Mr. Houston's daughters.

"You're really going to sell your baby to Mr. Powell?" Nellie asked, overhearing their conversation.

"Today, I'll do what I gotta do."

"Giving away your baby for money. You can't do that. Give him to me. I'll take care of him."

"Girl, you don't have any money to pay me for him."

"I have lots of love to give."

"That doesn't buy Pampers or milk. Take me to the estate. Let's first crash the old fart's barbecue."

Vehicles lined up one to get past security into the gates of the Powell Estate. Nellie drove up when it was her turn at the security checkpoint. Again, she flashed her old badge.

"You no longer work here," the guard announced, handing her back her badge.

Aniyah reached across Nellie and hollered, "I'm here to see old man Mr. Powell. He knows I'm coming. My name is Aniyah."

"Sorry, but you'll have to wait until I check with Mr. Powell," the guard informed.

They waited for verification.

"I hope that old jerk don't flip on me," Aniyah mumbled.

"We can go ahead to my barbecue. Plenty of finger-lickin' ribs and chopped barbecue," Nellie said, smelling the aroma of grilled food in the air.

The security guard came back to them. "Mr. Powell wants you to come to the main house. Someone will see you to his study."

"You thought I was lying." Aniyah stuck her tongue out at the guard.

Nellie pressed her foot on the gas, going in the direction of the home, while other vehicles followed the path where men in yellow polo shirts directed them to where Mr. Powell, Sr. designated the parking for his guests. Some attendees came by limos or in their own luxury vehicles while others traveled the lake by their boats.

The estate was decorated in red, white and blue. In the front, an American flag flew high on a pole.

Aniyah jumped out of the vehicle. A servant met her to escort her to Powell, Sr.'s study.

Down a long corridor on the first floor, the servant opened the door to the study. Aniyah saw her way in.

The walls were lined with books. Deep red drapes hung on decorative rods. The room was barely lit. Behind an office desk, Aniyah made herself comfortable in a high-back leather chair. She closed her eyes. She felt superior in the seat.

While she was deep in the emotion of feeling powerful, Powell, Sr. interrupted her. "Get your ass out of my chair," he yelled, entering his study.

She jumped. "Knock before you enter."

"This is my office, Tramp."

Aniyah switched places with him, watching him settle in the seat, while she made her way back around the desk.

"I need you to sign these papers." He handed her the document and pen.

Aniyah started to read what he hoped she would sign. Immediately, she saw Attorney Chavis had drawn up the document.

"I don't have all day. I have guests to entertain. It says you're signing my grand-heir over to me."

"I'm not a fruitcake like you and others think I am. This is a lot of writing. I'm reading every word." Aniyah sat down in a nearby chair. She read word for word of the document.

"Go ahead and read the damn thing. I'll be right back," he growled, as he stood to his feet. "Have it signed by the time I return."

As soon as he left, Aniyah tore the papers in half and threw them in a trashcan. "I'm not signing my baby over to anyone."

There was silence from outside the door. She hurried to join Nellie, who sat in her vehicle awaiting her. "It's firework time."

"You signed the papers."

"Girl, heck no. That pig gets no kid of mine. This is the deal." Aniyah explained to her what she wanted her to do.

"That won't get me in jail."

"Girl, no. Help me for my baby's sake."

Nellie decided to go along with the plan. They took their places in the parking area where guests parked.

Aniyah headed into the entrance to the backyard, while Nellie went ahead and followed her instructions.

Guests walked on the stone patio and grass, wearing plenty of designer sandals and sneakers. Music from a live band entertained them. Caterers stood at their selected stations on the lawn. Two top barbecue chefs smoked up two stainless steel professional grills. One chef prepared chicken, ribs and steaks. Others prepared hamburgers and hot dogs. At the far end, a black kettle pot filled with oil heated up for fried fish.

Down-home hash and rice was prepared for the pork eaters and corn on the cob, potatoes, shrimp, and sausages boiled in a big pot with plenty of Cajun seasonings. The bar station housed all kinds of bubbling beverages for the guests. And, at the last station, a chef stood behind a table with watermelons, ready to be sliced.

Servants dressed in black pants and white short-sleeved shirts walked around with trays of shrimp, veggie and fruit kabobs on skewers.

Aniyah looked around to see if she saw any familiar faces. She spotted Baron among the guests, and she sashayed over to him. Her Aunt Tessa was nowhere in sight. Aniyah tapped him on the shoulder. "No date." She laughed.

Baron turned to see her. "Get away from me."

"You're a guest like me. I leave when I'm ready."

"Then stay your distance from me." Baron turned to a servant carrying a tray of wine. He grabbed two glasses and drank the both of them.

"I'm sure you'll be getting divorce papers in the mail." Aniyah laughed.

"Your aunt is smarter than you think. She's at home in our bed suffering with sinuses. We're strong as a couple."

"She's weak. And, so are you."

In truth, Aniyah hated that her aunt had stayed with Baron. She looked across the lawn and spotted the youngest Houston. She wanted to run and strangle Kenley Houston. Aniyah noticed Kenley wore the Houston women's favorite summer wear—linen.

Baron watched Aniyah staring at her. "Stay away from Kenley and her sisters," he warned.

"I'm free. Them bitches don't dictate where I walk."

"You're headed back to jail sooner than you think," he argued, moving away from her to greet Kenley Houston.

Aniyah browsed the area, delighted when she saw Jarvis at one of the grill stations. He held a plate in his hand. The chef placed a juicy well-done steak on it. She watched Jarvis head over to the fish station.

Walking up to him, she gave him a tap on his broad shoulders. "I'll share a piece with you."

Jarvis turned to face her. "Baby, why are you here? You know how Dad is."

"I came to get my son. He needs to be with me. Not some nanny."

"Dad will come around. You being here will only make him angrier."

At times Aniyah wished Jarvis would man-up to his father.

"Gosh, Dad already sees you," Jarvis said, spotting his father.

As Powell, Sr. trotted toward them, Aniyah was quite aware he had been to his study and seen that she had vanished.

"Leave us alone, Jarvis. I need to speak to Aniyah," Powell, Sr. said to his son.

"Dad, promise me, please, no trouble." Jarvis walked away but steadily looked back.

Old man Powell whispered in Aniyah's ear, "Where are the papers? Did you sign them?"

She smiled. "I left them signed in your office desk drawer."

"You're a smarter tramp than I thought. I'll throw you a few bucks."

As Powell, Sr. walked away from Aniyah, Jarvis caught up to him. "Is there something I should know?" he wondered.

"Son, stop worrying. Everything is under control." Powell, Sr. smiled. He patted Jarvis on his back. "Go on and get your woman a plate of food to go."

"That's nice of you, Dad," Jarvis said confusedly. He hoped maybe things were turning for the best.

Aniyah picked up two plates, not letting the smell of free food go to waste. At the fish station, she fixed food for her and Nellie.

Jarvis came over to her. "I see you've already got started."

"It's BBQ time."

They walked to the meat station. They waited in line behind guests being served.

"I see the bee has stung you, again," a voice whispered in her ear.

Aniyah turned around to once again see her past stood in her face. Kenley Houston stood behind her. "Jarvis, she's a devil."

He turned to Kenley. "I understand how you feel. But Aniyah isn't the same woman that everyone talks about. She's changed."

"Time will tell." Kenley turned up her nose. "I think I'll skip the meat. I prefer fish."

"Bye." Aniyah waved her hand at her.

Kenley hollered back at Aniyah. "The skunk smell went away since we got rid of you out of the Houston Estate."

Aniyah went to go after her, but Jarvis threw his hand around her waist, pulling her back. "She's not worth it."

In place of the music from the band, Powell, Sr. stood at the microphone, his voice echoing throughout the lawn. "Hello. For those of you who don't know me, and that might be one or two of you." He chuckled and so did his guests. "Today is a grand day. You'll get to meet the second heir of the Powell family. You know my first heir." Powell, Sr. pointed at Jarvis, who handed his plate to one of the chefs for safekeeping. He left Aniyah and went to be near his father. "My son, Jarvis Powell, Jr."

Jarvis took the microphone. "Hello, everyone. Thanks for being here today." He returned the microphone to his father. He had no need for the attention that his father had sought.

"Eat and drink. I'll be right back with my grand-heir," Powell, Sr. said. He did not understand what took the nanny so long to bring the baby to him as he had instructed her to do.

Before Jarvis could make his way back to the food station, the other two Houston sisters and their husbands surrounded him. They conversed about the baby.

Aniyah rolled her eyes at the sight of the rest of the Houston sisters, dressed in their white linen summer pantsuits. She didn't bother to interfere in their conversations with Jarvis; instead she chewed on a piece of fish, praying Nellie had done what she had instructed her to do.

She took another bite of fish and eased her way to the band, which had yet to start playing again. She lifted the microphone off its stand. Everyone focused on her, including Jarvis.

"Hey, everybody. Papa Powell forgot to mention me. I'm Aniyah, the mama of his grandson, Jarvis, Jr.'s baby boy."

"Get off that microphone," Powell, Sr. yelled, heading toward her, after being informed by one of his servants that the baby was not in the nursery where she had left him. "Tell me where my grand-heir is," he shouted.

Aniyah did not let go of the microphone. Too tickled, she kept speaking. "Hey, ya'll. Old fart Powell has no grand-heir. Nor does he have a damn son," she said with pleasure.

Powell, Sr. did not respond to her announcement, but sweat had formed around his neck. He wondered how much more information she had on him. He kept his cool, staring at Jarvis, who did not know what to make of what Aniyah said. "She's delusional," his father responded.

"You'll do whatever it takes to have your way," Aniyah cried. "And you know what I'm talking about?"

Powell, Sr. tried to snatch the microphone from her, but Aniyah ran a few feet away from him. "I'm not finished. I'm not giving my baby to you or anybody else. He's not for sale."

"Aniyah, no one is selling our baby," Jarvis informed. "It's a family tradition for the heir to have a celebration and be introduced to family and friends. Dad had one for me when I was born."

"Jarvis, listen to me. He's trying to pay me off for our baby. And he's not your papa," Aniyah blurted.

"She's a conniving liar," Powell, Sr. screamed. "Call the police. She's trying to steal from us. The same way she'd tried to steal from the Houstons."

"I believe you," Milandra Houston said, voicing her opinion.

"Call whoever the hell who you want. I'm not lying," Aniyah shouted. She turned to Jarvis. "You're the biological son of Rupert Houston."

"You need a psychiatrist," Kenley said, making her way to Aniyah. "You don't bring my dead father into this. You're sicker than I thought."

They stood eye to eye.

"Ask your lawyer over there." Aniyah went around Kenley to confront Baron. "Tell them empty-headed sisters the truth. You know Jarvis is dead man Houston's son. Tell them how their papa sold his son to Mr. Powell so that he could have an heir."

Baron dropped his head down. He was too shocked to answer Aniyah's theory. He thought of all people, Aniyah was the one to discover the secret.

Kenley watched Baron stroke his forehead several times. She came eye to eye to him and spoke. "Is what she's saying true? Is Jarvis Father's biological son?"

"Is it the truth?" Milandra Houston questioned their lawyer, as well.

"Let's speak in privacy," Baron said to the sisters, noticing all eyes were on him.

"No secrets," Noelle Houston added.

"It wasn't my choice to keep it undercover. It was your father's wish," Baron admitted.

The Houston sisters and everyone on the lawn, as one, took a deep breath from the confession.

Jarvis stared at his father, recalling the numerous years his father never let him play. Banking was all he had heard about. He was groomed to carry on the business. His eyes filled with water. "Dad, you say, be a man. You tell me out of your own mouth."

Powell, Sr., defeated, became deranged. "I owe you no explanation. You're standing on my property I sweated for. So be grateful. I took you in to be my heir. You've been enjoying the fruits of it."

With teary eyes, Jarvis said, "Dad, I'm a bank deal you had negotiated. Have you no shame?"

"He thinks more of a dollar bill than you," Aniyah said.

"Thanks to me, Tramp, you wouldn't have a baby if I didn't tell him to knock you up so I could have a grand-heir." Powell, Sr. laughed.

All the time she thought the packs of condoms were defective, Jarvis intentionally had damaged them to get her pregnant. She turned to him. "Is that true?" She hated being played.

"I only agreed to it so that we could be connected, and maybe Dad would come around and let us be with each other."

Kenley laughed right along with Powell, Sr. "Aniyah, or Rosie, whatever your name is, you got tricked," she said, voicing her opinion.

"Tell me where my grand-heir is. Then, leave my property," Powell, Sr. demanded. He came toward Aniyah as if he were about to attack her, but Jarvis stood in his way. Powell, Sr. pushed him, but Jarvis forced him back away. "You're free now to leave with our baby, Aniyah," Jarvis said.

"Not yet." She confronted the Houston sisters. "Your papa wasn't crap. He took advantage of my Aunt Tessa and Jarvis' mother, Sina."

Kenley leaped after Aniyah. "Leave my father's name out of your trashy mouth." She grabbed Aniyah's hair.

"No Kenley, no fighting," Noelle Houston shouted at her sister. She went to separate her sister, but her other sister snatched her by the arm.

"Let Kenley sock her for us. Beat her, Sister," Milandra cheered.

Aniyah swung back at Kenley. They scrambled on the lawn until Jarvis and Baron pulled them apart. The guests stood back, watching the brawl.

"Aniyah, where are you getting this information from?" Jarvis asked inquiringly.

Aniyah and Kenley straightened their hair and clothing.

"Your mother, Sina, told me. She worked for Mr. Houston. He charmed his way under her skirt and got her pregnant. She gave the baby to him…paid her ten thousand dollars, then Mr. Houston sold you for twenty thousand to that pig over there," she said, pointing to Powell, Sr..

"Shut your trap up," Powell, Sr. roared.

"More to tell. The light is green. I'm going to keep going." Aniyah placed her hand on Jarvis' scar. "Your mama never hurt you. Your face was ruined by either a Houston or a Powell. Mr. Houston wanted to buy you back for double the money, when he saw you were a bright kid. That one over there," she pointed again at Powell, Sr., "he didn't want to give you back. So they struggled right in front of you. Mr. Houston pulled out a knife. Two pigs fighting caused you to get hurt. Mr. Houston didn't want to cause you any pain when he heard you calling the old fart, Dad. Houston didn't put up a fight anymore."

"Wow." Jarvis sobbed.

"Your mama is closer than you think. She never ran away with a man. Mr. Pig over there has been paying her off with checks for years."

"It's true, Son," Sina said, entering the lawn, being pushed in her wheelchair by her neighbor. She could not rest after Aniyah's visit. The guilt rose in her. She wished she'd had the fight in her years ago that Aniyah had to keep her child. She had read in the paper of Powell's event to introduce his grand-heir to the community. It was the perfect time for her to redeem herself.

Stunned to see his mother, Jarvis dashed to her. He kneeled down in front of her. "Mom!"

Sina placed her hand on his scar. "I'll never forget that day." She cried. "Please forgive me, Son, for not fighting for you. Jarvis, Sr. and Rupert may have taken you from me, but I won't let your son be taken from you and his mother. He's not a Monopoly piece."

Flushed from the sight of Sina, Powell, Sr. growled. "No one asked for your opinion."

Kenley confronted Sina. "I want to know did my father, Rupert Houston, take advantage of you."

Sina fanned herself with her hands. She confirmed Aniyah's allegations. She explained that she had worked long shifts at the Houstons. She remembered serving breakfast to Powell, Sr. when he paid visits to see the late Houston from time to time. She overheard one particular conversation, where Powell, Sr. wished for an heir to carry on the banking business. No woman Powell, Sr. bedded had ever produced a child for him.

The following day, Houston demanded she served him personally a fresh cup of coffee to sip on while he read his newspaper during his morning breakfasts. Black coffee, two sugars and heavy on the cream, Houston would say. And he demanded the brew be fresh or he would send it back. Houston knew what he wanted. He eyed her. No other servant could serve him. He insisted on the "sexy one," as he had called her. One morning, Sina was late bringing him coffee. Not feeling well, she decided to go back to the servant quarters, where she lived. She had come to tell him that another servant would bring him his drink. He wanted to know where she was off to, and had not served him as of yet. She turned to him with watery eyes and informed him she was a bit under the weather. He shocked her when he got out of his seat and patted her eyes dry with his white handkerchief. He rested his arms on her back and insisted his private doctor see her. She convinced him that a doctor would not be necessary. But, Houston would not take no for an answer and offered to escort her to the servant quarters. At his disposal, she loved the attention he gave her as his employee. What harm? she thought.

He walked her to the quarters. Once she opened the door and was ready to say thank you, Houston shoved her inside. He kicked the door closed with his foot. He wasted no time, ripping her uniform to expose her undergarments. He tossed her around, shoving her against the door. With soggy kisses, he wet her neck. She tried to slide from around him, but Houston became enraged, throwing her on the floor. Before she could get to her feet, he leaped on top of her, and took her to satisfy his male hormones.

In disbelief, Kenley covered her mouth. "I'm so sorry." She wept.

"I forgave your father a long time before his death," Sina said.

"Thanks for your forgiveness to Father," Kenley said.

"We don't know if what she says is true. Father is not alive to defend himself," Milandra argued.

Aniyah targeted her attention to Milandra. "Believe it, Snob."

"Enough!" Jarvis intervened. He directed his attention to his mother. "I want to hear it from you. What's the truth about me?"

"Tramps don't tell the truth," Powell, Sr. said sarcastically.

"Dad, no name-calling," Jarvis said.

Sina took a sip of cold water from a green straw inside of a to-go cup. "Time goes by so fast." She recalled how it did not take long before she began to show that she was with child. Houston ordered her to leave her job, even putting her up in an apartment. He made sure she had the proper clothes to wear. He took care of her in every sense of the way. She no longer slept on a twin-sized bed; he lavished her with a king-sized one. His attentiveness to her made her suppress his negative behavior, and she began to have feelings for him. She thought maybe he would make up his wrongdoing to her by leaving his wife and marrying her.

Delivery day came and Jarvis was born—Houston was there by her side. He held the baby before she did.

After coming home from the hospital, Sina signed some documents, unknown to her that she had signed her baby away. Houston gave Powell, Sr. possession of her son. Houston paid her money and then he tossed her on the streets.

After six years, Houston got in touch with her. He wanted Jarvis back and needed her help. He convinced her he would leave his wife for her, and they would become a family.

As a couple, they visited Powell, Sr.'s office. Houston demanded their son back. It was the first time she had seen her son since he was born. She was introduced to him by her first name. It hurt her when he called Powell, Sr., Dad, with high respect. Her son wore suits, not play clothes, before he could barely walk.

Unhappy, Sina decided to turn on Houston. She made it clear to both men that she was leaving and taking her son with her. Houston claimed he wanted Jarvis for himself, but Powell, Sr. wasn't hearing it from either of them.

Jarvis, a little boy, stared as grown folks argued. He wept for the only father he knew. Powell, Sr. heard his voice. To quiet him, he snatched him up in his arms.

Furiously, Houston reached for Jarvis, but Powell, Sr., struggled to hold on to him. Without hesitation, Houston pulled out a blade from his pocket, flipped it open, and then swung it at his once close friend. Powell, Sr. grabbed Houston by his left wrist but held on to the tearful Jarvis in his arms. The men struggled. They stopped once the knife accidentally cut Jarvis in the face. Blood gushed from him.

Powell, Sr. took a handkerchief from his pocket. He held it against Jarvis' wound, but at the same time, he ordered Houston and Sina to leave or he would call the police and point the finger at them for Jarvis' injury.

Neither Sina nor Houston wanted to leave Jarvis. But she left for the sake of her son. In her heart she did not want her son to live the life she could only give him—struggling to make ends meet. Houston left, not to be entangled with the law, and he was married.

Both parents worried. They hoped Jarvis was okay. Sina called every hospital in town to learn the outcome of her son's injury, but none had records of a little boy coming in for a facial cut.

Hopeless nights of not being able to sleep and missing meals made her too sick to do anything. Her body trembled every time she thought of Jarvis. She could not bear it anymore and took a chance contacting Powell, Sr. He spoke to her in a tone like a torch of fire as she requested for him to give Jarvis back, but all he did was made her feel guilty for the permanent scar left on his son's face. She needed to live and she somehow convinced Powell, Sr. to give her money in exchange for her son. Houston decided not to pursue custody for Jarvis as he was a married man. He, too, had some guilt for the damage on Jarvis' face.

"I've watched you grow, Son." Sina wept, sipping the water.

Aniyah took her by the hand to stop Sina from shaking. "They put you through hell. Bastards."

"I'm older. You could have come to me." Jarvis walked back and forth in disbelief.

"She's a liar," Powell, Sr. grumbled. "She wanted the money for you."

"Your head was filled with so much lies. I thought you wouldn't believe me," Sina explained to Jarvis.

The way Sina broke down gave Jarvis a sense of the pain his mother had endured not having her son as a part of her life.

Kenley, with tearful eyes, said, "You're a Houston. My sisters and I have a half-brother."

"It's unreal to know I have siblings." Jarvis embraced Kenley.

"We must confirm it with a DNA test, before I'll believe this craziness," Milandra said, darting her eyes at Attorney Chavis.

"I believe it," Noelle admitted. She embraced her new-found brother.

Jarvis focused his attention on Milandra. "I understand how you feel. We'll do a DNA, right away."

"I don't have to watch or listen to any of these lies," Powell, Sr. roared. Headed away, he ran into Nellie, carrying Baby Jarvis in her arms. He snatched him from her and hurried across the lawn to the microphone. "Everyone, I introduce you to my new grand-heir, Jarvis Powell, the Third."

"He's a Houston," Aniyah hollered, running to get her baby.

"Get away from me. You signed him over to me," Powell, Sr. said.

"I signed nothing. The papers are torn up in the trash. Give me my son," she ordered. She tried to take her baby from Powell, Sr.

Emotions high, Jarvis took charge. He stormed at his father, rescuing his son from him, and he handed Baby Jarvis to Aniyah.

Powell, Sr. again tried to force his way in taking the baby away from her. Jarvis gripped his polo shirt by the collar. "I'm in control from now on. I say my son stays with his mom."

Powell, Sr. jerked away. Never had Jarvis defied him. He straightened up his shirt. "You're dead to me," he grumbled, breathing heavy. He became overheated from the pressure of the situation on hand. The hot sun beaming down on him, old man Powell fainted with Jarvis catching him before he could hit the ground.

Despite his father's harsh words, Jarvis lifted him up into his arms. He turned and looked back at his mother. "We'll keep in touch." Jarvis carried his father away from the guests with his mother's friend escorting her home. A doctor attending the event immediately followed him.

Baron took charge as the host. "Everyone, I'm sure Jarvis, Sr. will be fine. On his behalf, he thanks you for coming. There's plenty of food. Feel free to take a plate home with you," he said and turned to Aniyah. "Leave."

Aniyah laughed. "I'm waiting on my husband. You go home to your weak wife."

"Husband?" The Houston sisters asked in unison.

Aniyah held her baby close to her bosom. She continued to laugh. "I'm your sister-in-law."

Kenley stepped up to her with no fear. "Mrs. Half."

"No, mouthy, I think I'll ask Jarvis to add Houston to our name. Let's see…should I go by Mrs. Aniyah Houston Powell or Aniyah Powell Houston? Either way, I think they both sound grand." She giggled.

Before Kenley could swing at her, her sister, Noelle caught her by the arm. "I think it's time we leave."

In unison, the Houston sisters rolled their eyes at her.

"Bye, sisters-in-law." Aniyah smirked.

With their heads held up high, the Houston sisters paraded off to their boats to head home.

Aniyah hurried to the pool cabana, where she located Jarvis.

She witnessed Powell, Sr. lying flat on a lounge chair. The doctor had put smelling salts up his nostrils.

Powell, Sr. immediately woke up. He looked up at Jarvis. "Get away from here. Take the tramp with you." He coughed, cutting his eyes at Aniyah.

Jarvis did not let his words bother him. He pulled the polo shirt over his father's head, to expose his sleeveless tee shirt. Powell, Sr., steadily gasping for breath, struggled to knock his hands away.

"What do you think, Doc?" Jarvis asked.

"Your father needs to go to the emergency room to be further examined," the doctor suggested.

"I'll call nine-one-one," Aniyah offered, showing Jarvis she wasn't heartless.

CHAPTER 34

It hurt Aniyah that Jarvis had gotten her pregnant on purpose. Any other time she would have made a man pay for betraying her, but Jarvis wasn't any other man. Her heart was his.

Lifting baby Jarvis from his car seat, she headed into the emergency room, while Nellie went and parked her vehicle inside the parking lot.

She spotted Jarvis in the far corner of the waiting area, leaned over, with his hands rested on his forehead. She headed straight to him. "I'm here, Honey."

He looked up and she gave him a peck on the lips. "My brains are on speed dial."

"I'm sorry about all this. But I couldn't keep the truth from you." Aniyah took a seat next to him, resting the baby on her lap.

"It's so unreal. I can't get mad at him. The man's sick. And I'm wrong for the way I got you pregnant. Dad wanted me to do it. I thought it was a perfect way to keep you in my life."

"I won't hold it against you. Our son is the best gift you could give me," she smiled, admiring their baby. "You're nothing like the old fart or Rupert Houston. You're a nice guy."

"I have to do better by my son." He watched Baby Jarvis sleep.

"Hold him." Aniyah placed the baby in his arms.

Jarvis kissed his son's tiny hands. He whispered, "My son." He turned to Aniyah. "I'm going to be a good dad."

"I know you will."

Not caring about the other people who were in the waiting room, she locked lips with her man more than once.

Aniyah pulled out the DNA test from the diaper bag. She handed it to him. Jarvis read the results. It was clear in writing that he was no match for the man he called "Dad." He crushed the paper in his hand into a ball. "Damn! I was a business deal."

"I hate to say it, but the pig loves you."

"Anyone here for Mr. Jarvis Powell?" a volunteer asked, interrupting their chat.

"I'm...his son." This was the first time it was uncomfortable for Jarvis to answer as Powell, Sr.'s relative. He handed Aniyah back the baby.

The volunteer took Jarvis to his father, where he learned of Powell, Sr.'s severe panic attack. The on-duty doctor had ordered for Powell, Sr. to stay overnight for observation.

Jarvis returned to the emergency room. Together, he, Aniyah, baby and Nellie went up to the floor where his father would make his residence for the night. They waited until the nurse arrived. She gave them permission to visit him.

To keep Powell, Sr. from not getting excited, Jarvis went in to see him alone.

Jarvis watched the nurse place pillows under Jarvis, Sr.'s head so that he could get into a comfortable position.

He became irritable when he saw Jarvis. "You don't need to be here." He coughed.

Jarvis teared up. "In spite of everything I've learned today, you're the only dad I've known."

"That baby is still my grand-heir," Powell, Sr. insisted.

"Okay, relax. He'll be your grand-heir," Jarvis said but wanted to tell him it would be on his terms. He would not let his son fall victim to his father's need to mold him into who and what he wanted Baby Jarvis to be.

"Bring him to me."

"He's not here," Jarvis fibbed, not wanting him to get riled up.

"You gave him to that tramp," Powell, Sr. roared, trying to lift up but Jarvis helped lie him back down.

"You need to relax. I'm going to leave so you won't get too excited." Jarvis headed to the door.

"Get my grand-heir from that tramp."

"Calm down, Mr. Powell." The nurse noticed his chest pumping at a rapid pace.

"Let me out of here," he roared. Again, he tried to get up but continued to gasp for breath. He felt relief once the nurse covered his nose with an oxygen mask. Then she administered him a sedative.

"Goodnight...Dad," Jarvis whispered.

Jarvis headed back into the waiting room, and took Aniyah in his arms.

"I love and hate the man."

"He's bullheaded."

"I need to leave here." Jarvis wiped his watery eyes. "Let's go."

"You know you don't want to go now. Take a walk."

"You're right." Jarvis went to let off steam.

Down the hallway with the baby in her arms, Aniyah hurried to old man Powell's room. When she entered, she went to the head of the bed. "You get no pity from me, old fart. I pity Jarvis for having to put up with a creep like you. I have love for him. Something you never gave him."

Powell, Sr. grumbled. He tried to lift his hand to point at her, but the sedative had mellowed him out.

"You won't have power over him, my baby or me. You accept me or lose your so-called heir."

Once she mentioned Baby Jarvis, Powell, Sr.'s eyes widened. He saw she held the baby in her arms. He had an urge to choke her. He grunted, "My grand-heir."

Aniyah whispered in his ear, "Your new daughter-in-law is in control."

The sedative went into full effect—her words were a bad dream to him.

"You shouldn't be in here," Jarvis said, returning back to visit his father. "Dad is not supposed to get upset."

"The pig doesn't know I'm here. He's asleep."

"No name-calling, Aniyah. He's the only dad I know. Let's leave and let him rest."

Jarvis put his arms around her waist, escorting her out of the room.

All the tension accumulated since Aniyah had met Jarvis had faded away. As his wife and mother of his child, he had given her what she had always wished for—the key to fortune and power.

About the Author

Christine Young-Robinson is the author of *We Didn't See It Coming* and the short story "Miss Amy's Last Ride," which was featured in the anthology, *Proverbs for the People*.

A wife, mother, and grandmother, Christine resides in South Carolina. She is the co-chairperson of the Eleuthera Book Club. Follow her on social media. On Facebook and Twitter: @christineyr, and on Instagram: christineyoungrobinson

Chapter 1

Rupert Houston must pay, Aniyah, twenty-eight years old, thought as she stared at the number on her cell phone of one of the wealthiest self-made businessmen in South Carolina. She was his mistress—until he decided that she was no longer of use to him.

Without hesitation, Aniyah tapped the touch screen with the tip of her middle finger on her right hand, allowing the call to go through. As she paced the kitchen floor of her apartment, three rings chimed in her ear before his voicemail came on.

"Bastard!" she yelled; she knew he was avoiding her call.

His home phone was next on her list to call. Aniyah did not care who answered. Extremely frustrated with him, she called the number. To her surprise, Rupert picked up.

"Kenley is not home, call back later," Rupert said, assuming that the call most likely was for his youngest daughter.

"Why didn't you answer your damn cell phone?" She startled him.

"How did you get this number? This is a private line. How dare you call my home?" he yelled.

"Obviously, it's not too private. I got it. Again, answer my question: Why didn't you answer your cell phone?"

"What if my wife or one of my girls had picked up? Have you lost it or what?" Rupert was furious.

"I'm one of your girls, too. Don't I count for anything?"

"Aniyah, okay, you made me aware of that. I've left you in my will. I'm willing to give you any money you need right now to take care of yourself, but that's where it ends. My wife has medical problems, and I don't want to do anything to upset her. Her doctor's orders are to keep her calm."

Aniyah listened to him. She had convinced him that she was his illegitimate daughter from his pregnant Mexican servant, Tessa Sanchez, whom he fired years earlier.

"I don't want your pity story. I could bust up your happy home anytime I want to."

"I know that, Aniyah, and that's what I'm over here fighting for you not to do. My girls and my wife think the utmost of me," he said as he pulled a handkerchief out of his pocket. He wiped the sweat that began to moisten his face.

Aniyah giggled. "They won't be thrilled to hear that you slept with me. Your family will flip over the shocking news. I'm the daughter that knows the real truth about you."

Rupert played the situation over and over in his mind, how she was supposed to be his treat for one night on a business trip that ultimately turned into an affair. How was he to know that she was the child of the Mexican servant that he had impregnated and then fired?

"What kind of creature are you? You knew I was your father, yet you still slept with me."

Aniyah laughed out loud. "Get over it. You want a better story than that one? I do have one."

Puzzled, he asked, "What are you talking about?"

"I'm talking about one of your other precious daughters."

"Which one?" Rupert said, wishing he could reach through the phone to grab and shake her for the way she was talking about his daughters. "Just say what you have to say."

"I don't know those damn high-class bitches' names. But one of them is banging your dear lawyer friend." Aniyah laughed wickedly.

Rupert stood up and yelled into the phone, "You're lying."

"Don't call me a liar, you poor excuse for a damn papa. I know what the hell I'm talking about. I may not be one of your high-class daughters, but I can find out shit when I want to!" she shouted back. "If I say one of them is banging the damn lawyer, then she is. Call the bastard and find out."

Rupert slammed the phone down in her ear.

"Oh, no he didn't!" she hissed as the dial tone rang in her ear.

Aniyah tried to call him back but he did not answer. Infuriated, Aniyah began to throw whatever was within her reach across the room. As much as she hated the way that he treated her, there were redeeming factors about Rupert. She admired his natural hair with salt-and-pepper waves. The suits that Rupert wore were tailored for his muscular body. His skin was as flawless as hers. They used to endure facials when they were together, when she was all that he thought about. All she thought about now was that he had to pay. She sat on a plush white loveseat and began polishing her toes in a deep beet-red shade.

Rupert was relieved that he would have some time to himself. After all, his favorite girls were out having a day of their own.

Stepping inside his walk-in closet, which was filled with his collection of designer suits, ties, shirts and shoes, he removed his silk blue tie and tossed it onto an ottoman, followed by his blue pin-striped suit jacket.

Too exhausted from a long day at his construction company, Rupert walked out of the closet and made his way to the double-pane plate glass window. He looked out at Lake Murray to relieve himself of the tension from work and the personal problems that dominated his mind. The water always kept him calm when work became too stressful, but now his personal life was in turmoil, like the choppy waves of the water in the wintertime.

Leaving the vision of the lake, Rupert picked up his cell phone and called his attorney.

"Baron Chavis' office," the secretary answered.

"This is Mr. Houston. Get Baron on the line, Sara." he ordered.

He waited for a moment until his attorney picked up.

"What can I do for you, Mr. Houston?"

Instead of bringing up Aniyah's gossip, even though it baffled him about the accusations she made about one of his daughters, he simply asked, "That new will I had you to draw up…you better still have it on hold. You didn't file it, did you?"

"I have it right here on my desk in front of me. It won't go any further until you give me the okay."

He sighed. "Thanks, Baron; I don't know what I would do without you. I'll get back to you soon enough. I wanted Aniyah to see me give it to you. Talk to you later, buddy."

Rupert hung up and went back to stare out of the window. His cell phone rang, distracting him from a sailboat going by. He looked at the number displayed. No way was he answering another call from Aniyah. The last ring grew silent and he was relieved.

Once again, the gossip that Aniyah shared with him ran across his mind like a marathon runner. *It can't be true.* Everyone who works for him knew the Houston Rule. Plain and simple—nobody dealt with any of his girls. Period! It was his duty to pick the right men for them.

Baron was his longtime attorney for all of his personal and work business. Rupert trusted him like he was his son, but to clear any doubts he called the Chavis Law Firm again.

"Sara, get Baron on the line immediately."

Baron again picked up. "Mr. Houston, you needed something else?"

"Are you or are you not messing with one of my girls?" he asked calmly.

Mr. Chavis hesitated. "Noelle and I only met up one time at a coffee shop. We chatted over a cup of hot coffee," he said, speaking of the second of Houston's three daughters.

"You son of a bitch." Rupert realized that Aniyah's gossip was true. "What happened after that?"

"Absolutely nothing," Baron fibbed to cover himself.

Rupert marched back and forth on the white carpet below his feet; tension etched furrows in his forehead. He didn't believe a word that his attorney was saying.

"I'm warning you, Baron, there better not be anything else."

"I promise you, Mr. Houston, it was a brief encounter."

"Get off my phone." He hung up and called Aniyah back.

"I spoke to Baron and he swore to me that he and my Noelle only met for a cup of hot coffee."

"Your precious girl is your lawyer's whore," Aniyah insisted.

Rupert yelled, "No one bad mouths one of my girls. Aniyah, you're despicable!"

"Your lawyer is lying to protect his ass. He's banging her and I can prove it." The phone beeped.

"Hold on, I'm not finished with you. I have another call," Rupert said as he switched over to another line.

"Yes, Kenley."

"Dad," his youngest daughter said, but was corrected in the background by her oldest sister, Milandra.

"I mean, *Father*, I need to talk to you."

"I'm busy. Make it quick. What is it?" he asked abruptly.

Kenley talked a hundred miles per minute. "My sixteenth birthday is coming up. I realize my sisters had their parties at the yacht club," she explained. She sat across from her mother and two older sisters as they waited on their lunch. "Father, it's a new day. I want to have my party by the pool at home. Can I please break this crazy tradition?"

"Damn it, you called me for that? Speak to your mother!" he yelled and hung up.

Rupert switched back to the other line. "Aniyah, take back what you said about my Noelle."

"Get your ass to a computer."

Rupert went to the far end of the east wing of the house to his study. He logged on to the Internet on his laptop that sat on a desk with a gorgeous cherry finish.

"What's your email address?" she asked curiously.

He was hesitant about giving Aniyah any of his email addresses, but Rupert gave up an email address he barely used.

"You better not be playing around. I have no time for foolishness."

"Shut up! Just get ready to see with your own cutie eyes," she flirted.

The email finally came through to his computer screen. He clicked on it and downloaded the image. There, in vivid color, was his daughter, Noelle, in the arms of Baron. Her breasts were partially exposed.

"Now who's telling the truth, dear Papa? My half-sister looks great in that position." Aniyah laughed. "I'm sure your friends would love to get a copy. Don't play with me; I'm no one to mess with." She threatened and hung up on him.

Rupert called the Chavis Law Firm again. The secretary picked up and turned the call over to her boss.

"Yes, Mr. Houston."

"Baron, you're lucky you're not here right now. I would strangle you to death."

"You can't be serious. You're not still sweating me about Noelle and me having a cup of coffee together, are you?"

"I saw it with my own eyes. I've got the email to prove it. You're sleeping with my Noelle. No one touches my girls, you bastard. You're fired! Send over all the files from my company and my personal files, too. Do it right away and stay the hell away from my Noelle or I'll strangle you with my bare hands."

"Okay, I admit, we had a little kiss. Is that any reason to fire me?"

Houston saw the email image in his mind. "Liar!" he yelled and threw the cell phone across the room, smashing it against the wall.

First Aniyah, now you, Baron, and my precious daughter have betrayed me behind my back. Rupert started to get up and felt lightheaded. He gasped for breath and his chest tightened. He grabbed his chest, attempting to unbutton his shirt, as blood rushed to his head. Trying to make his way out of the bedroom, he tumbled onto the floor.

There Rupert lay with his right hand on his chest. He mumbled, "My life is over."

Chapter 2

On the third Friday of every month, the Houston daughters had lunch with their mother. This was their time to bond.

After they dined on baked chicken parmesan and a Caesar salad, Milandra Houston, the oldest daughter of Rupert and Alana Houston, led the way out of the Italian restaurant. Wearing a two-piece, soft-pink linen pantsuit, she strutted in her open-toe pumps. Her handbag coordinated beautifully with her outfit. Each tap from the heels of her pumps was like a melody being played by a pianist. Her dark-brown hair was combed back off her face into a French roll, enhancing her glowing caramel complexion.

Walking by her side was her youngest sister, Kenley, dressed in a mint-green, sleeveless linen dress. She would have preferred wearing a pair of casual shorts and a tee shirt. Her hair, pulled away from her face, showed off her golden complexion.

Noelle, the middle daughter, took a bite out of a walnut cookie. She fastidiously brushed crumbs from her turquoise linen pant-suit. Her light-brown hair, which bounced against her shoulders, framed her warm milk chocolate complexion perfectly.

"You don't want to mess up that figure you worked so hard to obtain," their mother called as she caught up to them after taking care of the check. Pearl-colored polish gleamed on her perfectly manicured nails as she clenched her black-and-white clutch purse. She studied Noelle—her lookalike. She admired her daughter for shedding thirty pounds within the past year.

"Noelle, that's about five pounds you've added back onto your waistline or hips," Alana said as she watched Noelle devour the cookie in two bites.

"Unbelievable," Milandra said, noticing her sister, too.

"I'll work it off playing tennis or swimming a few laps around the pool," Noelle said as she and Milandra had taken time out from their tennis games to join their mother for lunch.

They made their way through the door to see that the limo had arrived to pick them up. The driver tilted his black hat as if to say hello. He opened the door.

"What did Father say about your birthday party?" Milandra asked Kenley as she was the first to get into the limo.

"He screamed at me," Kenley whined.

"That's not like Father," Milandra said.

"He's a busy man. He's probably on a construction site," Noelle said in her father's defense.

"You can talk with your father this evening when he comes home," their mother said.

Kenley mumbled, "Discuss it with Mother. That's the last thing he said."

Her sisters giggled.

"It's not funny at all. You two are way older than me. Yacht club parties are not for today's teenagers. A pool party at home is the best. At the yacht club, my friends and I will have to listen to boring piano music. At home, we can listen to current hip-hop and pop music."

"Mother, see what happens when you have an 'oops' baby?" Milandra teased.

"You're plain old mean." Kenley pouted.

Alana Houston was startled when the doctor told her that she was pregnant with Kenley. She knew exactly what day she had conceived. Her husband had not touched her in months. She felt he was going elsewhere to satisfy his sexual hunger. But one night, his so-called meeting must have ended earlier than he expected and he came to bed craving her, as if he was a wild animal starving for food. He awakened her from her sleep. Alana felt as if he was raping her instead of making love to her. He ripped her silk-lace gown from her body. Plunging on top of her, he entered with force. After three humps, he ran out of gas. Kenley was born nine months later. She saw to it that Kenley was home-schooled by a private tutor.

Kenley made new friends with her busy schedule—taking tennis and piano lessons and belonging to social teen clubs. Her sisters coached her in piano and tennis. After all, they were skilled in the same activities. Unlike her family members, who were Harvard University graduates, Kenley's goal was to break the family tradition and attend Spelman College.

Mrs. Houston glimpsed down at her diamond watch. "We have a little time to go pick out Kenley's party dress."

"I'll need a new bathing suit," Kenley hinted.

"Nonsense. You must follow the family tradition. Every daughter of mine celebrates her birthday at the yacht club."

"That's awful! It'll be boring and my friends won't have any fun," Kenley cried.

"It's traditional," her mother reminded her. "Kenley Houston, you will not embarrass me in public the way you talk."

"Mother," Kenley said.

"No back talk." Milandra jumped in as they headed to their next destination.

Kenley looked out of the window as they drove off. She folded her arms and sat back in her seat, pouting.

"Why are you so quiet, Noelle? Is there something you want to talk about?" Alana asked, noticing her daughter was lost in her thoughts.

"No, Mother, I'm just not in a talkative mood. Kenley has a mouthful for all of us."

"Yes, she does," Milandra agreed.

Noelle wanted to spill her thoughts. The secret she held would overshadow her baby sister's argument about a party. It would be a long lecture about what a Houston should do or not do. She wanted no part of hearing the Houston book of rules, and she dared not share her secret. Her mother would be furious. After having a heart attack a year ago, her delicate heart might not be up to p

"Mo   elle
asked l

"No   art
taking

"Mo   'll
take th

Alan   er.
Their   en
more.   ny
daught

Littl